Cinnamon Twisted

Books by Ginger Bolton

SURVIVAL OF THE FRITTERS

GOODBYE CRULLER WORLD

JEALOUSY FILLED DONUTS

BOSTON SCREAM MURDER

BEYOND A REASONABLE DONUT

DECK THE DONUTS

CINNAMON TWISTED

Published by Kensington Publishing Corp.

Cinnamon Twisted

GINGER BOLTON

Kensington Publishing Corp.
www.kensingtonbooks.com

KENSINGTON BOOKS are published by
Kensington Publishing Corp.
119 West 40th Street
New York, NY 10018

Special book excerpts or customized printings can also be created to fit specific needs. For details, write or phone the office of the Kensington Sales Manager: Kensington Publishing Corp., 119 West 40th Street, New York, NY 10018. Attn. Sales Department. Phone: 1-800-221-2647.

ISBN: 978-1-4967-4020-5 (ebook)

ISBN: 978-1-4967-4019-9

First Kensington Trade Paperback Printing: May 2023

10 9 8 7 6 5 4 3 2 1

Printed in the United States of America

ACKNOWLEDGMENTS

Writing could be a solitary or even lonely activity, but people in the mystery writing and reading community form a web of friendly and supportive connections, and I thank you all, especially Catherine Astolfo, Allison Brook, Laurie Cass, Krista Davis, Daryl Wood Gerber, and Kaye George.

My agent, John Talbot, and my editor, John Scognamiglio, have made Deputy Donut possible. Thank you! Like magic, Kensington Publishing Corp. transforms my manuscripts to books with adorable covers. Special thanks to Larissa Ackerman, Carly Sommerstein, Kristine Mills, and Mary Ann Lasher.

Sgt. Michael Boothby, Toronto Police Service (Retired) reminds me of how police investigations are run, and I thank him. Errors are my own.

Thank you to the organizers of the Maple Leaf Mystery Conference and to everyone else who lets me babble about writing.

A book would be nothing without readers, and I thank all of you for taking this latest journey with Emily and her friends.

Chapter 1

For the second afternoon in a row, the pinch-faced woman sat alone with her back to the wall at a two-person table in Deputy Donut. Our café was crowded and noisy, with locals and summer visitors teasing one another. The pinch-faced woman didn't join the fun.

She barely moved except to cross her ankles and tuck her feet close to the legs of her chair. She didn't need to try to hide her chipped neon orange toenail polish and once-white flip-flops. Fallingbrook was one of northern Wisconsin's many charming and hospitable tourist villages, and her flip-flops, blue denim cutoffs, and pink tank top weren't out of place here on a mid-June afternoon.

She had been at that table most of the afternoon, long enough to sip at her coffee and empty her mug twice, slowly eat a large serving of pesto and mozzarella twists, and order cinnamon twists to go.

Her eyes, heavily lidded and ringed by thick eyeliner and mascara, moved back and forth in a sort of tense watchfulness. Judging by the deep lines on her face, she had been miserable for months, maybe years. I couldn't pinpoint her age. She could have been anywhere from her early forties to her middle fifties.

Hoping to cheer her even a little, I smiled as I took her the bag of cinnamon twists and again refilled her mug with our coffee of the day, an almost chocolatey blend from Yemen. Her shoulder-length, wavy brown hair was tousled, as if she'd been untangling it with her fingers. A strand of it was caught in the hole in the middle of one of her gold earrings. The earrings were shaped almost like donuts, but flat and shiny like polished coins.

She turned her head and stared toward the large window into our office, which, like our kitchen, was at the rear of our building. As usual, I'd brought my shorthaired tortoiseshell tabby cat, Dep, to work. For health reasons, we kept the cat in the office. To prevent her from being bored, my business partner Tom, who was also the father of my late husband, had helped me build a kitty playground in our office. Ramps and mini stairways led to catwalks and tunnels near the ceiling. Large windows on all four sides of the office also provided Dep's entertainment. We'd painted her climbing structures and the office's walls in shades of apricot, peach, café au lait, chocolate, and vanilla.

At the moment, Dep was on the back of the office couch, a favorite perch where she could peer into our dining area. Although she sat up straight, her eyes were nearly closed. She was slightly smaller than the average house cat, and totally adorable.

The woman brushed crumbs off the glass tabletop and spoke in a voice so soft I had to bend forward to hear her. "That was a great late lunch." She smelled of woodsmoke. A camper?

I thanked her. "Are you in Fallingbrook on vacation?"

"I live here, but like, not in town. I'm renting a cabin on Deepwish Lake until I get settled." Red lines spider-webbed the whites of the woman's washed-out blue eyes.

I repeated, "Deepwish Lake. I should know where that is."

"It's out near Fallingbrook Falls."

I set the coffeepot down. "That's one of my favorite places near Fallingbrook. My parents stay there during the summers."

"Maybe they know the people who own the place I'm renting. The Peabody-Smiths."

"I don't know about my parents, but Summer Peabody-Smith manages the local artisans' co-op." I waved my hand toward the artwork on the peach-tinted white walls of our dining room. "We display some of their members' works. The Craft Croft is another fun place to visit."

"I did go there. Summer's the one who opened the cabin for me and showed me around. She said her parents are the actual owners, but they're on a cruise. She told me about The Craft Croft." The woman dug around in an off-white canvas tote bag and pulled out a faux-fur donut. It was almost identical to the ones fastened to the front of the fake police caps that Tom and I and our employees wore at work. Our summer uniforms were knee-length black shorts, white polo shirts, and aprons. The shirts and aprons were embroidered with our logo, the silhouette of a cat wearing a Deputy Donut hat. The woman nodded toward the office. "That torbie is beautiful with those tabby stripes and tortoiseshell colors."

"She's my cat, and I agree that she's beautiful. Not everyone knows that we call tortoiseshell tabbies 'torbies.'" It wasn't difficult to show admiration for the woman's knowledge.

"An ex had one. I love cats, but I'm allergic, so I'm glad you have a place where I can look at one, but she can't come in here and make me sneeze. I noticed her yesterday, so I brought her a catnip toy. Can she have catnip?" Like her toenails, the woman's fingernails had been polished orange, but not recently. The polish was almost entirely scraped off her left thumb.

"Yes, and she'll love it."

Fiddling with her wallet, the woman didn't return my smile. "Can you give it to her?"

"Sure."

The woman put bills on the table. She glanced toward the front windows, and the blood seemed to drain from her face. She quickly turned her upper body and again faced our office. She asked in a hoarse and almost breathless whisper, "Can I give it to your cat, Emily?"

How had she known my name? By watching and listening during most of two afternoons in Deputy Donut? And why had she changed her mind about who would give Dep the toy? She had also turned her back to the front windows as if she didn't want someone in the sunlit street to see her.

I didn't see anything remotely alarming on our section of Wisconsin Street, the main street running north and south through Fallingbrook's downtown.

Tourists window-shopped.

Diana, a blond-haired, goddess-like woman whose name suited her perfectly, strode along the sidewalk toward Thrills and Frills, the bridal boutique where she worked, across the alley from Deputy Donut. As if she didn't want anyone on our side of the street to notice that she wasn't at her job while Thrills and Frills was open, Diana shielded the right side of her face with her hand. A gust blew the skirt of her yellow chiffon sundress against her legs.

A compact, sandy-haired, twentyish man in cutoffs, loosely tied work boots, and a dark green T-shirt jaywalked across the street toward our patio. I felt like I'd seen him recently, but not in Deputy Donut, and I couldn't place him.

Another man hesitated beside one of our patio tables and peered toward our front windows. His black suit looked too hot for the warm afternoon, but it was Sunday. Maybe he'd needed the suit, white shirt, and narrow black tie for morning services and afternoon meetings.

The most sinister-looking thing out there was the shiny black SUV creeping past. I was sure it was the one that Fallingbrook had purchased for our new police chief.

I asked the woman, "Will your allergies let you be in the room where my cat spends her days?"

The hand clutching the toy donut trembled. "A few seconds won't hurt." She slipped out of her chair and stood. Like me, she was barely more than five feet tall and had some serious arm muscles.

"Come meet Dep, then. It's short for Deputy Donut, partly because of the cute donut-like circles on her sides. She let us use her name for our shop."

Most cat-lovers laughed or smiled when they heard the connection between my cat's and our café's names. This one merely ducked her head and grabbed her tote bag. Shuffling behind me as if trying to walk quietly or keep her flip-flops from sliding off, she bumped into the heels of my sneakers. I detoured to our serving counter and set the nearly full coffeepot down, then let her into the office and closed the door.

My sociable cat bopped her head against the woman's extended hand. Scratching the orange stripey patch between Dep's ears, the woman offered the fuzzy donut. "Do you like catnip?" Her voice was still soft, but now she was cooing, a tone Dep understood. Dep sniffed at the toy and rubbed one side of her mouth on the fake fur.

The woman glanced toward the front door. The man in the black suit was opening it as if about to come inside.

The woman opened her hand and let the toy drop. It landed on the couch beside Dep. "Is it okay if I go out your back door to the parking lot?" The woman's voice rasped. Had Dep given her sudden asthma, or had the man in the black suit startled her into breathlessness?

"Sure." I tried to sound encouraging. The man in the black suit was now standing just inside the door. He was staring toward us. I asked the woman, "Are you okay? Is my cat bothering you?"

Gazing down toward her flip-flops, the woman shook her

head. "I'm fine. I just don't want to accidentally carry allergens where your other customers are sitting."

Without commenting on her hasty and not quite believable excuse, I unlocked the back door. Like our front doors, it was mostly glass. "Okay. Thank you for the toy for Dep, um . . ."

The woman didn't take the hint to give me her name. She rushed out onto the porch.

What had caused her to panic? I guessed it was the man in the black suit. But why? I closed the door and watched the woman through the glass.

She barely made it off the porch when Diana, still holding the palm of her hand against her cheek, showed up at the end of the alley between our shops. My customer halted for a second, stared toward Diana, and then pivoted away and hurried north, away from Diana and out of my sight but not out of Diana's, at least not right away. Diana stopped and gazed toward the woman. Diana's hand dropped from her face, and she looked perplexed, as if she recognized the woman but didn't remember her name, and then she might have called to the woman, but she barely opened her mouth, and I didn't hear anything through the glass. Diana must have spotted me watching her. Frowning, she pointed toward where the woman had disappeared and lifted both hands, palms up, in a gesture of puzzlement. Did Diana want to ask me a question?

I stepped outside. A gust nearly slammed the door.

Diana turned and walked quickly south, the opposite direction from the one the woman had taken. Like our shop, Thrills and Frills had a back door. I thought Diana might head inside and return to selling bridal gowns, but she almost ran to a car, got in, and sped north as if she were hoping to catch up with our fleeing customer. Her right hand again covered her cheek.

I walked farther from our building. The customer had disappeared, and Diana's car was turning toward Wisconsin Street.

Something glittered on the pavement next to our loading dock. I walked over to it.

The wind must have blown the customer's hair, and when she brushed stray strands out of her face, she hadn't noticed that the dangly part of one of her gold donut-like earrings had come loose and fallen to the pavement.

Wishing that the woman had told me her name, I called, "Hello?"

Nobody answered, and the woman didn't reappear.

Chapter 2

✤

I loped through the parking lot to the next street. The woman was nowhere in sight. I plunged her partial earring into my pocket in case she came back for it.

I returned to the office and glanced through the window between the office and the dining room. The man in the black suit had seated himself in the chair that the pinch-faced woman had occupied during the past two afternoons. He stared toward me as if he were hoping I would go out and serve him, but one of our assistants, Jocelyn, was taking his order. She cleared the woman's dishes and headed toward the kitchen.

The man in the black suit was still watching me.

Her pupils wide in bliss, Dep rolled around on the catnip donut on the couch cushion. I asked, "Aren't you lucky?"

Lying on her side, she flipped the donut into the air, caught it with her front paws, and kicked it vigorously with both back feet. I closed her into the office and went back into the dining room.

The man in the black suit suddenly became interested in his tabletop. Our tables were circular, and we had painted a donut on each one and covered them with glass. The donuts were all different. The one on the man's table was pale orange with white sprinkles.

With an uneasy sense that he had lifted his head and was watching me again, I turned my back and went between the serving counter and the half-height wall and then on into the kitchen. Jocelyn was pouring boiling water into a teapot. Standing at our kitchen's marble island, our other assistant, Olivia, coated old-fashioned fudge donuts with fudge frosting and topped them with sparkling flakes of edible gold. Tom lifted a basket of raised donuts from a deep fryer. "Who was that in the office with you, Emily?" Tom had been Fallingbrook's police chief, and before that, a detective like Alec, my late husband, Tom's only child. Tom couldn't help being curious. And protective.

"I don't know. She was here yesterday and then again today. She gave Dep a catnip-filled toy donut." I raised my voice to let Jocelyn and Olivia hear me. "If the woman I let out the back door just now comes in looking for a shiny gold earring shaped like a flat donut, I have it. She dropped it in the parking lot."

Tom nodded, Olivia smiled, and Jocelyn gave me a thumbs-up.

I went into the storage room and washed my hands. When I returned to the kitchen, I asked Olivia if the man in the black suit had his order yet. She pointed at a plate with one of her gold-decorated donuts on it. "That's it. And Colombian coffee."

"I'll take it to him. Jocelyn's chatting to that couple in sunglasses about their tea."

Unlike the woman who had previously sat at the table, the man in the black suit was smiling and talkative. "I'm Gregory," he told me. He pointed at the black briefcase he'd set on the floor beside his chair. "I'm a pharmaceutical sales rep."

I welcomed him to Fallingbrook. "I hope you enjoy your visit."

His smile caused his nose to wrinkle, almost hiding some of his freckles. "I just moved here. I'm killing time until my appointment with the head pharmacist at the Fallingbrook hospital. Do many of the doctors who work at your hospital take their coffee breaks here?"

I poured his coffee. "No. The hospital's about a fifteen-minute walk from here, not really close enough for breaks even if they drove. But a few hospital employees eat their lunches here."

"Are there lots of doctors in the area?"

"I guess so. Because of the hospital, we might have more doctors than other nearby small towns do."

"I figured."

Wouldn't an actual sales rep know? And it was Sunday, almost four thirty, a strange time for making sales calls. Returning to the kitchen, I reminded myself that I was lucky not to understand how doctors and hospital pharmacists worked. Still, I wondered why a pharmaceutical sales rep would move to a smallish town surrounded by forests, rivers, and lakes. How many potential buyers could he find around here?

I waited on other customers and cleared tables. It was nearly closing time.

Gregory finished his donut and coffee and paid me. Tucking his charge card into his wallet, he stared toward the office. Dep was again on the back of the couch, but she was disheveled, as if she'd finally managed to subdue the catnip donut and had not yet smoothed her ruffled fur. Gregory put his wallet into the chest pocket of his suit jacket. "I miss my torbie. She'll join me here after I get settled. Can I pet yours?"

I tried not to show how startled I was. Our customers loved Dep, but they usually merely admired her through the window into our office. In the past half hour, two customers had asked to meet her, and both of them knew she was a torbie. They'd also moved here recently and had used the term "get settled." And the man had said that he had a torbie, while the woman had said that an ex had one. And although they hadn't acted like they knew each other, she'd seemed frightened of someone, possibly him. It seemed like an un-usual number of coincidences.

However, I liked showing off my cute and friendly cat, and she appreciated attention. "Sure," I said. "Come meet her."

Unlike the woman, Gregory laughed at my explanation of Dep's name.

I opened the office door. Dep had shoved her toy donut between couch cushions. Waggling her head in a clownish way, she pawed at the donut as if she couldn't get it out, one of her favorite games. She looked up at us. "Meow!" Her pupils were huge, like she was imagining herself as a bigger, wilder cat.

"Uh-oh," I said to Gregory. "She might be in a playful mood."

He thrust a hand toward her. "Here, Dep, let me help."

"Watch out!" My warning was too late. Reaching toward the donut, Dep grazed Gregory's hand with her sharp little claws.

He yanked his hand away.

Dep spun the donut off the couch, jumped down, grabbed the toy in her mouth, and trotted up one of her little stair-ways to the catwalk that circled the room just below the ceil-ing. She scooted into a tunnel up there and came out the other side. Without the donut.

I wanted to laugh, but a droplet of blood was beading up in the middle of a thin scratch on the back of Gregory's hand.

I apologized. "She's usually gentle, but catnip can make her silly."

"I see that. I should have known. My cat's the same."

"You didn't know she had catnip."

"I should have, from her eyes."

"Let me clean and bandage that for you." I opened a desk drawer. "We have first aid kits." I'd been a 911 operator until Alec was shot. After that, I had no longer been able to stand working at 911, but I had kept up my first aid training.

"It's nothing. I have all the stuff I need to clean it up in my van. It's out back. Mind if I go out that way?"

Another coincidence.

"Not at all." I unlocked the back door. "Are you sure you don't want first aid?"

His lopsided grin contrasted with his serious-looking outfit. "Don't worry. I'm on my way to the hospital."

I opened the door. His phone rang. Stepping out on the porch, he looked down at his phone and then turned back to me. His eyes were almost as wide as Dep's, and they were very blue. His smile was suddenly huge. "Maybe I'm not going to the hospital, after all."

"You made the sale?"

"Something like that." He ran down the porch steps and answered his phone.

I closed the door and watched him through the glass. The sale—or whatever—was apparently exhilarating. However, he didn't go far before he turned around and looked up toward our porch roof. His smile turned to a frown, then he strode north, the direction that the earlier torbie-loving customer had walked and that Diana had driven.

Chapter 3

✼

Our remaining customers left, and the four of us tidied the kitchen and dining room. Some time after midnight, four retired policemen who called themselves the Jolly Cops Cleaning Crew would come in and thoroughly clean everything.

I was meeting my friend Brent for dinner at my parents' site in the Fallingbrook Falls Campground, so I paid for leftover cinnamon twists and tucked them in their bag inside my backpack. My parents would undoubtedly share them with us.

Brent had been Alec's detective partner and also his best friend. After Alec was killed, Brent and I had spent years circling around each other and around our grief and our survivors' guilt. Finally, we had accepted that we meant more to each other than supportive friends. Alec would have been happy for us. Brent was more or less on call most of the time, and he occasionally needed to rush off to work, so as usual, we planned to drive separately to my parents' campsite.

First, I had to take Dep home. When she was a tiny kitten, Alec and I had trained her to wear a harness and walk on a leash. I snapped her into her harness, shouldered my backpack, said goodbye to the others, and started home. The wind had diminished, and the evening was pleasantly breezy and still warm. Dep hadn't quite come down from her catnip high and was extra frisky, especially when gusts inspired her to bounce and pounce.

We walked south on Wisconsin Street to our street and turned right. Maple was a pretty street, lined with Victorian homes, the older, larger ones close to Wisconsin Street. Farther along Maple, the homes were smaller and newer, but even the newest ones dated from around 1900.

Mine had been built in 1889. The sweet cottagelike home had never had a carriage house or garage, but finally, a detached garage was being built at the end of the existing driveway. The garage's fragrant lumber framework was nestled against the yellow brick wall surrounding the lawn and flower borders at the rear of my property. Work wasn't going as quickly as I'd hoped and, since it was Sunday, wasn't happening at all. The contractor had been trying to hire at least one more worker.

My small white SUV was in the driveway, along with a mess of construction materials in front of the partially built garage.

Turning up the walk toward my yellow brick home, I couldn't help smiling. With a covered porch spanning the entire front, ivory-painted gingerbread trim, and stained-glass panels over the front window and door, the house was charming. I took Dep into the living room and removed her harness and leash. "Your kibble and water are in the kitchen, and your litter tray is upstairs in the bathroom," I told her. She scampered toward the kitchen. I didn't take time to change out of my Deputy Donut shorts and polo shirt. Still wearing my backpack containing the paper bag of cinnamon twists, I grabbed a jacket from the closet on the landing two steps up from the living room and then went out to the front porch and locked Dep inside the house.

A new neighbor had moved in across the street. I hadn't met him yet. Most mornings when I left for work, a large dark green pickup truck was in his driveway. The logo on the door was a pine tree encircled by the words Ever Green Forestry, all in white. That truck wasn't there now, even though it was Sunday. Picturing the truck, I remembered why I'd recognized that afternoon's jaywalker, the sandy-haired man in the dark green shirt, cutoffs, and loosely tied work boots. He was the man I'd seen carrying boxes and furniture into the house.

I put my backpack and jacket on the passenger seat and started the car. Figuring that I would probably arrive at my parents' place before Brent did, I chose the longer, prettier route. Outside town, the road narrowed and wound through forests and between meadows in their fresh June greenery. I kept the car windows closed to prevent anyone who might be lurking in the forests lining the road from hearing my singing. I cringed each time I hit a wrong note, but I kept singing. It had been over twenty-four hours since I'd last hugged Brent. I could hardly wait to see him again. Maybe smiling while singing was throwing me off key.

I stopped singing when an Ever Green Forestry pickup truck passed, heading toward Fallingbrook. I didn't catch a glimpse of the driver, but the truck seemed identical to the one my new neighbor drove. I wondered how many pickups like that the company owned.

About a half mile farther on, I passed a small sign, a right-pointing arrow with the words PEABODY LANE hand painted on it.

It took a few seconds for the name to register.

I'd passed Peabody Lane on this route hundreds of times, but I'd never connected the Peabody on the sign to Summer Peabody-Smith, the manager of The Craft Croft.

The woman who had given Dep the toy donut had said she was renting a cabin from Summer's parents, and the cabin was on Deepwish Lake, near Fallingbrook Falls. Peabody Lane was only a mile or so from the falls, and I was almost certain the woods sloping downhill to my right were between the road I was on and Deepwish Lake.

Most likely, the sales rep, Gregory, was the person who had frightened the woman in Deputy Donut. However, one of the other people who had been outside when the woman had acted alarmed was my new neighbor.

And now he, or someone driving a truck like his, had been close to, I suspected, Summer's parents' cabin.

Was that only another of the day's coincidences, or could it have been a worrying non-coincidence?

Even before the woman had become pale and started trembling, I'd noticed that she hadn't joined the rest of the people at Deputy Donut in their fun. She'd looked tense, lonely, and sad.

I had a bag of cinnamon twists that I'd meant to give my folks. The woman had bought cinnamon twists. Maybe she would like more of them. They could serve as a housewarming gift or as a thank-you for Dep's donut. I patted my shorts pocket. I'd planned to leave the dangly part of the gold earring at work in case the woman returned the next day looking for it. I'd forgotten, and I had it with me. . . .

My parents didn't expect me for another ten or fifteen minutes. I could check on the woman and reassure myself that my concerns about her possible fright in Deputy Donut were due to my overactive imagination. And I could return her earring to her.

I slowed and signaled, planning to turn around in the next driveway, but it was blocked with a heap of brush. Maybe the Ever Green Forestry truck had come from there. A white-gabled house was tucked back among trees.

I turned around in the next driveway and returned to Peabody Lane.

Chapter 4

The packed-earth lane threaded through a green solitude of tall ferns, taller trees, and mossy boulders. Luckily, I didn't meet another vehicle coming toward me, and then Peabody Lane dwindled to possibly unnavigable tire tracks through wildflowers. I stopped. Another sign, PEABODY-SMITH, marked a driveway heading sharply downhill. Either Summer's family owned more than one cabin, or they had cabin-owning relatives, or I'd found the right place.

The driveway was narrower than Peabody Lane and had been carved into the side of a rocky hill. On the driver's side, those nearly bare stone cliffs rose as I descended. Beyond my passenger door, shadowy woods dropped into a valley. Negotiating curves, rocks, and eroded gullies, I slowed to a crawl. Finally, the cliffs on my left gave way to forest angling down toward the lake, and the driveway ended in a sunny, mown clearing. I parked behind a compact blue sedan with Wisconsin plates. At the base of a gentle slope to my left, a crescent-shaped beach hugged a small cove. Farther out, Deepwish Lake shimmered, blue like the sky and spangled with gold and silver beaming down from the still-high sun. To my right, a vegetable garden in its early stages was surrounded by chicken wire that might keep rabbits out but would not stop a hungry deer from munching on straggly leaf lettuce. Another stony hill rose beyond that little garden, and catnip grew, untamed and leggy, next to lichen-spotted rock. That nearly bare stone hill curved in front of me, shielding the clearing from the lake and forming a perch for a charming frame cabin with its rustic wood siding stained dark brown and its trim painted teal.

I grabbed my backpack, got out, stretched, and inhaled scents of pine, lake, and woodsmoke. Bees hummed among the catnip's minuscule lavender flowers. The *thunk* of my closing car door echoed through the otherwise quiet woods. I removed the slightly wrinkled paper bag of cinnamon twists from my backpack and waited with the backpack in one hand and the bag in the other in case someone had heard my arrival and might come to greet me.

No one did. A narrow path wound down toward the cove and the beach. Between trees, I made out a couple of kayaks, a yellow one and a blue one, overturned on sawhorses among weeds above the little beach.

In the forest above those cliffs, a woodpecker clacked into a hollow-sounding tree.

I called out, "Hello?"

Although the lake was wavy farther out, the water in the cove was still and silent, sand-colored in the shallows and almost black on the far side where looming pines cast their reflections. If the woman had told me her name, I would have tried calling it. With a backpack strap over one shoulder, I started up the hill toward the cabin.

Whoever had placed the flattish stepping stones to form a path must have been as tall as Summer. I had to lengthen my stride to land on the stones instead of between them. Higher up, between the cabin and the lake, the rocky ground rose to a point overlooking the lake. The pines near the point had straight trunks except for one next to a bench. Its trunk curved near the base, and then mostly straightened as if it were the only tree in the grove affected by prevailing winds.

The cabin's main door and a tiny front porch faced the cove. A beach towel, its stripes faded to pastels, hung over the porch railing. A squirrel chattered above me, and a pinecone fragment landed beside others on the towel.

The cabin's screen door was closed, but the teal-painted inner door was ajar. I pulled the partial earring out of my pocket, held it in my left hand along with the bag of cinnamon twists, and knocked on the screen door's wooden frame with my right. I called, "Hello?" Maybe the woman was out in a boat. I told myself I should turn around and go to my parents' campsite.

But in Deputy Donut, that woman's hand had trembled after she'd spotted something or someone outside. And I wanted to return her earring.

I called again.

An alarm inside the cabin blared a deafening warning.

I'd smelled woodsmoke when I first arrived. Now I smelled burning meat and grease.

Barely aware of the rich scent of cinnamon, I plunked the bag of twists onto a table beside the door. I heaved my backpack as far as I could into ferns where it should be safe from fire, pulled the screen door open, and shoved at the solid wood inner door.

To my left a living area was surrounded on three sides by windows overlooking the stony grounds and the lake. To my right was a small dining area.

Beyond that, on the stove, a cast-iron skillet glowed red. Smoke curled upward from it.

I tossed the earring onto the nearest love seat, pulled the button placket of my polo shirt up to cover my mouth and nose, rushed into the kitchenette, grabbed a silicone mitt from a hook, reached around the hot pan, and turned off the burner. With the mitt, I shoved the skillet off the burner. A charred lump in the middle of the skillet might have once been a burger. On the counter next to the stove, a bun lay sliced open on a plate. Ketchup and a few leaves from the garden's lettuce garnished one half of the bun.

The smoke detector continued screaming. Luckily, there was no fire, only smoke, and there wasn't much of that. Coughing, I fanned it away from my face.

No one came. Had the cabin's tenant forgotten she was cooking and gone off for a swim or a boat ride? The cabin's many windows were wide open. If I'd arrived seconds later, the grease in the skillet might have erupted into flames, and breezes might have fanned the flames and set the cabin ablaze. Glad that hadn't happened, I hoped the fresh air would end the shriek of the smoke alarm. My eyes burned and my hands shook. I pushed the oven mitt toward its hooked magnet on the fridge. The magnet slipped. The mitt fell off. Finally, I placed it where it belonged. Still holding the placket of my shirt across the bridge of my nose, I turned around.

The dining table was covered in crumbs, and there was a faint smell of cinnamon, probably not from the bag of twists I'd left on the porch. If I'd had any doubt that the crumbs on the table were the remains of some, if not all, of the cinnamon twists the woman had bought from me a couple of hours before, that doubt would have vanished when I accidentally kicked a wadded-up Deputy Donut bag out from under one of the chairs pulled up to the table. Why had the woman crumbled the cinnamon twists and spread the crumbs over the table? Maybe she'd wanted to dry them to make something. A crumb piecrust? Bread pudding? Rum balls?

Desperate to get away from the shrieking smoke detector, I headed toward the front door.

The alarm went suddenly silent. My head rang, my eyes watered, and my ears hurt. I didn't think anyone else was in the little cabin, but I called out, anyway, more of a croak than a shout. Again, there was no answer. I went into the living area where the air was fresher thanks to open windows on three sides. I let the neck of my shirt slip down where it belonged. The seating area was cozy, with teal love seats snugged against the walls beneath the windows, end tables in the corners, and in the middle, a coffee table that could be reached from all three love seats. One coaster had been removed from a stack on the coffee table, and a glass containing dregs of red wine was centered on the coaster.

Behind me, the skillet and stove ticked as they cooled. The cabin smelled of hot cast iron, burnt cooking oil, and charred beef.

A book lay facedown on one of the love seats with a check beside it as if the woman had been using the check as a bookmark. The check was made out to Pamela Firston and dated over a month before. I recognized the name of the agency that wrote the check. Happy Times Home Health Care supplied caregivers to invalids all over northern Wisconsin. The memo at the bottom of the check was handwritten in angry-looking thick black ink: *Final Severance.*

Was the frightened woman who had been in Deputy Donut Pamela Firston? Why hadn't she cashed her check?

More crucially, where was she now, and why had she left cooking unattended for what must have been a long time?

Again remembering her obvious anxiety, I steeled myself to search the little cabin.

I was in what I guessed was the original building. A bedroom wing had apparently been added later. The solid rock the cabin was on must have proved challenging. The addition, fronted by a balconied hallway, was four steps up from the main room. I climbed them. The bathroom was in the same end of the cabin as the kitchen. The door was open, and no one was inside. I started down the balcony past pretty handwoven blankets displayed on the railing.

I couldn't help tiptoeing. I poked my head into a room. A queen-sized bed took up most of it.

Costume jewelry and a dark blue and green Art Deco vase similar to one I'd inherited were in a heap on the handwoven bedspread. Who would keep valuables jumbled on a bed? Had I interrupted a burglary? My pulse, which had begun slowing after the smoke alarm quieted, sped again.

I pictured Gregory, the black-suited man who seemed to have caused Pamela—if that was her name—to rush away. Gregory had claimed to be a pharmaceutical sales rep, which might have explained his briefcase, but I could imagine a burglar lugging break-and-enter tools around in one. And like Pamela, Gregory had hurried away from Deputy Donut. He'd seemed happy about a call he'd received. Maybe it had been from an accomplice telling him where he might find a temporarily vacant summer home.

Was the burglar still here?

Whose car had I parked behind? Gregory had mentioned a van.

Maybe nothing he'd said had been true.

I was tempted to run outside, drive away, call Brent, and let my big strong detective friend check for burglars hiding in the cabin's other room.

But what if someone was injured or ill in that room, someone who needed immediate help, and couldn't move or call out?

Clutching my only possible weapon, my ring of keys, I went on, past another gorgeous handwoven blanket draped on the railing. Unlike the others, this one was crooked, as if someone had brushed by it quickly and hadn't bothered to straighten it. Afraid I might accidentally nudge it down onto the waist-high cabinet below it in the main room, I avoided it.

The other room was also a bedroom. It had a little more space at the foot of its queen-sized bed but was only slightly larger than the first bedroom.

The off-white canvas tote bag that had held the toy donut was on the bed, empty and flat, its contents dumped out on the handwoven bedspread.

There must have been a burglary.

The closet door had been wrenched off its hinges. A torn paper sign coming loose from the door said: OWNERS' CLOSET—KEEP LOCKED. Hard plastic boxes, loose clothing, cosmetics, and other personal belongings had been pulled out of the closet and abandoned, covering the floor between the closet and the bed.

Barely breathing, I started backing out of the room.

And then I saw it.

A hand.

Someone was lying underneath the landslide of owners' belongings and, except for that hand, was concealed by them.

It was a woman's hand.

The remains of neon orange nail polish contrasted garishly with skin that was much too pale for a living human.

Most of the polish was missing from the left thumbnail.

Chapter 5

✣

Against all logic, I had to find out if the woman might be alive and merely unconscious. I flopped down onto my knees and felt her wrist. I couldn't find a pulse. My hand was too clammy for me to judge her skin temperature. I tried my own wrist. It seemed warmer than hers.

I jumped up. My phone was in my backpack, which I'd thrown as far as I could when the smoke alarm went off.

Another phone, probably the woman's, was next to the emptied-out tote bag on the bed, but I wasn't about to try to guess her password or use her pale, cooling finger to open the phone. Her wallet had also been dumped out on the bed. With the back of a fingernail, I pushed a ten-dollar bill off a Wisconsin driver's license. The photo showed the woman who had given the catnip donut to Dep. Her name was Pamela Firston.

She would never cash her final severance check from Happy Times Home Health Care.

Or pet another cat.

I bolted, out of the room and out of the cabin.

On the front porch, I hesitated only long enough to grab the bag of cinnamon twists I'd brought, and then I dove nearly headfirst into lacy green ferns and plucked out my backpack. Leaping from flagstone to flagstone, I made it down the path to the sunny lawn where I'd parked behind the blue car. Feeling like a thousand eyes were watching from the woods, the lake, and maybe even the cabin, I unlocked my car, yanked the door open, fell into the driver's seat, and turned on the ignition. Using the car's hands-free connection to my phone, I called 911 and gasped, "I found a woman with no apparent vital signs." After I told the dispatcher where I was, I added, "Detective Brent Fyne is probably nearby."

I wasn't sure which emergency vehicles could make it down that driveway, but if any did, I didn't want them to block me in. The grassy patch gave me just enough room to turn around. If I hadn't been nervous, I could probably have done it in fewer than four backups.

I crept up that bumpy driveway. Twigs and grasses tapped at the sides of the car. Lips pinched together, I turned onto Peabody Lane and stopped with my right wheels on the grass, almost tight against a boulder.

Minutes later, Brent pulled his black SUV to my side of the road and parked with his car facing mine. I told the dispatcher that the detective had arrived, and the dispatcher disconnected. Brent got out of his SUV. Breezes nudged at his short, light brown hair. Sunlight slanted through trees, sending leaf shadows dancing across his jeans, his heather gray polo shirt, and his handsome but solemn face. I leaped out of my car and ran to him.

His eyes, the same gray as his shirt, were full of concern. "The dispatcher told me you called. What's going on?"

I threw myself into his arms and spoke into his hard chest. "A woman. She's dead."

"You're sure?"

"Positive. And that driveway is treacherous. I didn't want to be blocked in, so I drove up here, but you be careful." I was babbling.

Pulling me closer, he kissed the top of my head. "Is the driveway wide enough for my car?"

"I think so."

"You can leave your car up here and ride with me."

A bigger black SUV stopped in the road beside us. I hadn't heard a siren, and his strobes weren't flashing, but if he'd come from the Fallingbrook police station, the new police chief must have driven at race car speeds. He powered down his window. His heavily jowled face was ruddy. Like Brent, Chief Agnew wasn't in uniform. Chief Agnew's polo shirt was black. He greeted Brent with a curt statement of Brent's last name. "Fyne."

Brent kept one arm around my back and turned me so that both of us faced the SUV. "Chief Agnew, this is Emily Westhill. She found the body."

Chief Agnew aimed an index finger at me. "You two look awfully friendly. Fyne, do you know how to reach your friend?"

Brent dropped his arm from my shoulders but placed one reassuring hand in the middle of my back. "Yes."

Chief Agnew glanced in his rearview mirror as if expecting other emergency vehicles to careen into this narrow tree-lined lane, and then he glared at me. "Okay, Ms. Westhill, you can go. Be at the police station first thing in the morning to give me your statement."

"I can give it to you now." My voice came out sounding small.

Agnew barked, "No time for that. It seems you've arranged other work for us."

I offered, "I can come with you."

"You're to stay away from the scene."

A mosquito whined near my ear. I brushed it away. "It . . . it looked like it could have been an accident."

"We'll decide that." His window began rising.

"Wait!" I called. "What's 'first thing in the morning' at the police station?"

"Nine thirty." He scowled at Brent. "What are you waiting for, Fyne? Get down there and secure the scene."

Brent guided me to my car. Opening my driver's door, he whispered, "Talk to you later, Em. I was already at your parents' place when the call came in. I'm sorry, but I probably won't make it back there tonight. Can you apologize to your folks for me?"

"Sure." I sounded less in shock than I felt. *That cold hand . . .*

Brent watched me lock myself in, and then went to his car, inched around the far side of Chief Agnew's SUV, and started down that perilous driveway.

Chief Agnew didn't move his unmarked SUV. It wasn't in my way, but I was shaking too much to drive. I clutched the steering wheel and sucked in breaths that were meant to be deep, but ended up fragmented and shallow. *That woman, Pamela Firston, cooing over Dep, but now dead . . .*

Meanwhile, Chief Agnew didn't start down toward the sad scene in the cabin perched on rock above a glittering lake.

I muttered, "Nine thirty might be 'first thing' for you, but it isn't for me." Except for Sunday mornings when we opened later, Tom and I usually arrived at Deputy Donut around six thirty. Thinking about our little café calmed me, and I eased into the center of Peabody Lane. Tree branches arched over me in a green tunnel.

Before the first curve, I glanced into my rearview mirror. Chief Agnew's SUV was still there.

No one came toward me on Peabody Lane. I stopped at the paved road that would take me to the Fallingbrook Falls Campground. Far to my left, emergency lights flashed and sirens wailed, coming closer.

Tires squealing, I turned right.

Chapter 6

✺

Leaving before giving a statement felt odd. I knew I should write it all down immediately, but I longed for the distraction of watching my parents putter around their campfire the way they probably did nearly every evening whether they were at Fallingbrook Falls, at their winter campground in Cypress Knee, Florida, or on one of their meandering journeys between the two sites.

Forests, the deep green of pine dotted with the grass-green of poplar and aspen, crowded both sides of the road, and I could no longer hear sirens. Finally, after five minutes of tensely gripping the wheel, I came to the comfortingly familiar sign for the campground.

My fingers began to relax. I crept along groomed dirt lanes, following a route I'd learned long before I could drive. I stopped for people walking dogs and kids playing ball. Smiling at a dog who wore one ear up and the other down, I opened my windows to let in the sounds of cheerful voices and laughter and the aromas of fresh, piney air, woodsmoke, and grilled foods.

I tried not to think about the nightmare I'd left behind in Summer's family's cabin.

The site my parents had leased all of my life was large and

grassy, sheltered beneath tall trees. On one side, my parents' RV and car took up most of the parking pad. An awning extending from the side of the RV sheltered a wooden picnic table, the traditional style with built-in benches. It was covered with a blue and white checked tablecloth and set with my parents' sturdy blue picnic plates and wineglasses. Surrounded by log seats, their fire circle was near the center of the grassy site. In the fire pit, coals smoldered underneath a grill. The boulder that I had learned to climb when I was five years old was on the side farthest from the RV. Over the years, I'd spent hours up there, settled into a comfy niche, almost hidden from the rest of the world while I surveyed my kingdom, read, and daydreamed. There had been no RV in our early years at the Fallingbrook Falls Campground, only a tent. Until my parents retired, the three of us had spent most of our time in a large Victorian home in the neighborhood where I now lived, and we'd come out here for vacations and weekends. I'd loved the place then, and I still loved it.

Hoping that the forest here would once again surround me in its peaceful embrace, I parked on the side of the road and scrambled out of the car.

My tall, gray-haired father settled another log underneath the grill, and then straightened and waved, his smile warm. Smoothing her floral knit tunic over her jeans, my mother came out of the RV. I'd inherited my lack of height, bright blue eyes, and dark curls from her, but her hair was now salt-and-pepper. I'd been a happy surprise when my parents were already heading toward middle age and had given up on ever having a child. They'd spoiled me with love but hadn't coddled me. They had treated me like another adult who would automatically make excellent decisions. I had never wanted to disappoint them.

They wouldn't fuss over me now with insincere sympathy, but they would listen calmly to whatever I said. Simply being around them was comforting. Knowing how lucky I was with

these parents, I hugged them. "Brent apologizes. He'll probably need to work late and won't be back tonight."

My mother gave me a peck on the cheek. "At least we got
to see him for a few minutes. He said you'd made the call
to 911, so he wasn't sure you'd be able to make it. I'm glad
you did. And you turned up even earlier than we could have
hoped!"

I handed her the bag of cinnamon twists. "Fallingbrook
has a new police chief. He didn't want to wait for me to give
my statement."

"Not even to Brent?" My mother's eyes twinkled. She had
loved Alec and she loved Brent. She sniffed at the bag and
opened it. "Thank you! One of our favorites."

I teased, "You like them all. And you almost didn't get
these." Sitting at their table with them while we nibbled sweet
potato crackers and cubes of Wisconsin cheddar, I gave them
an abbreviated version of the reason for my call to 911.

My mother patted my hand. "Are you okay?"

"It's shocking and unnerving, but at least I don't have to
stay and investigate. I wish Brent didn't have to."

She squeezed my hand. "He's strong. Like you."

My father put marinated chicken and spears of fresh asparagus on the grill. "And you'll both let us know if we can
help in any way, right?"

"Right. And I hope he can make it here tomorrow evening
for the rehearsal dinner."

My mother grinned. "He has to! He's the best man!"
Misty and Scott's wedding was Tuesday, one day after the
rehearsal dinner.

My father prevented an asparagus spear from rolling off
the grill and into the coals. "How's the garage construction
going, Emily?"

"Not as fast as I'd hoped, but it's going."

My mother poured us each a glass of my father's refreshing

fruit punch. "I understand why you're building it the way you are, with your brick wall as the back of the garage and a hole punched through that wall for a people-sized door. Going to and from your yard without having to go through the house will be convenient, but I'm still a little sad that you're breaching the wall that's been there since 1889. Alec was thrilled when you two found that place with the totally secure yard."

I took a sip of punch. It was delicious. My father had concocted it based on sangria, but made with juices instead of wine for those of us who would need to drive home later. "We were both thrilled with that wall. After the garage is built, I'll keep the overhead door, the side door, and the rear door through the wall closed and locked whenever I'm not using them, and the yard will still be secure. Did either of you ever meet one of the sisters who built that wall and those houses?"

My mother gave me a fake shocked look. "How old do you think we are?"

Turning the chicken and asparagus, my father called back to us, "We heard about them. They were a Fallingbrook legend." He returned to the table. "Supposedly, they were going to build one house and live in it together, but they quarreled with each other and built two identical houses back to back and surrounded their yards with high walls so they wouldn't have to actually see each other."

Picturing the sweet little house that was now mine, I smiled. "I heard that story, too. Do you know what they fought about?"

My mother tapped the rim of her glass. "No. I'm not sure anyone does. What were their names?"

I knew, but my father answered. "Harriet—only everyone called her Hattie—and Esther Renniegrove. Neither of them ever married or changed her last name. They were from somewhere else. Cleveland, maybe, Annie?"

"I think so. Which one lived in your house, Emily?"

"Hattie. I wish I knew more about her. About both of them."

My mother and I went into the RV's small but efficient kitchen. She handed me a beet salad in a fragrant lime dressing. I took it outside to the picnic table. She brought her signature mustardy potato salad. Together, we arranged the blue-handled cutlery and napkins at our places. My dad brought the chicken and asparagus to the table. Forty minutes earlier, the thought of eating might have made me queasy. Now, despite the appetizers and punch, I was ravenous. It was all delicious. It felt like home.

Light footsteps landed on the road beside the campsite. Jocelyn, now in red shorts, tank top, and running shoes, waved at us. Her parents also spent their summers in an RV in the campground while Jocelyn, home from college, stayed in their home, which was also in my neighborhood, and biked to and from Deputy Donut. Like me, she came out here frequently. By car, not by bicycle.

My mother called out, "Come on in, honey, we have plenty of food!"

Smiling, Jocelyn answered. "Thanks, I ate."

My mother answered, "Not enough, probably!"

Jocelyn laughed, waved again, and continued jogging.

My mother started stacking plates. "She does that nearly every evening. I think she runs around on the trails near the falls and then jogs back to her parents' place. She was heading away from the falls when Brent was arriving. She must have come here straight from work."

I was sure she had, while I was taking Dep home and then making a side trip that I almost wished I hadn't made. However, although I hadn't been in time to save Pamela's life, I might have prevented fire from destroying the Peabody-Smiths' cabin, which would have been a blow to Summer's parents and would also have destroyed evidence and made

Chief Agnew's and Brent's investigation more difficult. Wishing Brent was with me that very moment, I suppressed a sigh.

We all cleared the table. As usual, my mother insisted that since I needed to work early in the morning and shouldn't stay at their place late, she would do the dishes after I left. We all went outside again.

My father poked at the fire. The embers were perfect for roasting marshmallows. "What would you two like for dessert? S'mores, or . . ."

My mother glanced at me as if asking for permission. "How about the cinnamon twists Emily brought, even if she did change her mind briefly about giving them to us? They won't be as fresh in the morning."

I headed toward the RV. "You can have s'mores for breakfast. I'll get the cinnamon twists."

When I came out with the pastries arranged on a plate, my parents were snuggling together on one of their log seats. Despite having seen the crumbled remains of the cinnamon twists I'd sold to Pamela, I enjoyed these. At Deputy Donut, we never skimped on flavors, and cinnamon was a favorite with nearly everyone.

A vehicle passed. My mother looked up. "Oh, good, Kayla and Logan can join tonight's sing-along."

A twentyish woman driving a tan pickup truck waved. Behind her, a man in a small black sedan also waved. The couple pulled into the next site and sauntered to our campfire.

Kayla was tall and angular, wearing loose jeans that almost threatened to fall off and a blue striped halter top that showed off defined arm muscles, as if she spent lots of time in the gym. Logan must have exercised regularly, too, judging by muscles bulging underneath his tight black T-shirt. Although summer's official start was about ten days away, his deep tan contrasted with his white-blond hair and his light blue eyes. He was also in jeans. A pale blue dress shirt was flung over one shoulder and held in the hook of an index finger. He moved with economical grace that reminded me of Dep. Kayla flicked her long, dark brown braids down her back. "Are we too early for your campfire?"

My mother answered, "We're about to start." She introduced us, and we passed the cinnamon twists to the couple. Kayla shared one with Logan. She tasted her half and asked, "Did you make these, Emily? Your parents said you have a donut shop."

"My partner and I and our assistants made them, and we make lots of other fried and baked goods, too. Next time you're in downtown Fallingbrook, drop in."

Logan finished his half. "We will. We have the full summer ahead of us."

Kayla wiped her fingers on her napkin. "Speak for yourself. I'm still hoping to find a job."

My mother offered, "Logan's a chemistry teacher, starting at Fallingbrook High in September."

I smiled at him. "My mother-in-law teaches art there. Cindy Westhill."

His returning smile showed teeth that were almost blindingly white. "I met her when the principal took me on a tour. Your mother-in-law seems amazing."

I didn't have to fake enthusiasm. "She is. What sort of job are you searching for, Kayla?"

"I'm a carpenter."

I couldn't help opening my eyes wide. "The contractor building my garage could use some help. Drop in at 1212 Maple Street during a weekday and introduce yourself. Maybe if he hires you, the garage will be finished by winter." I was exaggerating. I hoped it would be finished by September, maybe sooner. My mother and I brought out marshmallows, graham crackers, chocolate bars, and roasting forks.

Other neighbors drifted in. I'd known the Kasses and Poulins for years. The two couples had begun looking and dressing alike, their gray hair short, and their plaid shirts untucked over colorful T-shirts and new-looking jeans. About a half hour later, Jocelyn and her parents joined us. Jocelyn had changed to jeans and a sweatshirt, and her parents wore almost dressy slacks and jackets.

Jocelyn smiled at Logan and Kayla. "It's nice to actually meet you." She explained to the rest of us, "We keep running into each other on the trails."

Kayla joked, "Jocelyn is the one running. Logan and I are strolling around enjoying the scenery."

Jocelyn defended herself. "I enjoy the scenery, too, but I have to look fast."

Mrs. Poulin quipped, "At your speeds and near those cliffs, you'd better be watching where you put your feet, Jocelyn."

My father retrieved his guitar and my mother's banjo from their RV, and the sing-along began. I didn't want to ruin the evening, so, wishing once again that I had inherited at least a little musical talent from my parents, I stayed quiet. We roasted marshmallows and ate s'mores. Logan stirred the coals and kept them perfect for browning the marshmallows without burning them, although Mr. Poulin blackened a few, on purpose, he claimed. "You get the best flavor that way."

No one agreed. No one argued, either. We'd had that conversation with him many times. I couldn't help smiling.

The campground was in the valley near the foot of Fallingbrook Falls, and deeply shaded, but the sky was still light at eight thirty when I said goodbye and told my parents, "See you tomorrow at the rehearsal dinner! And thanks again for hosting it."

"No problem," my father answered.

My mother added, "Misty's like another daughter. Samantha, too." All six of our parents treated all three of us like daughters. Misty, Samantha, and I had become best friends in junior high. Samantha was an emergency medical technician, and Misty was a police officer. Samantha had married Misty's patrol partner, Hooligan. Misty was marrying Fallingbrook's fire chief, Scott. Misty, Scott, Samantha, Hooligan, Brent, and I got together as often as our work schedules allowed.

I hugged my parents, said goodbye to the others, double-checked that Jocelyn had a car and could drive back to town, and headed home. Avoiding the scenic route and Peabody Lane, I chose the quicker, more traveled route into town. I hummed, slightly off-key, the song still rattling around in my head from the campfire, "She'll Be Comin' 'Round the Mountain." The sun set.

I planned to drive to work the next morning so I could easily bring my bridesmaid's gown home from Thrills and Frills after we finished at Deputy Donut. I would be leaving home in the morning before the builders arrived to work on my garage, so I didn't need to leave my driveway free. I backed into it and got out of the car. Darkness was overcoming the dusk except for the nearly full moon high in the sky.

Lights blazed in the one-story house across the street where my new neighbor lived. The Ever Green Forestry pickup truck was again in his driveway.

I retrieved my backpack and jacket. Lights on timers had already come on in my living room and in the front room upstairs. Smiling at Dep on the living room windowsill, I climbed up to my porch. Dep jumped down. I opened the front door and went inside.

Meowing, Dep wound around my ankles. I scooped her off the floor. Although Alec and I had refinished the pine planks and the natural wood glowed, Hattie Renniegrove would probably have been horrified at the bare floors. She had undoubtedly hidden them with carpeting and intricately patterned rugs. My similar, though probably less valuable, rug covered most of the living room floor. Its jewel tones of red, blue, gold, and off-white blended with the dark red velvet couch, the matching armchair, and the dark blue wing chair, all the same vintage as the house. I had inherited the rug and upholstered furniture. Their colors also went with the stained-glass panels above the door and the window and with my late grandmother's antique vases, displayed on clear glass shelves. I studied the Art Deco vase. As I'd thought during my quick and devastating exploration of the Peabody-Smith's cabin, my vase was almost identical to the one I'd seen on a bed there.

Now that it was too warm to build fires in the fireplace, I'd placed a bouquet of leafy branches on the hearth. With a last glance at the homey room, I carried Dep upstairs to the front bedroom, which I used both as my office and as a guest room.

With Brent's help, Alec and I had painted the walls in this room white. They were still waiting for the perfect artwork. A blue braided rug went with the couch that could be unfolded to make a guest bed. Dep hopped onto the windowsill in front of my desk. I turned on the computer. I was tired, but I didn't want to delay writing everything I remembered from when I approached Pamela's cabin until I ran, silently screaming, from it.

The words on my computer screen swam, and I kept having to go back and add details, but finally, I had a reasonable statement. I printed it, signed it, and folded it into my backpack.

And then I needed to know more about the woman whose body I'd discovered under a heap of things in a lakeside cabin. The only social media account I found for Pamela Firston was locked to strangers, but I was able to see her profile photo and a brief biographical statement. The photo was not of her. It was a cat, a torbie. Not Dep, but one with a striped, half-black, half-orange face and an adorable pink tongue. Pamela's bio read: *Better than Happy Times—living the dream on Deepwish Lake!*

Had I stumbled on how Pamela's murderer located her?

She seemed to have been making the best of possibly being fired. Saddened about the way her dream life had ended, I turned off the computer and followed Dep into the other bedroom.

It was no bigger than it needed to be. Another circular braided rug, in shades of blue that went with the Wedgwood blue of the walls, hid most of the gleaming pine floor. White piping decorated my Wedgwood blue duvet cover and the matching pillow shams. The room was pretty, and also calming.

My last thought before I drifted off to sleep was hoping that Brent and Chief Agnew had decided that Pamela's death was an accident, and Brent would be able to go home that night to his chalet on his own lakeside property northeast of Fallingbrook and get a good night's sleep.

And that I would see him when I took my statement to the police station.

My first thought in the morning was also of Brent. Actually, my first thought was *Why does my alarm sound so strange?*

It wasn't my alarm.

Outside, the sky was beginning to lighten, with a pinkish glow in the east. It was too early for anyone to call, but my phone was ringing.

Chapter 7

I sat up in bed and grabbed my phone off the nightstand. Dep stomped a nest in the duvet covering my shins.

Brent apologized for phoning early. "I'd have called you last night, but I got home late. I'm in a coffee shop, on my way to Green Bay to teach a course to police recruits. It starts at nine this morning."

I thought I was at least half awake, but none of what he said made sense. I managed, "I'm confused."

"You're not the only one. Agnew was supposed to teach the course, but after he saw you and me together, he took me off the Pamela Firston investigation and is sending me to Green Bay to teach as his substitute."

"But . . ."

Brent must have guessed what I'd been about to say. "I've already told Scott I won't make it to the rehearsal and the picnic tonight, but I'll definitely be back for the wedding. I'll reschedule tomorrow's classes to Saturday and stay in Green Bay over the weekend."

I was disappointed about the amount of time he would be away, but he was often on call, and we were always flexible about rescheduling plans. I loved him for his dedication. Among other things.

"Okay." I pinched a pleat into my duvet cover. "Does this mean that Pamela's death wasn't an accident?"

"It definitely wasn't. Maybe it was supposed to look like she fell, but nothing in the room could have done that damage to her skull."

"So, Chief Agnew will call in the DCI." The Wisconsin Division of Criminal Investigation was supposed to help investigate major crimes in smaller communities. The DCI had access to the latest forensics tools and equipment, and they sent experienced detectives who were called agents, like FBI agents, to supervise local police departments.

I heard a sigh. "I hope so, but Agnew is also a detective, and he's . . . confident that he won't need help."

I commented drily, "Or arrogant."

Brent laughed. "Your words, not mine."

"Is he any good?"

"He's been with the department for all of two weeks. Fallingbrook's only crime during that period might have been someone jaywalking. Agnew's strength so far seems to be holding meetings."

"Your favorite thing." I stared at Dep, now stretched across my ankles and apparently no more willing than I was to roll out of bed. "Brent, something bothers me about Chief Agnew. I understand how you got to the scene quickly. You were nearby, at my parents' campsite. But Chief Agnew arrived at almost the same time. If he drove from the police station in Fallingbrook, he must have nearly flown."

"He has a reputation for driving fast."

"I think I saw him drive very slowly past Deputy Donut yesterday afternoon."

"Hunting for jaywalkers, maybe?" I heard the smile in Brent's voice.

"There was at least one at the time. I don't think he stopped and ticketed him."

"You know, there's another reason why he might have arrived quickly at the cabin Firston was renting."

I thought, but didn't say, *Maybe he knew Pamela before they both moved here, and he needed to silence her.*

If Brent figured out what I might have been thinking, he didn't admit it. He only said, "He could have been nearby on another call. I wasn't on duty at the time, so I don't know."

I tried it from a different angle. "It's strange that he would send the department's other detective out of town during a murder investigation."

"Not really, since you found the body. He doesn't know me well. He might think I would corrupt evidence to protect you."

"He could pay attention to the fact that I was the one who reported the murder. No murderer in their right mind would stick around in an isolated place like that, where escaping unnoticed would be easy, merely to call the police in an attempt to appear innocent."

He repeated, "'In their right mind.' Listen, Em, be careful around Agnew, okay? You're used to trusting Misty, Hooligan, and me. Also, most of the DCI agents you and I have encountered in the past few years have been decent, hardworking, and trustworthy. This Agnew, though, I don't know. I think he's more ambitious for promotions and power than for serving the people who pay our salaries."

Even though Brent couldn't see me, I made a face. "He didn't exactly make a good first impression on me."

"He's not trying to make good first impressions. He wants to make tough first impressions. Don't be as open and trusting as you usually are, okay?"

"Okay. I should tell you what I didn't get to say yesterday and what I'll tell Chief Agnew later this morning. The woman who died, Pamela, was in Deputy Donut yesterday until around four. We might have been some of the last people to see her."

He exhaled in a quiet whistle. "I'm not trying to corner you, but where were you yesterday between when you last saw her alive and when you found her body? Were you with anyone? Did anyone see you?"

"I was with Tom, Jocelyn, and Olivia at Deputy Donut until about five twenty. I don't know who might have seen me walking Dep home. It was Sunday, so the builders weren't working on my garage. Not counting people in vehicles or walking around while I was still in town, the next living person I saw was you."

"I believe you, and I know you wouldn't hurt anyone—"

"Unless they deserved it!"

"Not even then."

"Ha!" I must have said it too forcefully. Dep raised her head and gave me a baleful kitty glare.

"Not seriously. Agnew will be looking for quick answers, so don't tell him anything he can twist into one."

"I won't."

Brent gave me the warning that, thanks to some of my previous experiences, I was expecting. "And don't ask sketchy people questions, and don't try to find out who killed her."

"I won't. When I talk to Chief Agnew this morning, I'll tell him about the people who might have made her nervous yesterday afternoon when she was in Deputy Donut and they were outside."

"Let me get a pen and paper." I heard scrabbling noises, and then he was back. "Tell me about them."

Knowing he needed to drive on to Green Bay for that morning's class, I quickly described Diana and the pharmaceutical sales rep named Gregory. "And my new neighbor was the jaywalker that Agnew, who was also going past and who might have been the person who alarmed Pamela, didn't stop to ticket. I saw an Ever Green Forestry pickup truck like my new neighbor's near Deepwish Lake shortly before I found Pamela. I'll give Chief Agnew all of the details at nine thirty." Which was still five hours away.

"Try not to accuse our new police chief of murder." I could tell by Brent's joking tone that he knew I wouldn't. He added, "Not to his face, anyway."

I answered primly, "I'll do my best."

After some affectionate teasing, we disconnected.

My alarm went off. Dep's feet hit the floor before mine did.

I showered and went downstairs. The house had no hallway on the main floor. I walked through the living room and then through the dining room. Alec and I had painted the cozy dining room white and had furnished it in white, chrome, and glass to reflect light. The only windows in the room were stained glass ones high on the wall flanking the chimney above the dining room fireplace. The house's original lighting had been gas. I didn't know why Hattie hadn't put larger windows in the east-facing dining room. During the daytime, natural light filtered in from the living room and the kitchen, though the natural light in the kitchen came from the sunroom jutting into the lawn in back.

Dep waited for me in the kitchen beside the brown pottery dishes that my mother-in-law Cindy had made for her. Alec had been as fond of cooking as I was. We had splurged on our kitchen with a six-burner range and an extra-large fridge-freezer combination. Thick tiles in autumn shades covered the floor, and the counters were granite. As a nod to the house's age, we had installed simple pine cabinets. It was still my dream kitchen.

I fed Dep and made myself a gouda and asparagus omelette. Like my parents, I took full advantage of asparagus season, was sorry it was ending for the year, and didn't mind eating it morning, noon, and night. Dep finished her breakfast and stalked into the sunroom, which was separated from the kitchen by a half-height wall. Like the living end of the main room in the cabin that Pamela Firston had rented, the sunroom had windows on three sides. Dep surveyed our walled yard from the room's wide windowsills.

Before they left on Friday, the people building my garage had put plywood over the roughed-in entryway they'd cut through the wall surrounding my yard. That section of the wall would serve as the garage's rear wall, with a door I would be able to lock. I went outside. The screen door from the sunroom to the patio squeaked, reminding me to oil the hinges when I wasn't in the middle of something else.

The plywood was still in place, and the yard was safe for Dep. She couldn't scale the smooth yellow bricks of the wall, and she had learned the hard way that climbing trees and bushes was easier than figuring out how to descend in a graceful, dignified, and painless way, so she almost never tried. In case she forgot the rules she'd made for herself, I kept trees and shrubs pruned away from the wall.

I let her out, carried my plate to the patio table, and ate breakfast in the refreshing cool of early morning. Dep meandered around the yard entertaining herself. Above, wisps of cloud drifted through the otherwise blue sky. After we were both inside again and I was ready to leave for work, Dep thudded on her little cat feet to me. I picked her up and toed her soft-sided cat carrier out of the closet. She yowled in dismay.

I zipped her into the carrier and cooed through the mesh door, "Sorry, Dep, but I don't want to carry my gown all the way home from Thrills and Frills this evening, so we need to take the car today." I put on my backpack and took Dep out to the porch. As always, I turned the front door's dead bolt and double-checked that the door was locked.

The sun had been up for an hour already, and the morning was warming rapidly. I belted Dep's carrier into my car's rear seat. Dep grumbled.

Driving down my street toward work, I couldn't help

frowning. Caring about me and my safety, Brent had naturally reminded me not to interfere in this latest murder investigation. I did not plan to or want to.

However, during other investigations, Brent had been in
town and in charge until a DCI agent arrived to take over,
and then Brent had worked, usually well, with the detective
from the state. Whenever I'd learned anything that might
help solve the case, I'd been able to pass it along to Brent. I'd
felt protected from any DCI agents who might be looking for
a quick and easy solution, like blaming me or another innocent person for murder.

But this time Brent had been sent out of town for two
weeks, not counting the next day, when he'd promised to return for Misty and Scott's wedding. I would miss him and his
unwavering support.

I wouldn't be able to call Misty with ideas or clues, either.
She had already started her two-week wedding and honeymoon vacation. Not that I would be searching for evidence,
but sometimes people in Deputy Donut said or did something
that turned out to be important.

Only one of my close police officer friends, Hooligan,
would be on duty during the next two weeks, and he was also
attending the wedding. Maybe by the time the wedding was
over, Chief Agnew would have found the culprit or would
have brought in an impartial DCI agent, and I would be able
to relax.

In our Deputy Donut office, I unzipped Dep's carrier. She
scooted to her highest catwalks and into a tunnel. I called
to her, "Do you still have that catnip-filled donut up there,
Dep?"

Her answering meow was shrill with kitty excitement that
must have meant that she was already playing with the toy
and reveling in whiffs of catnip.

My colleagues arrived. Olivia and Jocelyn filled creamers
and put them on our dining tables along with bowls hold-

ing packets of sugar and other sweeteners. Tom and I started rolling dough and cutting out donuts while the fryers heated. Tom had not heard about Pamela's murder. I told him, "She was in here for a long time both yesterday afternoon and the afternoon before. She left late both days."

"The woman who gave Dep the catnip donut?"

"Yes. I found her body."

"You what?" Even though Tom kept his voice down, his question was emphatic.

"I didn't plan it. She liked cinnamon twists. I was taking some to my parents when I passed Peabody Lane. Since she was renting Summer's family's cabin, I detoured down there to say hello and bring her more cinnamon twists as a welcome to Fallingbrook."

Without looking at him, I could tell that Tom was staring at me. He said exactly one word. "Why?"

I concentrated on rolling dough evenly. "When she was here, she seemed lonely and maybe even scared. And I forgot to leave her earring here in case she came back looking for it. I still had it in my pocket."

Tom grunted.

I asked, "Does her name, Pamela Firston, seem familiar? She told me she only recently moved here, but she didn't say where she lived before. Do you remember any cases involving her from when you were police chief?"

"No, but I've been retired for a few years. And don't go looking for trouble, Emily. More trouble, I should say."

"I didn't go looking for it. She didn't answer when I knocked. I wouldn't have gone inside the cabin, but a smoke alarm went off, and the door was standing open." I recited a quick version of what I'd found inside. "Brent was nearby, so he got there first. Our new police chief, Chief Agnew, arrived next. Do you know him?"

"Haven't met him."

"Know of him?"

"Only that he was a detective for several years in Green Bay."

"I have to go to the police station and give him my statement at nine thirty."

"Why didn't you do that last night? Didn't you say Brent arrived first?"

I twisted a donut cutter in the dough, making certain that it cut all the way through. "Not in time to take my statement. Chief Agnew got there almost right away. He sent Brent down the driveway—it's a long and precarious one—to secure the scene. Agnew told me to leave the area and then go see him this morning. Not the way you'd have done it, I suspect."

"I'd have asked you to wait and give your statement to the next officer who arrived. I can understand why he wanted to process the scene immediately himself. Evidence is best when it's fresh."

"But he didn't go to the cabin right away. He stayed up on the road in his SUV at least until I was out of sight."

"Don't trust him, Emily."

"Brent said the same thing."

Tom removed a bowl of yeast dough from the fridge where we'd put it to chill overnight and stop its rising. "Brent knows him. I don't, and I haven't heard much about him. But I do know that a detective anxious to prove himself in a new job might suspect the first person on the scene."

I groaned. "I wish he'd heard my side of the story as soon as he arrived. By now he'll have pictured me as a murderer and decided that I am one."

"Maybe he wanted to wait for your statement because he planned that a DCI agent would arrive in Fallingbrook early this morning and take it."

"I hope that's it." I told Tom about Chief Agnew seeing Brent and me together and then sending Brent away.

Tom pointed his rolling pin at the office. "The rest of us can take care of prepping and opening the shop. Go in there to the computer and type up everything you remember from the time you arrived at the scene. Date it, print it, sign it, and take a copy with you. That way, even if this new chief puts words into your mouth, you'll have a signed and dated statement."

"I did that last night and brought it with me."

"Why am I not surprised?"

"Because you trained Alec, and he trained me." And Alec's father was almost as wonderful as Alec had been.

Chapter 8

✾

The police station was a short walk north along Wisconsin Street, then west on Oak Avenue, the southern border of our village square. The "square" was actually a rectangle, with the long sides on the east and west. Paths crisscrossed it, skirting small hills and tall trees. Benches lined the paths, and a fountain burbled in the middle, too far from Oak Avenue for me to hear the splashing water. I passed the newish fire station. Its big overhead doors were closed, and I caught glimpses of fire trucks through windows near the tops of the doors. Apparently, there were no fires at the moment, which always made Scott happy.

I climbed the broad stone steps to the covered front porch of our combination police station and village hall, originally Victorian and restored. The heavy oak door was easier to open than it looked. I went inside to the police section of the building.

I knew most of Fallingbrook's police officers. Many of them—excluding Chief Agnew and our previous chief—occasionally took breaks at Deputy Donut, all the while denying rumors that police officers ate dozens of donuts and drank quarts of coffee. They didn't, but everyone liked to pretend they did and then tease them about it. Brent, Misty,

Hooligan, and their colleagues were conscientious. They deserved a break now and then, and nearly everyone who tasted our donuts and coffee returned for more.

The serious-looking uniformed rookie at the desk had been inside Deputy Donut only a few times. I wasn't wearing my Deputy Donut hat and apron, but even though my white polo shirt was embroidered with our logo, the officer either didn't recognize me or acted like he didn't. He was already good at arranging his face into a noncommittal police officer expression. I gave him my name and told him I had an appointment with Chief Agnew. While he checked his computer, I wondered if Brent was teaching the police recruits down in Green Bay to look inscrutable. Brent would be an excellent teacher, not only about not revealing thoughts and emotions. Picturing Brent in front of a classroom of eager recruits, I couldn't completely suppress the twitch of a grin. I hoped the officer in front of me didn't think I was laughing at him.

He ordered in cool tones, "Come with me."

I followed him along a wide corridor on the opposite side of the police station from where Alec had shared an office with Brent, an office that Brent now had to himself. The officer's heavy boots resounded on the shiny terrazzo floor. The soles of my sneakers squeaked. Pale yellow walls, interrupted by honey-colored oak doors with frosted glass windows, lined the hallway.

The officer opened one of the doors. "Go on in and have a seat." His tone remained impersonal. "Chief Agnew will be along shortly. Help yourself to coffee." He left me and closed the door.

I'd been in this room one other time, and I'd been wearing my uniform shorts on that hot day, too. Even though the shorts ended almost at my knees, they'd ridden up, and the backs of my thighs had stuck to the sallow yellow vinyl couch cushion.

I chose one of the gray tweedy chairs. And waited.

And waited.

Gray tweedy turned out to be gray scratchy. It could be worse, I reminded myself. I could be sitting on a hard metal chair at a steel table in a basement room with concrete walls, a one-way mirror, and cameras and microphones aimed at me.

That could still happen.

The mugs in the drainer beside a coffeemaker reeking of scorched coffee looked like they could have been the same assortment that had been beside that sink the last time I'd been there.

I did not help myself to coffee.

Chief Agnew came in carrying a briefcase. When he'd been sitting in his SUV, I hadn't realized how big he was. Almost as tall as Brent and, I guessed, about ten years older, he wore a navy blue dress uniform that looked uncomfortably tight. Maybe he shouldn't have tried buttoning the jacket over an armored vest. The gold buttons down the front of the jacket strained the buttonholes. Without a greeting, he sat in the chair across from me, set the briefcase on the low table between us, snapped it open, and removed a notebook and pen like the ones all Fallingbrook police officers carried.

When he finally met my gaze, his eyes were cold. "Just so you know, this interview is being recorded."

"That's fine." I doubted that my agreement mattered to him. I unfolded my signed statement and laid it facing him on the table. "I wrote down everything I noticed at the scene."

He barely glanced at the stapled-together pages. They didn't stay flat, but sort of keeled over backward. Something like annoyance flickered across his face. "So, Ms. Westhill, what made you go to that particular cabin at that particular time?"

I resisted picking up my statement and bending the fold backward to straighten the pages and make them easier for him to read. "The deceased woman, Pamela, had been in Deputy Donut yesterday afternoon."

Chief Agnew held up a hand for me to stop talking and

scribbled in his notebook. Without looking at me, he asked, "When?"

"Between about one and four. She'd been there around the same time the day before, too."

"Can you be more specific than a three-hour timespan?"

"Sorry. She was there for approximately three hours, both days, but I didn't notice the exact times when she arrived. She left yesterday around four."

"So, you'd just seen her. Why did you go right out and visit her?"

I tried to hold still. I didn't want to look nervous. Even more, I didn't want to rub the backs of my thighs raw on upholstery that felt like random wooden splinters had been woven into it. "She told me she was renting a place from the Peabody-Smiths. I was driving to visit my parents at Falling-brook Falls Campground. The Peabody-Smiths' cabin is on the way."

"I'll reword my question, and maybe I'll get a straight answer. Why visit a woman you'd only met a couple of times when you'd just been with her?"

"After she left our shop, I found part of an earring I thought she'd dropped. I wasn't due at my parents' campsite yet, so I thought I'd return the earring to her. Also, she seemed lonely. She said she had just moved here, well, into that cabin until she got settled, so I dropped in with the earring and some cinnamon twists as a welcome to Fallingbrook."

Chief Agnew's squint made his eyes look tiny and beady. And malevolent. He demanded, "Is that what those crumbs were all over the table in that place?"

"They weren't from the ones I brought. They must have been from the cinnamon twists she bought at Deputy Donut."

"She bought some, and then you decided to take her more." His tone seemed to accuse me of committing a crime.

"I knew she liked them." I tried not to let it sound as lame as it was.

He looked at me from underneath thick, lowered eyebrows. "Then you and she crumbled them together?"

"I don't know who did that, but she was already dead when I found her, and her cinnamon twists had been broken apart before I arrived. The crumbs looked hard and dry, but that could have taken less than fifteen minutes." I told him about the smoke alarm and my rescuing of the red-hot skillet.

Apparently not interested in fires that hadn't occurred, he interrupted me. "Tell me exactly where you were yesterday from the time the deceased left your donut shop until you phoned us."

I knew that pinpointing the exact time of death was not possible, but I asked, "Do you know what time she died?"

"I'm asking the questions."

"Right. Sorry. I was at work at Deputy Donut until about five twenty."

"According to your website, you close at four thirty. Is that not true?"

"After four thirty, we tidy up." I gave him Tom's, Jocelyn's, and Olivia's names. He didn't seem to recognize Tom's. I guessed too many years had passed since Tom was police chief for Chief Agnew to have heard of him, although Tom's photo, labeled with his name, hung in the lobby along with portraits of other past chiefs. I added, "I didn't look at the exact time when we left, but we usually finish around five thirty, and yesterday, I think we finished early. Then I walked home."

"Alone?"

"Yes, except for my cat."

He said sarcastically, "Cats don't provide alibis. Did you talk to anyone on the way home, or did anyone see you?"

"I didn't talk to anyone, and I don't know who might have seen me. I let the cat into the house, and then I drove toward Fallingbrook Falls, the long way."

Still without referring to the statement I'd brought, he went back to asking for details about the cabin where Pamela had died. I gave him the best answers I could.

Those dark eyes drilled into me. "Can you tell me anything else?"

"When Pamela was about to leave Deputy Donut, she looked out the window toward Wisconsin Street, and something she saw seemed to scare her."

"Seemed to."

"She turned pale, started trembling, and asked to go into our office to give my cat a catnip-stuffed donut." I described Diana, Gregory, and my new neighbor. I added, "When this pharmaceutical sales rep, Gregory, started coming inside, Pamela asked to be let out the back into the parking lot. Later, Gregory also wanted to meet my cat. Gregory reached for the catnip-stuffed donut. My cat wouldn't let him have it, and then Gregory also went out the back, the same way Pamela had."

Agnew scoffed, "Coincidences."

"I thought so too, but Pamela had told me that her ex had had a cat similar to mine, and Gregory mentioned that he had one."

"Did they appear to know each other?"

"No, but they could have been hiding it."

Agnew made a scornful noise.

Hoping he wouldn't notice that I could be accusing him of something, I worded my next sentence carefully. "You might have seen Gregory, the bridal store clerk, and my new neighbor. When they were near the front of Deputy Donut, your SUV passed slowly, heading south on Wisconsin Street."

"I would have been watching traffic, not ogling pedestrians. And like it or not, coincidences happen. It's easy for civilians to look back and think they saw something that had a bearing on the matter when it didn't."

I conceded, "True." I didn't point out that the opposite was also true—people often didn't realize that a detail they'd observed could be important.

He leaned forward. "Now, when you were at the Peabody-Smith cabin, did you see anyone else near it, either on the lake or at nearby cabins?"

"No, and I didn't see any other buildings."

"They're not close. How about on Peabody Lane? Did you notice any people or vehicles?"

"No."

"How about out on the road before you first got to Peabody Lane?"

I spoke slowly, thinking it through. "This could be another coincidence, but I did see a truck like my new neighbor's before I reached Peabody Lane. I didn't see who was driving it, though, and when I got home around nine, my neighbor's truck was in his driveway."

"Where's this neighbor live?"

"Across the street from my house, but just slightly west. I don't know the street number."

"We'll find it."

I scooted forward on the scratchy upholstery and immediately wished I hadn't. "I noticed a paycheck that Pamela must have been using as a bookmark. It was from Happy Times Home Health Care and was made out to her, but it had been written about a month ago. Surprisingly, it hadn't been cashed. But the memo said something like 'final severance.' Could Happy Times Home Health Care have had, I don't know, a grudge against her, and they not only fired her, but they also killed her? Or was one of their clients or their clients' families looking for revenge for some reason?"

Agnew's fleshy cheeks reddened. "I didn't see a check. And it makes no sense. This was not an apparently wealthy person. If she had a check, she would have cashed it. There was no check. You're imagining things. Or someone took it before I got there."

I opened my mouth, closed it, and glanced at the statement I'd typed and signed. Would Chief Agnew change his story after he read my description of that check? Was he implying that Brent had taken the check? Brent wouldn't have removed anything from the scene before other investigators arrived, and he certainly would not have hidden the check or pocketed it.

I remembered not to squirm.

Chief Agnew gave me another piercing look. "Now, what about this part of an earring you say you found? Where did you find it and what made you think the deceased dropped it?"

"It was outside, near our loading dock. Diana, the clerk from Thrills and Frills who I just told you about, pointed at Ms. Firston as Ms. Firston walked away from the back of our shop, and Diana seemed to be asking me a question, but before I could find out what Diana wanted to know, she hurried away. I went out and found the dangly part of an earring like the ones that Ms. Firston had been wearing. It was shiny and gold, round with a hole in the middle of it like a flat donut, with a smaller hole near the edge for the ring that connects that part of the earring to the part that goes into the ear."

"Did you give the earring back to Ms. Firston?"

I couldn't help giving him an unbelieving stare. "No. When I located her, she was cold and had no pulse."

"What did you do with the earring or part of an earring?"

I tried to remember. "I think I was holding it in one hand, and I knocked on the door with the other. When the smoke alarm went off, I just kind of threw things. I think I dumped the earring onto the love seat closest to the cabin door. By then, I'd noticed the red-hot skillet, so I was concentrating on preventing a fire."

Chief Agnew's answer was another grunt. He pulled on a pair of investigators' gloves, removed a pale pink envelope from his briefcase, and slapped the envelope facedown on the low table between us. "What can you tell me about this?"

Chapter 9

What game was Agnew playing? I asked him, "What do you mean?"

"Just what I said. What can you tell me about this envelope?"

"It's about the size that comes with a greeting card, and it does not appear to be sealed." Since Agnew had put on gloves before handling the envelope, I knew not to touch it.

"Do you recognize it?"

"No."

He turned it over with the address facing me. "Now do you recognize it?"

"No. It's addressed to me at my home, but there's no stamp and no return address. It doesn't look like it was ever mailed." The handwriting was in purple ink and schoolgirlish, with extra loops.

He pointed out dismissively, "Letters can arrive other ways, like being hand delivered."

"I don't remember receiving one like that either in the mail or any other way in the past few years." *Pink*, I thought. *Who would send me a letter on pink stationery?*

"Did you, by any chance, leave this in the cabin that Ms. Firston was renting? Like you left the earring?"

"No." I said it firmly. "I've never seen that envelope before. Did you find it in that cabin?"

"I'll ask the questions." In other words, he had found the envelope in the Peabody-Smiths' cabin.

I steeled myself to maintain a bland expression and not let my annoyance show. "I have no idea why it would have been there. I saw her for the first time on Saturday afternoon." The loopy handwriting reminded me of the signature I'd barely glimpsed on Pamela Firston's driver's license. Why would she have addressed an envelope to me? Thinking about her odd request to give my cat a toy and the way she'd sat in our shop for two afternoons seemingly doing little besides observing all of us, I couldn't help wondering if she had been following me around.

I had no idea why she would have, but I wasn't about to suggest it to Chief Agnew. He might decide, if he hadn't already, that her possible stalking was a motive for me to harm her. Not expecting a satisfactory answer, I asked, "Is anything in the envelope?"

"Let's see, shall we?" There was a gotcha tone to his words. He slid a black and white photo out of the envelope.

It showed a woman wearing a polka-dotted, mid-calf-length dress, a white straw hat that didn't quite cover her gray curls, and white tie-up shoes with clunky, two-inch heels. The woman stood proudly in front of a small, two-story Victorian home with dark gingerbread trim. It took me a second to recognize the place. "That's my house!" The house number, in an older style than the one Alec and I had installed, was 1212. And the gingerbread trim matched what was on my house. Before we'd painted it ivory, we had removed layers of paint. The earliest had been dark green.

"I know. I drove around there this morning to check."

"Why would Pamela Firston have a photo of my house?"

"That's exactly what I would like to know." He said it like I was hiding the answer from him.

I wasn't. I remembered to lean rather than scoot forward. "Does it say anything on the back?"

To my surprise, Agnew turned the picture over. In old-fashioned handwriting, it said, *Hattie Renniegrove, 1936.*

I couldn't help a little bounce. "That's the woman who built my house! I've never seen her picture before. That's exciting! Is there anything else in that envelope?"

He gave me a long, assessing look, and then he inched a folded sheet of stationery from the envelope. I didn't know what color the stationery had originally been, but it certainly was not pale pink like the envelope. Maybe it had started out as ecru. Now it was brownish, foxed with mildew and streaked with rust.

He unfolded it, but even before he spun it on the table so that it would be right side up for me, my excitement dwindled.

The handwriting was old-fashioned, cramped, and so faded that in places it disappeared into random stains. It slanted downward, and a couple of lines crossed the deckled edge and disappeared as if the letter-writer hadn't noticed she was writing on her desk blotter or a magazine instead of on her once-pretty stationery. The border trim might have started out as gold. It had gone dull and greenish.

I looked up at Chief Agnew. "It's not easy to read, is it?" That was an understatement.

"Want to try?"

I suspected it was a trick. If I read the letter with ease, he would believe I'd possessed it since before the damp had camouflaged the handwriting, but I was not about to pass up the opportunity to find out what was written on a letter that someone must have put into an envelope and addressed to me.

First, I looked for the signature. It was squeezed at the bottom right, the top of the name merging with the bottom of "Yours sincerely." I peered at the signature, and then looked again at the writing on the back of the old photo. Careful not to touch the letter, I whispered, "I think Harriet signed this letter."

I glanced up at Chief Agnew. His eyes narrowed, but he nodded, and I looked back at the letter. "The date's easy. *May 28, 1949. Dear*—" I stopped. "I can't read the name. Teller? Was Hattie writing to someone at her bank?"

Chief Agnew wasn't helpful. "You tell me."

I deciphered the first sentence aloud. "*Thank you for being such a delightful young lady.*" I plowed on, almost forgetting that Chief Agnew might be an adversary. If I were doing this with Brent, I would have enjoyed it, and together, we could have figured out more words and phrases. I wanted to haul out my phone and take a picture so I could examine the entire thing later and possibly decipher it, but I wasn't about to suggest it in case Chief Agnew might whisk the letter and photo out of my sight forever. I read aloud, "*Thank you for saving my gold-headed cane from that man who keeps trying to steal it.*" I looked up at Chief Agnew again. "Reading her writing is easier than I thought, since she keeps repeating what she said earlier." I read aloud, "*You are a delightful young lady. Thank you for chasing*—this can't be right—*Dopey One and*—oh, maybe it is right. The next words look like Dopey Two. *Thank you for chasing Dopey One and Dopey Two out of my*—" I stopped again. Whatever Hattie had meant to write must have landed to the right of the stationery.

The next sentence repeated the delightful young lady sentiment. Hattie again mentioned the man who tried to steal her gold-headed cane and Dopey One and Dopey Two trying to take her galoshes and sleep in her bed. Maybe not all at once. It wasn't clear.

In the next paragraph, Hattie complained about watery soup and some sort of junket—a trip?—she didn't like. Rust stains hid many of the words.

I kept hoping to read about my house, but the last paragraph only said, if I was reading it correctly, "*You are a delightful young lady. If I had a granddaughter, she would be like you, so I'm giving you a key. If you can unlock the chest in* . . . Oh, no, she wrote off the edge again. Something *will be yours. You are a delightful young lady, and you deserve it. Yours Sincerely, Harriet Renniegrove.*" I looked up at Chief Agnew. "That's frustrating. It hardly says anything. I was hoping she'd written about my house."

Gazing toward one of the framed waterfall photos hanging on the wall as crookedly as the previous time I was in this room, I thought about Hattie Renniegrove. When Alec and I had bought the house, we'd looked up her obituary. Hattie had been born in 1867. The woman who had fought with her sister, had a house built for herself when she was only twenty-two, and had stood proudly to be photographed in front of that house many years later, was long gone. And sadly, toward the end of her life . . . I murmured, "It sounds like she was institutionalized, and not particularly happy except for the 'delightful young lady.'"

Chief Agnew asked, "What happened to the key?"

Annoyed that he thought I might know, I only said, "Maybe Teller took it and unlocked the chest and found whatever she was supposed to find, years ago. If Teller was a 'young lady' in 1949, she might also be gone by now."

I didn't point out that if one studied the rust marks carefully, one might imagine that they were shaped like keys, one right side up and the other its upside-down twin because of the way the letter had been folded. If so, the key hadn't been as big as a car key or even a house key, but must have been closer to the size of the key to a padlock. The rust indicated that the key, a steel one, evidently, might have spent several years inside the letter. I hoped that Chief Agnew wouldn't decide that I had somehow put that letter inside Pamela's cabin but had kept the key.

He didn't suggest it. He inserted the letter into the envelope and slid it into his briefcase. "You can go now." He turned off his recorder. "I'll have this typed up for you to sign. We'll get back to you."

I stood and pointed down at the statement on the table. "My signed statement is there. I have nothing to add."

"We'll see," he said.

As I left, I glanced back into the interview room. Chief Agnew snapped the latches on his briefcase. Its stapled top lying flat and the other end of the pages still higher than the table's surface, my signed statement was where I'd set it. Would he take it with him, let alone read it? Although the letter he'd shown me hadn't given any of the information I'd hoped for, and Hattie's probable institutionalization and possible mental decline made me sad for her, the letter had given me an inkling about her personality, which was more than I'd known about her before.

Chapter 10

Walking back toward Deputy Donut, I thought about my promises to Brent and Tom not to meddle. I didn't intend to.

They had also told me not to trust Agnew. I didn't think I'd given him ammunition to use against me. I guessed I wasn't surprised at his eagerness to suspect me. Visiting Pamela and discovering her body had put me at the scene around the time of the murder.

Had Agnew actually found that envelope in Pamela Firston's cabin? And had the letter and photo been inside the envelope when Agnew picked them up, or had he himself put them there? Maybe Agnew had taken the missing key.

It was strange that he had denied seeing the check made out to Pamela Firston and had implied that another investigator might have taken it.

Something was definitely off about Chief Agnew and his investigation into the murder of Pamela Firston.

I wouldn't endanger myself by meddling or asking the wrong people questions, but I would have to pay attention to anything I saw or heard that might point to the actual murderer.

In addition to seeming to want to believe that I had committed a murder, Chief Agnew had not been interested in my information about Diana or Gregory, although at least one of them might have been responsible for making Pamela tremble, turn pale, and scurry away.

I would probably see Diana that evening when I went to Thrills and Frills for my bridesmaid's gown.

Learning more about Gregory could be a problem. Had he really made appointments at the hospital? Shannon Tredthorn, who was an administrator there, often ate lunch in Deputy Donut. . . .

I would have to find a way to meet my new neighbor. If he hadn't been the driver of the Ever Green Forestry pickup truck near Pamela's cabin shortly before I found her, he might be able to tell me who had been driving it or where he'd been when his truck wasn't in his driveway.

Meanwhile, what might Summer Peabody-Smith know about the murder? It was just after eleven. She would probably be at The Craft Croft.

On Deputy Donut's front patio, Jocelyn was serving an obviously honeymooning couple. I could see Olivia through the windows. She was talking to one of our regular weekday-morning groups, the Knitpickers, who always sat inside at one of our large tables next to the front windows. I suspected that they were, as usual, teasing the retired men who sat at the other big table. Aside from those two groups and a few other people inside the dining room and on the patio, Deputy Donut didn't seem busy.

I asked Jocelyn if she could spare me for another five minutes.

She studied my face. I was probably still steaming about Chief Agnew. "Take all the time you need," she said.

I thanked her and walked a few blocks south to The Craft Croft.

I loved visiting the artisans' co-op and seeing the new artwork and crafts on display in the white, glass, and brushed nickel showroom. As soon as I walked in, Summer beckoned to me from her office. I went in and shut the door. Summer stood and shook my hand across her desk. Even bending toward me, she was noticeably tall. Her usually generous smile was cautious, her distinguished, sculpted face looked worried, and strands of ruby red hair had escaped from the masses of curls piled on her head. "Have a seat, Emily. I have . . . unpleasant news." She heaved a sigh. "A woman was renting my parents' cabin. She was found dead in it last night."

Gulping, I nodded. "I . . . found her."

Summer sank down into her desk chair. "You what? Sit down. I'm staying at my parents' home here in Fallingbrook while they're on a cruise, and I've been looking after everything, including their cabin, not that there was much to do, we thought, because they rented it to this woman for the entire summer. Around two this morning, our new police chief pounded on my parents' front door and scared me half to death, just to tell me that my parents' property was a crime scene, the renter had been murdered, and I couldn't go there. He said that the person who found the body prevented the cabin from going up in flames. Then he gave me this squinty-eyed look, like he thought I'd committed a murder and started a fire. Did it look like someone killed her and then tried to burn the place down to hide the evidence?"

"Possibly, but it seemed more like she was interrupted while cooking, and the murderer didn't bother moving the skillet off the stove, if he even noticed it was on. There was no damage, except the skillet might never be the same. There was hardly any smoke, and the windows were open, so the smoke cleared quickly."

Summer nibbled at a perfectly groomed nail, the same red as her hair. "Here's the thing. The woman who was renting the cabin, Pamela Firston, was in here yesterday morning. I was just joking around and teased that she might be running from a boyfriend, and she kind of nodded. She told me her ex knew all about medicines, and therefore all about poisons, too. Then she gave me this sideways look, like she was watching to see if I guessed that she was afraid he might poison her, which I did, but I didn't say it."

All about medicines—like, maybe, a pharmaceutical sales rep. I asked Summer, "Did she tell you his name?"

"She started to and stopped. What came out sounded like 'Gray.'"

I suggested, "Gregory?"

"Could have been. What made you suggest that name so quickly, Emily?"

"She spent yesterday and Saturday afternoons in Deputy Donut, and ran out when this guy came in. She looked frightened. When I served him, he introduced himself as Gregory."

"Whoa! He sounds like the obvious suspect!"

"To me, too. In addition to looking scared, Pamela seemed lonely. She gave my cat a catnip donut. From what she said, I think she got it here."

Summer nodded, jingling her miniature-windchime earrings. "She bought a stuffed donut toy here." Summer glanced at my cap of curls. "Sort of like the ones we sew to fake police hats for you folks. She wanted to know if the seam would be easy to open so she could add catnip. We have catnip growing wild at the cabin." Sighing, Summer glanced down at her hands, and then she gazed at me again and said softly, "We could have lost that cabin if you hadn't shown up when you did."

"I wish I could have saved Pamela, too."

"Just as well you weren't there when her murderer was."

"I didn't see anyone else near there or on Peabody Lane. Could he have gotten away by boat?"

"Boat, car, ATV, on foot on trails behind the summer homes and cabins. Anything."

"Have you told the police chief what she said about the boyfriend and poison?"

Her nod set those windchime earrings jingling again. "I did. That police chief! He seemed annoyed that he couldn't immediately talk to my parents in person. They're on a cruise! He wanted to know if I had a key to their cabin. Of course I do. He wanted to know who else had keys. I told him that only my parents do unless other people they'd rented it to over the years made copies. He didn't seem to believe that I hadn't been there since I opened the place for Pamela. I told him what she'd said about her ex, but Agnew said poison didn't kill her. He acted like my information was useless."

I folded my arms. "Maybe her ex intended to poison her, but another method became available." I told Summer about the crumbled cinnamon twists. "Maybe he was adding poison to the crumbs."

"Who would eat crumbs after the ex who knew about poisons messed with them? I had the impression that Chief Agnew was going to rush through the investigation, and anyone who had a key to the cabin might be a handy suspect. But maybe you, the first person who acknowledged being there, might let me off the hook."

"I'm sure he's thinking I had the opportunity, or would have had it if she hadn't already been dead. I don't know what the means of murder was or what my supposed motive could have been."

Summer's smile returned. "Catnip donut. You were jealous of her because your cat liked her best."

"Or you were mad at her because she ripped out part of the seam of a toy donut that one of your crafters made!"

"Obviously, you and I had the strongest motives ever known for murder."

I heaved a dramatic sigh. "I have no alibi. I was alone part of the time when she might have been killed."

Summer made a phonily morose face. "I was, too." Suddenly, she brightened, snapped her fingers, and joked, "I could say you were with me."

"Thanks, but no thanks. We'd both end up in jail. You'd be a great roommate, but . . ."

Her big, happy laugh rang out. "So, not even your tall, handsome detective can save you?"

"We weren't together. But he was second on the scene."

"Oooh. I bet he's being very comforting."

"He could be. Could have been. Agnew sent him out of town early this morning."

"No! What an unromantic louse. Agnew, I mean."

I laughed. "I knew who you meant. Brent's driving back for tomorrow's wedding."

"Great! Give Misty and Scott kisses for me."

"I will. Did you happen to notice Pamela's earrings yesterday?"

"Yes."

"Did they come from here?"

"No. They looked mass-produced. Gold, but not fine jewelry. They didn't exactly go with the rest of her outfit."

I joked, "Maybe that's why she dropped the dangly part of one outside Deputy Donut and didn't pick it up." More seriously, I added, "I wonder where she got the earrings." I told Summer about the costume jewelry piled on a bed. "Do your parents keep jewelry and antique vases in their cabin when they have a tenant?"

"No, and not when they're staying there themselves. They go there to relax, not dress up. It's not like their house is far away if they want to go out in their best finery." Her eyes warmed with humor and affection for her parents. "Finery is not their thing, though."

I grinned. "My parents are the same."

"Speaking of our cabin, come see my latest paintings." She led me out of her office and into a corner of the gallery displaying only paintings. Woods, lake, the cute little cabin perched on its rocky plateau . . .

"They're lovely! You really captured the calm and woodsy feeling of the place. And I recognize that tree with the crooked trunk. It's near the bench on the lookout point." Beyond the trees, tiny patches of lake glittered. Summer was talented. I would have liked the paintings better if they didn't remind me of the previous evening's other scene, the dismal one inside the front bedroom. My favorite painting didn't show the cabin or the woods around it but was a scene of the lake at sunset, both the sky and water brilliant shades of orange, peach, and gold. Trees on the far shore were almost black, and so was the silhouette of a canoe far out on the lake. I couldn't tell if the person in the canoe was a man or a woman, but he or she looked totally relaxed, just sitting there with no paddle in sight.

After praising the paintings again and saying goodbye to Summer, I returned to Deputy Donut. The Knitpickers were certain that I'd been enjoying a romantic rendezvous.

I placed my hand dramatically over my heart. "If only."

As I'd hoped she might, Shannon Tredthorn, the hospital administrator, came in for lunch. I asked what I could get her.

"All this fried food is going to kill me, but I can't help it! Luckily, the way you folks cook, your food is never greasy. What do you have today?"

"Fresh asparagus spears and feta wrapped in puff pastry and deep-fried. And samosas filled with local spinach and potatoes." She ordered some of each.

I took her the plate and a mug of the day's special coffee, a mellow, fruity medium roast from Ethiopia. I asked as casually as I could considering that my question was strange, "Do many drug-company representatives make sales calls at the hospital?"

"A few, but we're kind of out-of-the-way. Most only phone

or email us. One was supposed to come in and talk to the head pharmacist yesterday, but he canceled at the last minute. Strangely for a sales rep, he didn't make a new appointment, maybe because the only day the pharmacist could work him into her schedule was yesterday. Why do you ask?"

I'd been afraid of that question, but I had a response more or less ready. "One was in here yesterday. He said he was heading over there later, which I thought was strange on a Sunday, but then he got a call and said that maybe he wasn't going to the hospital."

Shannon concluded, "It must have been the same man."

I asked, "Is our hospital popular with sales reps?"

My question was odd, but she answered. "Not really, and I'm sure the doctors and pharmacists don't mind."

I hoped that Shannon wouldn't connect my peculiar questions with Pamela's death.

After having spent some of the morning away from Deputy Donut, I didn't take time off for lunch except to go into the office and call my parents. "Brent can't make it to the rehearsal dinner tonight, but he promises to come to the wedding."

I could hear the fond smile in my mother's voice. "He called and told us. It's kind of shocking that the new police chief sent him away when there's a possible homicide for Brent to investigate, but Brent said the new police chief is also a detective, so I guess it will work out."

"Probably."

"Why would this police chief send Brent away? I mean other than wanting to investigate by himself and not let Brent steal his glory. Does the police chief suspect you?" She added in a mother-hen way, "He'd be wrong, of course."

Not wanting her to worry, or even worse, do some meddling of her own, I fudged. "I hope not. He doesn't know Brent yet and can't be expected to be certain that Brent wouldn't let friendships interfere with his work. I don't know if Misty has heard about this investigation. In case she hasn't, let's not mention it, okay?"

"I totally agree with you, and if anyone starts talking about it, I'll change the subject."

I smiled. I could count on my parents to make Misty's evening the best it could be. Besides, if they were focusing on that, they wouldn't be thinking up ways of interfering in Agnew's investigation. I thanked my mother and we disconnected.

Jocelyn and Olivia left with their deep-fried lunches. They were going to eat at picnic tables in the village square.

After they came back, Tom joined Dep in the office while he ate lunch, and then he went out. He returned with fresh strawberries from the Monday farmer's market.

The afternoon was fun, with tourists clamoring for our strawberry shortcake donuts topped with vanilla ice cream. Our iced coffee float made with chocolate or vanilla ice cream and nutmeg was also popular.

After work, we again tidied quickly. I left Dep in the office and walked down the driveway to Thrills and Frills. Reminding myself that I was going there for the final fitting of my gown, and I shouldn't be obvious about my curiosity over Diana's possibly having frightened Pamela, I opened the door and went inside.

Chapter 11

The first thing that met me in Thrills and Frills was the bridal boutique's almost overpowering fragrance of lavender.

The second thing that met me was the colossal amount of space the dresses took up, especially the ones meant for brides. The white gowns puffed out from racks on both sides of the long, narrow store. Each gown took up about as much space as about thirty-seven bulky sweaters would have, back when the shop sold casual clothes, before Madame Monique opened Thrills and Frills. The attendants' gowns, some bright, some black, but most pastel, were arranged in a row down the center of the shop.

The third thing that met me was romantic music winding around the room from speakers in the ceiling.

The fourth thing was Madame Monique herself, in all of her puce silk-swathed glory. "*Bonjour,* mademoiselle!" She nodded her head, bobbing her black curls.

I wasn't a mademoiselle, but I was happy enough not to be called a madame. "Hello, Madame Monique."

"You have come for your final fitting, *non?*"

"Yes."

She belted out in a voice more suited to a dockyard than to

the softly lit, lavender-perfumed shop, "Diana!" I managed not to jump. "Bring Mademoiselle Emily's gown."

Seconds later, Diana came out of the back of the shop. With a genuine smile, she carried the seafoam satin and chiffon confection on its hanger.

Madame Monique pressed her palms together near her heart. "Ah, but it is lovely, *non*?"

My smile was as genuine as Diana's. The dress was lovely, and I said so, but most of the smile was remembering the first time I'd come in here with Misty and Samantha to shop for gowns.

Diana, tall and slender with that Scandinavian blond hair, could almost have been Misty's twin. Diana had trotted out a succession of bridal gowns while Madame Monique lavishly praised them, praised Misty, and praised all brides everywhere. Misty had almost lost her police officer ability to keep a neutral face. Samantha and I had managed not to break into giggling fits reminiscent of our junior high days, but our grins at Misty's attempts not to laugh had been huge.

The gowns that Madame Monique had asked Diana to show Misty appeared to have been designed for extremely tall six-year-olds playing princess, with tiers of lace, puffy sleeves, ribbons, bows, bling, and in at least one case, an enormous bustle. None of them suited Misty's no-fuss personality, and her perfect figure did not have to be hidden in yards of bunched-up fabric. I had wandered to the rack and pulled out a simple and slinky ivory satin dress cut on the bias to show off curves while gently flowing over them. It was sleeveless with a boat neckline. The bias cut gave the neckline a light draping of soft folds. "Try this, Misty," I'd said.

With a grateful wink, she accepted it. When she came out of the fitting room wearing the dress, she beamed with satisfaction. "This one. It doesn't need alterations."

In her own long gown that did not quite hide her satin

shoes—they were chartreuse that day—with their sensible heels, Madame Monique had trundled to Misty. "But it is divine! Turn around."

Misty had, and Madame Monique had agreed that, as long as Misty wore the right heels, nothing needed to be done to the dress.

We'd found dresses almost as simple for Samantha and me, except that a layer of chiffon covered the satin underdresses, and a removable panel of chiffon floated from the shoulders all the way to the hem in back.

Since that day, my dress had been taken in around the hips and shortened. Diana helped me slip it on.

I twisted and turned, checking both sides and the back in the triple-fold mirror. "It looks perfect."

Madame Monique clapped her hands. "It is heavenly! Madame Samantha came in earlier, and hers is also perfect. You three will look like angels!"

I couldn't help it. "But angels are dead."

Diana turned away from Madame Monique, but I saw the smile.

Madame Monique clutched at her heart. "But *non*. Angels are alive. They fly unseen and unheard among us with their heavenly feathered wings." She shuddered and repeated my unfortunate word. "Dead! Did you not hear? There was a murder." She rolled the r's. "It was on the news this morning. A person who is not from here, Pamela somebody, was *murrrrdared* out near Fallingbrook Falls last night!"

"Pamela Firston," I supplied. "She was in Deputy Donut yesterday afternoon and Saturday afternoon, too."

Diana might have been studying how to be a police officer. As soon as Madame Monique had pronounced *murrrdare*, Diana had controlled her smile, and the lack of expression on her face was almost an expression in itself.

Madame Monique staggered backward. "*Non*, it is too

terrible! You see her one minute and the next one, pfft! She is dead!"

Wordlessly, Diana helped lift the dress off over my head.

I pulled my polo shirt on. "Diana saw her yesterday, too."

Diana carefully inserted the padded hanger into the dress. "I did?"

"Out back, around four." I stepped into my shorts.

Frowning, Diana shook her head. "I don't remember that." She didn't meet my gaze.

I zipped my shorts. "She was wearing cutoffs, a pink tank top, and flip-flops."

Madame Monique tut-tutted. "So not elegant!"

I added, "And nice gold earrings shaped like flat donuts. I think she dropped part of one, and Diana, you might have called to her about it, and pointed, but she didn't stop. I went out and retrieved it. She'd disappeared from view."

Diana looked less bewildered. "Okay, I do remember seeing a woman drop something. You were at your back door, and I couldn't make myself heard because I was biting down on a piece of gauze, so I signalled to you, Emily. I'm sorry I didn't help you try to catch up to her. I'd just had a tooth pulled, and I couldn't think of anything besides going home and lying down."

Madame Monique folded her arms. "I was swamped all afternoon. I expected the lovely Diana back here after her dental emergency—imagine, she found a dentist willing to do the extraction on a Sunday!—but she never showed up and never told me she wasn't coming."

Diana bowed her head. "I'm sorry, Madame. The dentist had told me I would have to go home and rest after he pulled that tooth, but I didn't believe him. I thought it couldn't be that bad. Working here is so easy that I thought I could do it. But he told me I couldn't. Something about a nerve possibly being exposed and causing what he said would be unbearable pain."

I remembered the way Diana had held one hand over her cheek. I thought she'd been shielding her face from view, but maybe the freezing made her want to touch her cheek to convince herself it was still there and not grotesquely swollen. I asked, "Does it still hurt?"

"It's not bad. But yesterday afternoon, I was afraid the freezing would wear off before I got home. And I couldn't talk. The dentist told me to keep biting down on that piece of gauze and then switch to biting on a tea bag when I got home." She turned a contrite face toward Madame Monique. "If I could have made myself understood, I would have either come in here or called you, Madame."

Madame Monique waved a puce-shrouded arm in dismissal. "All is forgiven, poor petite. Now, if you will be so kind, place the gown oh so carefully into its bag and then after Mademoiselle Emily and I conclude our little bit of business, you can help her take the gown to her car." Madame Monique smiled at me. I obediently reached for my charge card.

After we concluded our little bit of business, Madame Monique demanded, "And, *aftairrre*, you must bring me *peec-turrres* of the wedding and of you three angels in your gowns. And of the oh-so-gorgeous men, also!" She placed her hand over her heart. "That groom, the fire chief, he is a god, no? A dreamboat!"

Wondering who had been the first person to come up with equating attractive men to boats, I agreed. "And he's every bit as wonderful as he is handsome. They're a perfect match." I couldn't help adding, "I might have seen that they belonged together before they saw it."

From the speakers surrounding us, the strings reached a crescendo. Madame Monique appeared about to swoon. "And did you, mademoiselle, help bring about this match?"

"I don't think my help was necessary."

But Madame Monique did not appear to have heard me.

"*Pairrhaps* you will find the divine Diana a Nordic god of her own!"

From the look on Diana's face, I might have guessed her toothache had suddenly returned full force, but then she smiled back at me.

Warning that we must not carry my gown far and *pairrhaps* drop it, Madame Monique let Diana and me out through the rear of the shop. Diana and I tenderly placed the garment bag in the rear compartment of my SUV, and then Diana headed toward Thrills and Frills, and I unlocked our office door.

Fortunately, Dep was right there, not in her playground near the ceiling. I picked her up. Apologizing, I zipped her into her carrier. She didn't yowl at full volume. Quite.

Driving home with her carrier belted into the rear seat, I couldn't help wondering about Diana and her emergency dental appointment. When I'd seen her, she'd been walking from the north. My dentist had an office two blocks north of Deputy Donut. I had never needed him on a weekend, but it didn't surprise me that he might come in on a Sunday, even on a beautiful afternoon in June, if a patient was in pain.

As Summer had said, Gregory was an obvious suspect.

But was Chief Agnew considering anyone besides Summer and me?

Not surprisingly, especially if he had committed a *murrr-dare*, Gregory had not returned to Deputy Donut.

I wondered where he was.

Chapter 12

❁

A block from home, I heard hammers and drills. I called over the back of my seat to Dep, "I think they're working on our garage!"

Apparently still annoyed at being confined in her carrier, Dep's only answer was a plaintive request to be released. I parked behind a lineup of workers' vehicles on my side of the street. Cooing that we were home, I took Dep into the house and let her out. She raced to the living room windowsill, sat down, and licked the back of a wrist. I returned to the car for my gown. Fearing I might wrinkle it, I stretched my arm up and carried it by the hanger. I was glad I hadn't needed to park even farther away.

Wearing a leather carpenter's apron plus a harness and tether over her T-shirt and jeans, Kayla scrambled over two-by-fours framing my new garage's roof. I smiled and waved with my free hand, but she was watching her footing, and I didn't want to distract her by calling out to tell her I was happy that she'd joined the crew building my garage. On the porch, I checked the mailbox. It was empty. I carried the bridesmaid's gown upstairs, hung it in its garment bag in my guest room closet, and put on the dress I'd bought for the rehearsal.

It was disappointing that Brent wouldn't see me, at least not this time, in the long, shimmery gown. I'd chosen deep green in case I ended up sitting on a log or the ground. Also, the bluish shade made my eyes appear even bluer. The spaghetti-strapped dress came with a matching jacket, perfect for when the evening cooled in the shady woods. Because of the uneven ground I'd be walking on, I put on black patent flats. I'd bought a black patent bag that was only a little larger than an evening bag. Since my short, curly hair had a mind of its own, I simply combed and fluffed it.

I fed Dep and told her goodbye. Not wanting to be reminded of the previous night's too-eventful detour, I took the faster route, but after I left Fallingbrook's outskirts behind, that route was scenic, too, with forests dotted with boulders lining both sides of the road. Guessing that caterers might need to keep their vehicles close to my parents' site, I parked on the next loop in the campground. My parents must have had the same idea. Their car was already there. I walked the rest of the way, past families eating at picnic tables, kids playing ball, and neighbors calling out that I looked fantastic. Cooking at their barbecue, the Kasses waved.

At my parents' campsite, lanterns in Misty's wedding colors, white and seafoam, hung from tree branches. My folks had replaced the logs around the firepit with an assortment of lawn chairs that they must have borrowed from neighbors. The fire was built but had not been lit. Near the huge boulder, caterers milled around barbecues and tables they'd hauled to the site.

My mother ran down the steps from the RV. "Emily!" She wrapped me in a hug and then backed up. Long strings of colorful beads in shades of ruby, turquoise, sapphire, and emerald hung around her neck and matched the colors of her handwoven caftan. "You're more gorgeous than ever, Emily. Do I look too hippy-dippy?"

"You're perfect."

She pinched my cheek. "So are you."

My father came out in a ruby red shirt, his usual loose jeans, and a black leather tie that he had probably owned since his hippy-dippy days. He hugged me, too, and I again thanked them for holding this party for Misty and Scott.

My mother nestled against my father's side. "When we found out that Misty and Scott were holding their wedding at the chapel here, we wanted to do this. Her parents made all of the arrangements with the caterers and helped set everything up—all we had to do was borrow lawn chairs and get dressed. The caterers will clean up afterward. It's the best way to throw a party! And the weather cooperated."

"Hello!" Scott's voice, even more cheerful than usual.

Misty and Scott must have also parked on another loop. Waving, they strode toward us. Both of them tall, slim, blond, blue-eyed, kind and caring, they were adorable together. Misty was elegant in white slacks and tunic. She must have known that for once we wouldn't be sitting on logs. Scott, too. He wore khakis and a white dress shirt. Thanking my parents, he handed my mother a box of handcrafted chocolates.

Misty's and Samantha's parents showed up together, and Samantha and Hooligan arrived only moments later. They'd come almost straight from work, but Samantha had changed out of her EMT uniform into a long navy linen dress, and instead of his police uniform, Hooligan wore a checked blazer over his T-shirt and jeans.

Scott's parents arrived and gave Misty a big hug. Scott's mother wiped away a tear. "It's joy," she explained to me. "We love that girl."

I answered, "And everyone loves Scott, too."

Servers in black pants and white shirts passed platters of appetizers. I chose two: a mini caprese salad—a tiny olive oil-soaked bocconcini ball, a cherry tomato, and a basil leaf on a toothpick—and a parmesan crisp topped with goat cheese and a sundried tomato.

Naturally, Hooligan agreed to be what he called "second best man" in Brent's absence, earning a playful mock punch from Scott.

We feasted on ribs and pulled pork sandwiches with all of the fixings including tangy coleslaw and crisp dill pickles. Dessert would be later, after the rehearsal.

My parents' site was near the eastern edge of the campground, the one closest to the falls. The chapel was near the western edge. Scott, Misty, Samantha, Hooligan, and I decided to walk to the chapel for the rehearsal. In case the evening cooled before we returned, I put on the pretty green jacket.

As soon as we were out of sight of the party, Hooligan stopped to retie a shoe. Samantha and I waited. Misty and Scott kept going.

Hooligan stood and put a hand on my arm. "Let's not catch up, Emily. I don't want to discuss this latest investigation when Misty can hear. She deserves a break from police work."

Samantha skipped ahead. "I'll catch up with her."

Setting a slow pace beside me, Hooligan said, "I'm really sorry about Agnew sending Brent away, but there was nothing I could do."

"I wouldn't expect you to try. Were you at the scene?"

"Yes. I'm sorry you had to see that."

I tried to look like I wasn't remembering finding Pamela. "I'm sorry that any of us did. I'm sorry it happened."

"Yes, but some of us chose a career that, despite its many rewarding features, has downsides. Brent was already there."

"Agnew, too."

Hooligan corrected me. "Sort of. When I arrived, Agnew was in his vehicle on Peabody Lane near the top of the driveway. I'm not sure what he was waiting for, but he sent Tyler and me down to the scene."

"Tyler?"

"Tyler Tainwright is my patrol partner while Misty's on vacation."

I thought about the police officers who had been in Deputy Donut recently and guessed, "Tall guy, barely says a thing, but there's a twinkle in his eyes?"

"That's him. He's a good officer." In the glow of the setting sun, the red highlights in Hooligan's auburn hair were almost gold.

I hugged my bag closer. "Did you happen to see a check made out to Pamela Firston? I saw one, but Agnew told me I was mistaken and there was no check."

Hooligan cast a worried look down at me. "Tyler pointed it out to me. It was on the love seat next to an open book lying facedown. I guarantee you that Brent, Tyler, and I did not touch it or the book or the piece of an earring on the cushion next to the one where the book and the check were."

I groaned. "That earring will have my fingerprints on it. My fingerprints have been on file for years, ever since I applied to work as a 911 dispatcher. Pamela's earring came apart outside Deputy Donut, and one of the reasons I stopped in at the cabin was to return the part she lost. When I realized I needed to move the red-hot frying pan off the burner, I must have tossed the earring onto the nearest piece of furniture and then, with everything else going on, I forgot about it, not that I'd have taken it with me. I'm nearly a hundred percent sure that it was hers. I'll probably end up in trouble with Agnew over it, especially if Pamela was still wearing its mate."

"She was. Maybe Agnew won't check the fingerprints on the one you touched."

"He will. I told him I took it there. He'll use my fingerprints as evidence that I killed her." I wasn't completely joking. "I'm sure he thinks I took the check, too, but if I had, I wouldn't have mentioned it to him."

"Brent, Tyler, and I were in the bedroom with the . . . with her when Agnew arrived. Brent called out and told him where we were and where she was, but Agnew spent a few minutes in the main room before he joined us. Maybe he accidentally slid the check underneath the book and forgot he saw it, and one of the investigators who came in later put it somewhere."

"Did you notice the name of the company that wrote the check?"

Without pausing, Hooligan answered, "Happy Times Home Health Care. I was surprised to see an uncashed check, especially one that had been written over a month ago."

"That's what I saw. It said, 'Final Severance Pay.'"

"I noticed that."

I skipped a step to keep up with him. "I wonder what happened to that check."

"So do I." Hooligan could be playful in social situations, but his voice was steely.

While I had his attention and no one else was within earshot, I went on with my questions. "Did you see a pink envelope in that cabin? It was addressed to me, in purple ink."

"I didn't. I would have remembered that." Frowning, he repeated, as if he wasn't sure he'd heard me correctly, "Addressed to you?"

"Yes. The writing was similar to Pamela Firston's signature on her driver's license. And no, I'm not the one who emptied her tote bag and wallet. They'd been dumped out before I found her, and her driver's license was plainly visible."

Hooligan laughed. "I didn't suspect you." He said, not accusingly, but admiringly, "You noticed a lot of things in that cabin."

"I sort of had to. In addition to returning the earring, I'd gone there because, earlier that afternoon in Deputy Donut, Pamela had seemed frightened, and her fear worried me. I wanted to make sure she was all right, and if she wasn't, maybe I could help her."

"That sounds like you."

"Well, maybe. Then I found the place was nearly on fire from unattended cooking, and I naturally went into check-everything mode. I didn't touch things or open cabinets or closets, so I didn't notice everything, like the envelope addressed to me. Agnew claimed he found it at the scene. He seems to want to believe that I accidentally left it, but the first time I saw it was this morning when he showed it to me at the police station."

"What was in it?"

I described the photo and the letter. "The envelope hadn't been sealed and there was no stamp. I don't know how Pamela got hold of the picture and the letter, but I guess she somehow knew that I own that house, and she figured, correctly, that I'd be interested in anything about the first owner. It's sad that this stranger, who has now been murdered, might have been doing something like working up the courage to talk to me." I told him about her long, nearly silent visits to Deputy Donut and the gift she'd given Dep.

Hooligan agreed that all of it was sad. "Did Agnew say where he found that envelope?"

"Only that it had been in that cabin."

Hooligan glared straight ahead. "Agnew knows I'm taking tomorrow off for Misty's wedding, though he seemed to think it was weird for patrol partners to attend each other's weddings."

I muttered, "Agnew probably doesn't have friends."

Hooligan made a mirthless attempt at a laugh. "I hope he doesn't figure out that Misty's and my circle of friends includes you and Brent, or he might send me out of town, too. I need to keep an eye on that guy and how he runs the investigation. I don't want him jumping to the conclusion that because you were first on the scene, you must be a killer."

"Thank you. To be fair, he doesn't know me and he barely knows Brent. He'll ask for help from the DCI, won't he?"

"He should, but none have shown up. Maybe no agents are available at the moment."

"How likely is that?"

"Not very."

We were crossing one side of a grassy play area where teens were playing catch. A girl made a gasping shriek, and a boy yelled, "Watch out!"

Chapter 13

❦

Something flew toward me. Automatically, I reached up and grabbed it out of the air. It was a flat blue and white plastic disk with a hole in the middle.

Hooligan laughed. "That was quick, Emily. You snatched that almost out of my hands."

"Ha," I teased. You didn't have a chance." Luckily, my long dress and matching jacket were stretchy. I broadened my stance and backhanded the flat plastic donut toward the girl, who stood still with one hand over her mouth and her eyes wide and frightened.

Behind her, two boys were obviously trying to control their snickers, and another girl appeared to be almost as concerned as the first. They all looked about fifteen.

The plastic disk soared in a gentle curve toward the girl who had accidentally launched it in our direction. It slowed, nearly hovering. She raised her hands, clapped both hands over the disk, yelled, "Thanks," and threw it. It didn't land near us or any of her friends. One of the boys picked it up, took it to her, and suggested, "Try again."

Ahead, Misty, Scott, and Samantha had turned around and were watching. Misty yelled, "You haven't lost your touch, Emily!"

Beside me, Hooligan asked, "Do you practice a lot or something?"

I pointed at Misty and Samantha. "We three used to toss those things around, but we haven't done it in years. Don't ask me to repeat either the catch or the throw."

"Must be all the donuts you fling around. I hope you don't throw them at your customers."

I pretended to complain. "Didn't you see how I made it float so that girl could easily catch it? That was a perfect backhand toss. I would never harm a donut."

He grinned. "Not on purpose, but real donuts might splat against walls and be wasted. Let's catch up to the others."

The quaint white board-and-batten chapel was tucked into the forest next to another grassy area. The Gothic, pointed curves at the tops of the chapel's clear glass windows added charm. The small steeple held a bell that was visible to anyone, and, I knew, a set of hidden speakers.

Reverend Christopher, one of Hooligan's boyhood friends, had also officiated at Hooligan's and Samantha's wedding. Reverend Christopher met the five of us at the double front doors of the chapel. We discussed our roles, and then the three men went inside.

After a minute, I opened one of the doors. The chapel was rustic wood inside. Beyond the windows, golden beams of late sunlight slanted between trees. The men stood facing us near the front of the chapel. Samantha started slowly up the aisle toward them.

When Samantha arrived at the front, I walked up the aisle past pews that I knew from trying not to squirm in them had been carved for comfort, at least for adult comfort. Reverend Christopher, Samantha, Scott, and Hooligan all smiled at me. I turned, stood beside Samantha, and watched a broadly smiling Misty attempt to maintain a dignified pace up the aisle.

Reverend Christopher discussed what would happen next,

and then we all recessed down the aisle in the order we would use the next day. Reverend Christopher needed to go home and look after his baby and toddler so his wife could enjoy what he said was a much-needed girls' night out. He'd already told Misty's and my parents that he would miss dessert and the campfire.

My friends and I walked back. The teenagers were still flinging the plastic toy around their circle. The girl who'd had trouble before was improving.

Being with my two best friends and their significant others, I missed Brent more than ever.

We joined Misty's, Samantha's, Scott's, and my parents around the campfire. Servers brought us plates of strawberry pie. We finished the delicious dessert, and then the caterers cleaned and tidied while my parents brought out instruments and we all sang. Well, I didn't, but I enjoyed listening to the others.

Kayla and Logan pulled into their campsite next door. Again, Kayla was driving a tan pickup truck and Logan was driving a small black sedan. They waved, but like my parents' other neighbors, they didn't join the party. People in that campground were happy to be sociable but also able to give others privacy and space.

Trailering the barbecues and smokers behind vans, the caterers left.

My mother jumped up. "Now we can have s'mores without offending the caterers."

Samantha, Misty, and I stood, planning to help gather everything.

My father headed toward the RV. "Sit down, Misty. For once, we'll let you act like an honored guest. But Scott can look after the fire. Just don't extinguish it, Scott."

Nothing besides firewood, not even a marshmallow, burst into flames.

I was sure that Scott didn't mind.

* * *

I arrived home too late to call Brent. And after Dep's bed-time.

However, in the morning, my sweet little cat kindly made certain that I woke up around our usual time.

I stretched and told her we had the next two days off. "Misty and Scott are getting married today." I didn't tell Dep that she'd be home alone again that afternoon and evening, or that I would see Brent and she probably wouldn't. I got up and moved my car out of the driveway long before I expected the day's work on the garage to begin.

Dep ate her breakfast in the kitchen, and I went out to make certain my walled garden was safe for her. The ply-wood covering the hole in the wall for the door to the garage was still firmly attached, and I let Dep outside while I ate. The sun rose, warming the morning, and turning the irises and lilacs into mini-gems sparkling with dew.

The builders arrived. Power tools whirred. Kayla's voice joined the good-natured shouts and laughter. I drank coffee and read. Dep pounced on bugs. Bees buzzed in apple blossoms.

After a lazy hour, I went inside and mixed up pizza dough and bread dough. They rose, and I whipped through house-cleaning and laundry.

I shaped the bread dough into rolls and set them aside to rise again. I grated cheeses, sliced pepperoni, and chopped tomatoes, peppers, and mushrooms. I dusted single-size card-board pizza rounds with cornmeal and stretched portions of pizza dough onto each one. I spread my homemade pizza sauce on the dough, sprinkled half the cheese over them, dis-tributed the pepperoni and veggies, and sprinkled the rest of the cheese on top. I slid the mini-pizzas into plastic freezer bags and lay them gently on shelves in the freezer. I would have baked one for my lunch, but the sauce and pepperoni probably contained more garlic than was polite to eat right before a wedding. I had a salad.

I baked the rolls until they were beginning to brown and then left them on a rack to cool.

Finally, I showered and put on a linen-cotton blend turquoise sleeveless dress and a pair of silver sandals. My curls dried in the sunshine during my short walk—by myself—to Deputy Donut. I popped into the kitchen and asked Tom, Jocelyn, and Olivia, "Are you folks okay without me?"

Jocelyn slapped the back of a hand against her forehead, knocking her Deputy Donut hat askew. "No! You'll have to stay." She glanced at my outfit. "You won't need to change into your bridesmaid's gown before the wedding. You look perfect. You can work here this afternoon, and then race out to the falls and go straight to the wedding in that dress and those shoes."

Olivia must have been afraid I would take Jocelyn seriously. "We're fine, Emily, honestly."

At his usual spot at the fryer, Tom grinned. "How are you surviving without fresh donuts?"

I pretended to stagger. "I might starve."

They all told me to have a wonderful time and to give their best wishes to Scott and Misty, both popular customers in Deputy Donut.

Outside, I unlocked the garage where we kept our delivery car. The 1950 Ford had been painted black with white doors to resemble a police cruiser. Our Deputy Donut logo was on the doors. The bullhorn-shaped siren above the windshield was actually a loudspeaker. We could broadcast a wailing siren if we wanted to, or music, or announcements. If that loudspeaker was all anyone saw, the car might pass as a vintage police car. However, it would have been hard to ignore the large donut lying flat on the roof with white plastic "frosting" dripping down the sides. The frosting was dotted with "sprinkles" that were actually lights. Not many people would be fooled into believing that huge plastic donut was a light bar like the ones on new police cars. The donut also didn't resemble the single flashing light that might have graced this car if it had ever actually been a police car.

I pulled the Ford out of the garage, locked the garage door, and fiddled with the controls for the lights in the big plastic donut. They could be programmed to flash all at once, twinkle, dance to music we played through the loudspeaker, and change color. I got out to double-check that I'd set the lights to white with random twinkling. I had.

Pleased with our slightly goofy delivery car, I climbed back into it and turned off the donut's lights. I drove home and parked as close to my house as I could.

Walking the rest of the way home past the builders' vehicles, I couldn't help smiling. Brent might already be at the campground.

Inside, I put the partially baked rolls into the freezer and made certain that Dep's food and water bowls were filled. I carried my gown in its garment bag to the donut car and then returned for my shoes and everything else I would need, including decorations for the car.

Dep meowed.

"Sorry, Dep, I'm leaving everything in your capable paws for a long afternoon and evening again."

She jumped up onto the living room windowsill, obviously ready to watch for my return.

I blew her a kiss, went out to the porch, and carefully turned the dead bolt. Arms full, I returned to the donut car.

As soon as I pulled up in front of Samantha and Hooligan's house, Samantha ran outside with her gown in its garment bag on a hanger and a duffel bag in her other hand. She'd highlighted her brown curls with touches of seafoam and silver. I opened the back door, and we laid her gown on the seat on top of mine. "We'll have to keep track," I joked. "The garment bags from Thrills and Frills are identical."

"And the dresses are probably almost exactly the same size."

"Probably. Would you like to drive?"

She opened those big brown eyes. "You'll let me drive your donut car?"

"Anyone who can drive ambulances can drive this."

"Okay, but I haven't driven a standard in a while. I might stall a few times."

I gave her the keys and got into the passenger side. She didn't have to adjust the seat—it was a bench—or the rear-view mirror. For safety, seat belts had been added to the old car. We fastened them. She turned the key, eased forward, and released the clutch. The car barely bucked. "This is fun!" She chose the scenic route. My heart rate sped as we neared Peabody Lane, but the narrow road looked entirely peaceful with no vehicles entering or exiting it.

Samantha pointed at the pile of brush in the driveway beyond Peabody Lane. "I wish people wouldn't do that. I could squeeze an ambulance past all that debris, but firetrucks might have problems. Maybe the driveway doesn't lead to anything."

"There's a house back among the trees. That entire driveway was blocked Sunday night when I wanted to turn around in it."

The rest of the way to the campground, Samantha crowed about the fun of driving the old car. She had no trouble shifting gears.

She backed into my parents' driveway, and we scooted out.

In jeans, plaid shirts, and sneakers, my parents greeted us with hugs. By the time they'd helped us carry everything we needed into their tiny bedroom, a troupe of small boys had abandoned their bikes in the dirt road and were peeking into the donut car's windows, stroking its glossy finish, and outdoing each other with where they would go in that car and how fast they would drive it.

The hairstylist and makeup artist arrived. At the picnic table in the natural light, the makeup artist started with Samantha.

My parents and I took the boxes of decorations from the donut car's trunk. To reach the top of the car, my mother and

I opened the doors and stood on the sills. My father didn't need the extra height. The three of us draped frothy white tulle over the plastic donut on the roof and tied it on with seafoam satin ribbons. We fastened a bow to the siren-shaped speaker and placed tulle wreaths embellished with ribbons and bows over the Deputy Donut logos on the car doors. We tucked plastic roses into ribbons.

Not hiding their disgust, the small fans of vintage police cars hopped onto their bikes and raced away.

My parents and I stood back to admire our work. Samantha clapped her hands and called out, "Perfect for a police officer bride." My parents went into the RV to dress for the wedding.

At the picnic table, the makeup artist did my face while the hairstylist arranged Samantha's curls, and then the hairstylist combed and styled my unruly curls. "There," she said when she finished. "I tried to keep you two from looking like twins, but we could quickly spray some silver into your hair, too, Emily."

Thinking about my parents' hair, I said, "Bits of silver will probably appear soon enough, all by themselves."

My parents came outside, my mother in a long, pale blue gown, and my father in a light gray summer suit. They both looked wonderful.

In jeans and a T-shirt, Misty arrived with her parents. Her mother's gown was teal. Her father wore a navy blue suit, a white shirt, a teal tie, and a proud smile.

Misty laughed aloud at the donut car's decorations. "I can't wait to ride in it!" She, Samantha, and I shared a smile. We knew about the secret wedding present that Misty had arranged for Scott. He was going to love it.

My mother offered limeade. "You can't say no. Walt squeezed limes all morning."

Samantha and I went into the RV and helped each other with gowns and shoes while Misty's face and hair were being done outside and Misty's and my parents toasted each other with limeade.

Misty brought her gown and shoes into the RV and smiled in the doorway of my parents' compact bedroom. "I'm glad none of us wanted poufy dresses. We couldn't have come here to put them on!"

Samantha agreed. "We had some great times in this campground with your folks, Emily."

I gave both of these friends high fives. "And we'll continue to."

We helped Misty into her gown, and then all three of us went outside. Misty and my mother went all teary-eyed. Open-mouthed, three small girls watched from across the road. The hairdresser lowered fragrant circlets of roses and lily of the valley on Misty's, Samantha's, and my hair and pinned them in place. Instead of a veil, long white ribbons trailed down Misty's back from her crown of flowers. Shorter seafoam ribbons were attached to Samantha's and mine.

Four slightly bigger girls joined the trio across the road.

I reached into the donut car, made my planned adjustments to the sound system, and started the white lights twinkling through the tulle wrapped around the donut on the roof. With an expression of glee, my father got into the driver's seat and pushed the bench seat back. Misty's parents helped her into the passenger side of the front seat. Trying not to nudge any part of our hair or gowns out of place, Samantha and I clambered into the back. My mother and Misty's passed our bouquets of roses and lily of the valley to us and closed the doors. At the rate the two mothers were going through tissues, they would need an entire box before the wedding began.

I knew that if Brent had showed up early, he would have joined us at my parents' site. He hadn't arrived.

My father started the car. "Here Comes the Bride" played softly, both inside and outside the car. Misty burst out laughing.

My father quickly said, "Don't blame me. That music must be Emily's doing."

I hoped that no one was napping in tents or trailers. I rolled down the window a tiny bit. The music outside the car was as gentle as I'd planned. I closed the window.

Waving at friends and neighbors, my father drove slowly along the campground's dirt roads. I turned and peered out the rear window. Misty's parents were behind us, bringing my mother. Samantha's parents were scheduled to arrive at the last minute.

Chapel-goers were encouraged to park on a vast grassy field between the chapel and the recreation hall where the reception was going to be. My father parked the donut car where we'd planned, beside the chapel. Beyond the car, the lawn sloped down gently toward the woods. Also as planned, my father left space for at least one car to park beside the donut car, but downhill from it. He turned off the engine. The lights stopped twinkling and the music ended.

Carefully, we all slid out of the tarted-up car. The organist inside the chapel must have been playing Handel's *Water Music*. It chimed from the speakers in the steeple. My parents headed into the chapel. Misty's parents joined Misty, Samantha, and me beside the donut car. Above us, the sky was brilliant blue with a few puffs of clouds that seemed too lazy to move.

Among the vehicles in the field, I saw Hooligan's and Samantha's car, which meant that Hooligan was here and probably already waiting near the altar.

Scott's parents' car was also there, which meant that Scott would also be inside the chapel.

Brent's black SUV should have been easy to spot among the smaller cars shimmering in the sunlight. I scanned the field and then checked again more slowly.

Brent's car wasn't there.

Chapter 14

Hearing a vehicle behind us, I turned around. Even though it wasn't Brent's SUV, I couldn't help a big smile.

The car was a bright red 1950 Ford with FIRE CHIEF written in gold on the door. Samantha's father eased it into the space where the donut car would hide it from Scott's view even after he came out of the chapel and stood in the reception line.

Samantha's mother opened the passenger window. "Is this where you want us to park, Misty?"

Misty beamed at the car and at Samantha's mother and beyond her at Samantha's father, happily in the driver's seat. "That's perfect. Scott still thinks Emily's donut car is our getaway car, and he won't catch a glimpse of this one until he heads for the driver's side of Emily's car."

Samantha's father saluted and turned off the engine.

"I think," Samantha commented delicately, "it's called a going-away car, not a getaway car."

"Going-away?" I repeated. "Wouldn't come-hither be more appropriate for a wedding?"

Samantha's parents got out of the bright red car, told us we all looked wonderful, and headed toward the chapel's front door.

The red Ford's curves gleamed in the sunlight. I told Misty, "It's beautiful!"

"I figured you'd like it."

"You only said you were giving Scott an old car. You didn't tell me it's almost identical to the donut car, but painted red, and no donut on top. It's even a Fordor like mine!" Both sedans had four doors. Ford had named their 1950 two-door sedan a Tudor.

Samantha waved her bouquet toward the almost-matching cars. "Misty's been having fun with her secrets."

I accused Samantha, "You knew and didn't tell me!"

"I only found out what model it was and how it was painted this morning after it was safely hidden in my parents' garage. Isn't it wonderful?"

"It is," I said. "Scott's going to love it. He still doesn't know?"

Misty's grin couldn't be wider. "No. I've told the photographer to station someone out here to capture the look on his face when I hand him the keys."

It was almost time for the wedding to start, and the best man hadn't arrived.

Brent wouldn't have been late unless something delayed him.

Our gowns had pockets just big enough for our phones and a tissue or two. Samantha's phone must have vibrated. She pulled it out of her pocket, shielded the screen from the sunshine, and told us, "Hooligan says that if Brent's here, send him in."

My phone vibrated with a message. I read it and breathed a sigh of relief. "He's turning in at the entrance to the campground."

Samantha texted that information to Hooligan and told us, "They'll wait." The organist's interpretation of "Ode to Joy" from Beethoven's *Ninth Symphony* sounded from the chapel speakers.

Two minutes later, Brent's SUV came into view, driving slowly past the grassy field where children were racing around. Brent obviously caught sight of the bright red 1950 fire chief car. With a questioning expression, he pointed at it. All three of us put fingers up to our lips. Smiling, he parked and got out. His black suit fit him perfectly and showed off his broad shoulders. Straightening his tie, he strode to us. "Sorry I'm late." He gazed at my face for a second. "I'd give you a kiss, but I don't want to mess up your makeup."

I held my hand out in as dainty a gesture as possible considering that I felt like laughing, dancing, and maybe even singing. He planted a big smooch on the back of my hand, hurried to the far side of the chapel, and disappeared around the corner.

To keep our heels from sinking into the lawn, Misty, Samantha, and I tiptoed to the chapel's front door. The organist inside began the transition from "Ode to Joy," and the outdoor speakers went silent. In the grassy field, the children giggled and shouted. Closer, blue jays teased one another.

Two of Scott's firefighters opened the chapel's front doors. Samantha walked into the entryway. The organist started Pachelbel's Canon, and Samantha started slowly up the aisle. I stayed just inside the door.

The chapel was packed. Both Misty and Scott had grown up in Fallingbrook and had spent most of their lives here. Scott had been three years ahead of Misty, Samantha, and me at Fallingbrook High. The congregation looked almost like they'd strayed from a high school reunion. Off-duty police officers were also in the crowd, along with volunteer firefighters and Misty's and Scott's friends from college. Members of Misty's and Scott's extended families attended, too.

The chapel smelled of roses and lilies of the valley. Many of the windows were open, letting in sun-kissed breezes. The organ nearly drowned out the blue jays' cheerful discussion.

At the front, Reverend Christopher stood looking down

the aisle. To his left and the congregation's right, Scott waited for his bride. Beside him, Brent stood perfectly composed as if he hadn't just dashed into the chapel. He'd even managed to button the middle button of his jacket. Beside him, Hooligan was also standing still and grinning as his own recent bride walked toward him between flower-bedecked pews. All four men, like the ushers, wore black suits and white shirts. Reverend Christopher's tie was black. Scott's, Hooligan's, Brent's, and the ushers' ties matched the seafoam color of Samantha's and my gowns.

As Samantha reached the front and turned to face the congregation, I started up the aisle. I smiled at the people in the pews, but the only person I really saw was Brent, steady, reliable, comforting, all of those things to other people plus loving when we were alone. Those gray eyes never wavered from me while a little smile played around his lips. I knew I should try to be in the moment, celebrating every second of Misty and Scott's wedding, but it was difficult to focus on anything besides wanting to throw myself into Brent's arms. And placing my feet where they were supposed to go at the stately pace without tripping over the long gown and possibly pitching myself into the laps of startled former classmates.

I reached the front and took my place beside Samantha.

The congregation rustled. The organist began Beethoven's *Moonlight Sonata.* Ushers opened both front doors, and Misty entered with her parents.

All brides are beautiful, but Misty was almost ethereal in the 1930s-inspired satin gown and the Nordic crown of flowers. Her romantic side totally eclipsed the no-nonsense police officer personality. That afternoon, she was Misty, and she was misty.

Her parents were also misty, but obviously fiercely proud. Eyes shining, they slipped into the pew with Samantha's and my parents. My mother and Samantha's dabbed at their faces with tissues.

Misty and Scott faced Reverend Christopher and joined hands.

Watching them and listening to Reverend Cristopher, I started thinking about Dep and hoping she was okay and wouldn't miss me too much during what would seem, to her, a very long afternoon and evening.

And then, in all the beauty, romance, and love of Misty and Scott's wedding ceremony, memories of finding Pamela underneath the contents of Summer's parents' closet intruded.

I reminded myself to pay attention to the ceremony, and the next thing I knew, Misty and Scott were wife and husband, the organist was playing "Ode to Joy" again, and Misty was walking down the aisle with Scott. Even from the back, they looked perfect together.

Samantha recessed down the aisle with Hooligan, and I placed my hand on Brent's arm and walked with the best man.

We formed a reception line in the sunshine outside the chapel. From where I stood between Hooligan and Brent, I couldn't see the red fire chief car hidden behind the donut car and its tulle-frothed donut topknot. I didn't think that Scott had caught a glimpse of the red 1950 Ford.

Most of our Fallingbrook High classmates had no reason to know a Fallingbrook detective. Standing next to him, I introduced him to them simply as "our friend, Brent."

One of our classmates shielded her mouth from his view and mouthed *Wow* at me. I smiled so much my face hurt.

After the reception line, guests could wander around while the photographer took pictures of the wedding party. We trooped back into the chapel for formal shots and then came back outside.

As far as Scott knew, he was going to drive the donut car, Misty would ride with him, and the rest of us would pile into other cars for the short drive to the base of the falls for more pictures.

Arm in arm, Misty and Scott headed toward the donut car. In our strappy heels, Samantha and I nearly galloped after them, our phones up, ready to capture the moment. With a long-lensed camera on a tripod, a photographer lurked near the edge of the woods.

We were near the trunk of the donut car when Scott opened its front passenger door for Misty.

Her voice rang out, "I'm not riding in that!"

Poor Scott. For a second, he looked appalled, then he noticed Samantha and me, now joined by Hooligan and Brent, all of us aiming our phones at him. Scott quirked an eyebrow and looked down at Misty. She led him toward the back of the donut car.

We scurried to the far side of the fire chief car and stopped where we wouldn't be in the way of the photographer near the trees.

Misty took Scott around the back of the donut car and pointed. "Let's go in that."

Scott's smile became almost wider than his face. "Okay!"

Samantha's father handed Misty a thick, cream-colored envelope with Scott's name in calligraphy on the front. She held it out toward Scott. "Open it."

He removed a card. A set of keys fell out onto the grass. He picked them up, read the card, blushed, and swept Misty into his arms. "For me?" He patted the brilliant red roof. "This is mine?"

"Yes. Let's go for a ride."

He stared at the car in something like wonder, let out a whoop, and then gave Misty another prolonged kiss. Finally, he ushered her into the passenger seat of his "getaway" car and slid into the driver's seat. The engine started with a throaty purr. Scott's smile was bigger than ever.

Brent slung an arm around me and pulled me close to his side. "Does this mean that we get to ride in your donut car?"

"Clever detecting, Detective Fyne. You and I and Samantha and Hooligan are now scheduled to ride in it. Would you like to drive?"

"No, thanks. I was behind the wheel for hours today. A truck rolled and dumped hundreds of cases of beer."

I offered Hooligan the donut car's keys. "Samantha already drove it today."

Hooligan and Samantha sat in front. Using the rear seat's middle belt, I cuddled up to Brent. "Mmm," I said. "This is nice. And it's okay if you mess up my makeup."

His face came closer. "We're going to be in more pictures."

"I don't care."

Neither, it seemed, did he.

Chapter 15

Hooligan drove Samantha, Brent, and me to the base of the Fallingbrook Falls and parked beside the bright red 1950 fire chief car. Brent and I disentangled ourselves and scooted out into the fresh air.

In our teens, Misty, Samantha, and I had entertained ourselves exploring the falls, the woods around them, and the banks of the river above them. In those days, we'd worn sneakers. Now, we minced in our heels to the pool's stony bank. Roaring water tumbled off the rocky lip high above us and splashed into the pool, churning the water into mist.

Unable to hear the photographer and one another except when we yelled, we posed for traditional, romantic wedding party photos with the background of water falling in veil-like sheets between rocky cliffs dotted with saplings and leafy green ferns.

And then we posed with the two 1950 Fords. Some of these photos would not be traditional or particularly romantic. Comfortable together, we couldn't help clowning around. Misty and Scott seemed unable to stop smiling, and the rest of us were as happy. Brent and I kept brushing against each other and trading laughing, affectionate glances.

When it was time to return to the sunny meadow between

the chapel and the recreation hall, Brent and I again used Hooligan's services as a chauffeur while we snuggled together in the rear seat.

While we'd been posing for photos, Scott's firefighters had removed the decorations from the chapel and arranged them inside the recreation hall. The flowers, bows, and ribbons contrasted with the rough-sawn planks of the hall's interior. Rustic-chic, Misty called it.

White tablecloths, bouquets of flowers, sparkling glassware, dishes, and cutlery added to the chic. Misty, Scott, Samantha, Hooligan, Brent, and I had enjoyed what we'd fondly referred to as "planning parties." Sometimes, there had been more partying than planning, but the end result of our design was stunning.

Misty, Samantha, and I tucked our bouquets into water-filled vases at the head table on a raised dais. Brent's place card was beside mine. While we ate, the floor-length tablecloth kept people in the lower section of the room from noticing how often my knee touched Brent's. The delicious meal was prepared by the previous night's caterers.

We kept our speeches short, a combination of teasing and praising Misty and Scott. Several people mentioned the hobby that Scott and his firefighters shared, restoring pedal cars and giving them to kids who might not have had many toys. Misty's wedding gift to Scott had been perfect—a grown-up, restored car painted bright red.

The dance band was made up of first responders, many of whom had been part of a garage band when we were at Fallingbrook High. Although none of the band members had become professional musicians, they were good. I danced with Scott, with my father, with Misty's, Samantha's, and Scott's fathers, with Hooligan, and with classmates from Fallingbrook High. Whenever the band played slow, romantic tunes, I danced with Brent.

I knew I should have forgotten all about Pamela Firston

and the investigation into her death, but I couldn't. I asked Brent, "Did you see a check made out to Pamela Firston when you were at the murder scene?"

He loosened his grip on me enough to look down into my face. "Yes. Why?"

"Chief Agnew said there wasn't one."

"Hmm." He guided me around another couple.

"He implied that you or one of the other investigators might have taken it. Hooligan says that he, his partner, and you were in the larger bedroom when Agnew arrived in the cabin, and although you called, Agnew didn't come in right away."

"That's right."

"Hooligan wondered if someone had accidentally slid the check underneath the book, and that's why Agnew didn't see it."

"Hooligan, Tyler, and I were the only ones there before Agnew arrived, and none of us touched that check."

"Agnew must have hidden or discarded that check. Maybe he wants to accuse one of you three of taking something from a crime scene."

Brent pulled me closer. "We can look after ourselves."

I hoped so, but I couldn't help wondering what Agnew was up to. He was already Fallingbrook's police chief, so if he wanted a more powerful position, he would have to move to a larger community. Did he want to force officers like Brent and Hooligan out of his department? That would not make sense. Good detectives and police officers could only bolster his reputation. Maybe he didn't want to be compared to them.

I told Brent, "There's something else. Did you see a pink envelope at the scene, addressed to me?"

"No, but Agnew stayed in the cabin after he sent the rest of us out."

I described the photo and the letter. "Agnew seems to think that the envelope proves that Pamela and I had a connection. We didn't, other than she'd been in Deputy Donut that afternoon and the one before, and she gave Dep a toy donut. I'm afraid Agnew wants to believe that I murdered her. I don't have an alibi for between when I left work and when I called 911."

"I know you're innocent."

"Thanks, but you as a witness for my character might not help. But on the bright, but not very bright, side, Agnew also suspects Summer Peabody-Smith because the cabin wasn't broken into, and Summer has keys to it. She has no alibi, either."

"Firston might not have locked herself into the cabin after she got home that afternoon, or maybe she locked it, and then unlocked it to let someone in. Maybe it was someone she knew, or maybe she only thought she recognized someone. Or she was too trusting."

I described what Summer had said about Pamela's ex who supposedly knew all about medicines, and then I explained why I thought the sales rep I'd told Brent about over the phone early Monday morning was Pamela's ex. "Summer and I both told Chief Agnew about him, but Agnew didn't seem interested."

Brent grinned down at me. "Sometimes we just pretend."

The song ended, and the toastmaster announced that it was time for all of the single women to come to the front, and Misty would toss the bouquet. "Whoever catches it will be the bride at the next wedding."

Naturally, Misty made certain that I was in the prime position to catch the bouquet, although I had lots of competition, including from children of family members and classmates, whose weddings, we hoped, wouldn't be for years. Misty looked at me, turned around, and tossed the bouquet behind her. It came straight toward me. I reached up.

A girl who looked about twelve but was, not surprisingly, taller than I was, reached over my head and grabbed the bouquet. Squealing with pleasure, she dashed to her parents. The mother looked dismayed. I gave her a reassuring smile. The girl would not be under nearly as much pressure as I would have been if I'd caught that bouquet, and I didn't want anyone pressuring Brent, either. We were notorious for taking our time.

My father gave me the donut car's keys. "We took off the decorations and put them in the trunk with your change of clothes."

"Do you need a ride?"

"We'll walk. There's a full moon tonight."

"That's why Misty and Scott chose this date." I kissed him and my mother. "Have a good night, and thank you for everything."

They went off to say goodbye to Misty and Scott, and Brent and I returned to the dance floor.

Too soon, the music ended and the lights in the hall brightened. We all went outside. The full moon painted silver edges around puffy clouds. Brent put his arm around me. "Warm enough?"

I nestled closer. "Not quite." Actually, it was a lovely evening. The air felt soft against my skin. Waving, Scott and Misty got into their fire chief car. The full moon reflected off the red roof. The single light on top of the car swooped around three times, sending streaks of scarlet through the woods, and then they were gone.

Brent walked me to the donut car and opened the driver's door for me. "I'm heading back to Green Bay."

Gown, heels, and all, I slid in behind the wheel. "It's late."

He leaned down, brushed a ribbon from my flower crown off my face, and kissed my forehead. "If I postpone the drive, I'll risk getting into another traffic jam and miss my morning classes."

I touched his cheek with the palm of one hand. "Take care."

"You, too." He kissed my hand, tucked it inside the car, and closed my door. Seconds later, he pulled up behind me. I started down the winding campground road. He followed me along the shorter route to town until we came to the intersection leading to the road that would take him to the main highway heading south. He flashed his lights and turned.

Already missing him, I kept going. "Well, Dep," I muttered to myself in the lonely darkness of the vintage car, "at least we'll have each other."

I parked on the street behind my own car, left the decorations inside the trunk, and carried my change of clothes and shoes into the house. The timer had already turned off the light in the living room.

Blinking sleepily, Dep plunked herself at my feet and meowed.

"Sorry for being away so long, but I had a wonderful time, and you would not have enjoyed it."

"Merrow."

She obviously expected me to pick her up, but I couldn't risk little kitty claws coming into contact with the chiffon and satin of my gown. She plodded upstairs behind me. I carefully removed my circlet of flowers, my gown, and my makeup. Dep and I went to bed.

I was dancing, warm in Brent's arms. The band was playing. The drummer pounded.

SCREECH!

Screech?

My heart took over for the drums. My eyes opened, searching the darkness. I was warm, but not in Brent's arms, and not dancing. I was in bed at home, alone except for Dep at my feet.

And something had screeched like no instrument in a dance band ever should have.

Chapter 16

Willing myself to meander back into the dream, back to dancing with Brent, I closed my eyes. I told myself I hadn't heard a screech or even a loud creaking noise.

Scrape.

The noise was so slight that I probably wouldn't have heard it if I'd still been asleep. I lifted my head. A slight brightening edged the bedroom curtain in the east window, but it was only about three. Dawn was an hour away.

Scrape.

I could just make out Dep at the foot of the bed. Instead of being curled up as usual at this time of night, she was sitting straight and staring toward the north window, the one overlooking the walled garden behind the house.

Did a stripe of light move across the ceiling? My breath caught in my throat. I tried to focus on the moving light.

It was gone.

Could a car have driven past on the street and cast a beam in a strange way, maybe from a headlight pointing up instead of ahead? Both of my bedroom windows were open, and I hadn't heard a car.

Scrape. Now I was sure the noise was coming from inside my walled garden.

My heart started its drumming again. Had a raccoon managed to scale the wall and invade our previously secure little paradise? I sat up. A drift of air ruffled the curtains.

I wasn't likely to sleep again until I figured out what I'd been hearing.

Thump.

That noise came from behind the house, too.

Dep jumped off the bed and onto the back windowsill. She parted the curtains and slithered through the gap between them. The gap closed behind her. She made a sound like a kitty growl.

As if I hadn't been groggily wishing, only moments ago, to fall asleep again, I flapped the duvet off, rubbed at my eyes, and padded barefoot to the window. I inched one of the curtains back. Dep stood, rubbed against my forearm, and purred.

The full moon was still high enough to turn most of my yard into an etching of gray and charcoal, with the peak of the roof casting a darker triangular shadow near the house. High in the oak tree, young leaves rustled.

Nothing was out there. No marauding raccoons or cats. Dep and I could go back to bed.

Creak.

It was a faint imitation of the original screech. My waking mind must have magnified a slight *creak* into a full-blown *screech*.

And the scrapes and the thump? They could all be explained by—I didn't know what. Maybe by my staying up hours later than usual and then dreaming of the evening's fun?

But Dep had growled, something she seldom did.

An engine started. It wasn't close. It was probably farther down the block, past my garage, or even on the next block. I seldom needed to go anywhere at three in the morning, but neighbors could be outside that early. Maybe a family was leaving for their summer vacation. The engine sounds dwindled, and then all was quiet except for the eerie hooting of an owl and an answer from farther away.

From this window, I could see all of my walled yard except the area behind the sunroom. The patio and that triangle of the yard in the shadow of the roof were too dark for me to see much. The open patio umbrella was a paler circle in that triangle.

I was the widow of one detective, the daughter-in-law of another, and the girlfriend of a third one. They would have gone outside and investigated.

I was the only one here.

I put on my slippers and robe and slid my phone into the robe's pocket. Dep tiptoed downstairs with me. The soft terrycloth robe warmed me against some of the morning chill. I tied the belt tighter.

I didn't turn on lights. Moonlight illuminated the street, the front yard, and the porch steps, and cast a glow through the living room. I eased into the dining room and through the kitchen to the sunroom where windows on all three sides overlooked my yard and my shadowed patio.

I turned on outdoor lights. They flooded my entire walled garden.

No one was there.

Keeping Dep inside, I opened the back door. The screen door's hinges squeaked. I was so used to the sound that until then, I barely noticed it. Could those squeaking hinges have awakened me? I closed and opened the screen door again. Unable to cause those hinges to make sounds anything like what I'd heard from upstairs in my bedroom, I went out onto the patio, and then around the sunroom to the once-solid brick wall where plywood had been fastened over the new opening to keep Dep in and intruders out.

The plywood had been replaced by the steel-clad door I'd requested. It was closed. I'd ordered a dead bolt that required a key no matter which side you were on. I didn't have a key. I reached out a tentative hand. The knob turned.

The door had not been locked.

Great. Until the contractor gave me the key or finished enclosing the garage, anyone could come and go from my yard. By having a hole cut in the wall, I had betrayed Alec's trust that Dep and I would stay safe behind high walls.

I pulled the door slowly toward me.

SCREECH.

I jumped, but opened the door the rest of the way.

Moonlight filtered between the garage's rafters and studs and lit the concrete floor beside the big empty square where the overhead door was to be installed.

Shadows moved and jittered in the light from my phone, but no one, not even a cat or a raccoon, was inside the garage among the ladders chained to the stands of large power tools.

I stepped over the doorsill into the garage and ran my beam over the yellow brick wall nearest the unlocked door. The second people-sized door, the one leading to the pathways to the front of my house, had also been installed. It was locked, for all the good locking it did when the front of the garage was open. The same key was supposed to turn the dead bolts on both of the people-sized doors.

At about shoulder height, short horizontal two-by-fours were attached to the vertical studs, strengthening the framework and resembling little shelves.

On one of them between the door and the window opening, brass gleamed.

A shiny new set of keys.

I picked them up and returned to my walled garden. As if I could shut out imaginary intruders as well as real ones, I quickly shoved the door shut. It made a creak like the one I'd heard more faintly from upstairs. I opened it slowly. *Screech.* I fanned it back and forth at different speeds. The screech was loudest and most prolonged the more slowly I moved the door.

I locked it with the key, and then tried the knob. The dead bolt held. My yard was once again safe from intruders.

I stood for a second in my yard, looking at the lawn. By inadvertently knocking dew off the grass, I'd made a visible pathway from the back door.

I wasn't the only one.

Someone had circled part of my yard, passing the flowerbeds on the east side in a sort of scalloped pattern like they were stopping to smell certain flowers before returning to the new door in the wall.

Whoever it was had left, and I had locked the door.

I went inside, turned off the outdoor lights, and climbed up to my bedroom.

I took off my wet slippers. Although Dep obligingly snuggled next to my duvet-covered cold feet, I didn't fall asleep right away.

Why had someone come into my yard? Was it simply because for over a hundred years the yard had been inaccessible, and now someone wanted to take advantage of the door in the wall to tour my garden in the moonlight?

Whoever it was had probably been disappointed. It might have been a secret garden, but it didn't harbor secrets.

I woke again to hammers pounding, power tools whirring, and full daylight. I'd managed to sleep until eight, and the builders had obviously started working on my garage.

And I had another day off.

I yawned, stretched, and checked my phone. Shortly after four, Brent had texted that he had arrived safely at his hotel and was planning to catch a few hours of sleep before his first class.

I showered and dressed in a denim skirt, white eyelet blouse, and sandals. I fed Dep and ate my own breakfast. I slid one of the new brass keys onto the keychain I always carried and stored the other one with my stash of spare keys. Belatedly, I became anxious about the donut car, which I'd parked on the street. We seldom left it outside and unattended. Now was a little late to worry about it. . . .

To my relief, it was fine. I removed the box of decorations that my parents had packed, took it inside, and put it in the basement that Alec and I had planned to finish, someday. And maybe I would, someday.

When I headed for the front door again, Dep looked hopefully toward the closet where I kept her halter and leash. "Sorry," I told her, "I'm going without you this morning. But this time, I won't be long."

I drove the donut car to Deputy Donut and backed it into its garage. I went into our café to say hello to Tom, Jocelyn, and Olivia.

They didn't need any help from me, but they wanted to hear about the wedding. I showed them the pictures I'd snapped with my phone, including photos of Misty's surprise gift to Scott.

Tom's eyes widened. "What this town needs is an entire fleet of fifties cars."

We all agreed that would be fun. Jocelyn clutched at her heart. "Think of the parades!"

Olivia added, "Especially if some of the old cars are convertibles!"

The Knitpickers called me to their table. They adored Scott and had been helping Misty learn to knit. They wanted to hear about the wedding. I poured myself a mug of the day's special coffee, a flavorful and almost nut-flavored medium roast from Peru, and sipped it while I answered their questions and showed them the photos. Cheryl patted her white curls and sighed. "You're all so young and beautiful."

Priscilla demanded, "Where's Dep, Emily? Didn't she attend the wedding as a flower girl or something?"

Imagining Dep sitting quietly in the chapel, I nearly choked on my coffee. "No."

Priscilla's eyes gleamed. "Did you bring her with you today?"

"I left her at home. We have the day off."

The often-serious Priscilla became even more impish. "Monster! You'd better go keep her company."

I laughed. "I think I'm being dismissed." I took my mug to the kitchen, but I couldn't leave the dining room without greeting our other customers, especially the retired men who would never have forgiven me if I'd spent time with only the Knitpickers and not them.

Relaxing in the shop as if I were a customer gave me a new appreciation for how welcoming and comfortable Deputy Donut was. Jocelyn had fit in with the customers right away, but Olivia, who was older, had been shy at first. Now she was self-confident and outgoing, and she was having fun talking to customers and watching their faces when they bit into our pastries and tasted our beverages.

However, Priscilla was right. Dep was probably miffed. As if I were a customer, I left via the front door, but I chatted to diners on our patio before heading south on Wisconsin Street.

It was another glorious June day. On Maple, the fragrances of privet and mock orange were almost overwhelming.

I started up the walk to my house. Kayla was fastening sheathing to the side of the garage. The contractor lifted a hand for me to wait. He strode to me. "The overhead door hasn't arrived, but your other doors came, so we installed them to keep your yard private." He turned and waved toward the garage. "Like them?"

"Very much. Thank you."

I couldn't figure out how to tell him in a nice way that I wished he had locked the door into my yard, but he went on talking. "Did you find your keys?"

"Yes, I—"

He pointed to my front porch. "I hoped you would. You weren't home, so I locked both of the doors and put the keys in your mailbox. I figured you'd find them when you got home."

Chapter 17

The contractor beamed at me, proud of his work and proud of locking the garage's two entry doors and of placing the keys where he thought I would find them.

But that wasn't where I'd found them. They'd been inside the garage. Confused, I asked, "Did you put the keys in the mailbox yourself? Or did you ask someone else to?"

"I did it personally."

"Thank you." My smile felt brittle, but confessing that I hadn't checked my mailbox before someone else did wasn't going to help anything. I also didn't want to appear to scold him for not putting those keys directly into my hand. He might discover that other commitments would delay finishing my garage. I added, "The garage is looking good. I see you hired Kayla."

"Yes, thanks to you, and, I gather, your parents, for sending her to me. She's skilled, and she works hard. I hope to keep her on for other projects." He gave me a friendly nod and headed back to the garage.

On the porch, I checked my mailbox. It was empty. People no longer wrote letters like they did back in Hattie's day. If Pamela had mailed the letter that she must have addressed to me, it could be arriving about now, after her death. That would have been weird, but thinking of the possibility made me wonder if she had mailed anything to me before she died. I would keep checking, probably long after I could logically expect anything to appear from her.

Dep greeted me in the living room and led me through the house to the sunroom door leading to the patio. "Great minds," I told her, "but wait. You can't come out until I make certain that the new door in the wall is closed." Even though it was daylight and I was wide awake, I couldn't help jumping a little when the hinges on the back screen door squeaked.

I strode to the door in the brick wall. Workers were clambering over the garage roof, but the door was still locked. I let Dep outside.

No one appeared to have tampered with the back door and windows. Whoever I'd heard in my yard must not have tried to break into the house.

I could explain the screech that had awakened me and the squeak a few minutes afterward. The hinges on the new door did that, screeching when the door was moved cautiously but merely creaking when someone moved the door quickly.

What had caused the scraping sounds and the *thump* like someone dropping a heavy object on the ground?

Above the sound of the builders working on my garage, I heard an excited kitty chirp. I turned around.

Dep batted a scrap of paper into the air.

"What's that, Dep?" My voice was almost as squeaky as unoiled door hinges.

She subdued the piece of paper with one paw. The scrap was obviously already torn. Hoping that Dep wouldn't shred it completely, I pretended I wasn't interested in it and strolled casually toward her.

She jumped up, left the paper behind, and ran underneath a peony plant, its buds still coiled in tight spheres.

Crouching, her pupils huge, Dep peered out at me.

I picked up the piece of paper. It was thick, like from an

old book, and varying shades of ivory and ecru. I set it on my patio table underneath the umbrella. With the afternoon sun no longer glaring on the paper, I recognized that it was part of an old map of a neighborhood.

I could barely make out the thin, old-fashioned, and originally hand-printed letters.

Owners of properties were printed diagonally inside the outlines of the lots they owned. *Harriet Renniegrove* had been printed across one lot. The square north of that one was marked *Esther Renniegrove*. The "Waln" of Esther's Walnut Street showed, and the name of my street, Maple, ran neatly along where the sidewalk was now.

My street number, 1212, was circled. It took some refocusing, but I determined that the number and the circle were not part of the original map. They had been added, in pencil. Lightly. Maybe years ago, or maybe recently.

Fingering the thick scrap of paper, I studied the top of the yellow brick wall surrounding my yard. The piece of paper felt too heavy for anything weaker than gale-force winds to lift it over the wall. Possibly, it had risen on an updraft of hot smoke if a neighbor had been burning papers. I smelled only flowers and grass. I didn't see char marks on the scrap, and it wasn't damp or dirty.

Had this morning's prowler brought it into my yard?

Dep had moved from the peonies to the forsythia, where green leaves had replaced the yellow sunburst of blooms from only days ago. Dep had her back to me. I anchored the piece of map with my phone on the table and walked across the grass toward her. "Where did you get that scrap of paper, Dep?"

She didn't answer, except to switch her tail while staring at something underneath the forsythia.

I stooped, and then I noticed something I should have already seen.

There were holes in my flower borders.

The holes had not been there the day before. I asked, "Dep, did you do all this digging?"

She backed out from under drooping branches and gave me a disdainful look as if to remind me that she always filled the holes she dug. Besides, these new holes were almost straight-sided, as if made by a trowel, not kitty paws.

"Mrrrp." Tail up, Dep padded underneath the forsythia again. She crouched, wriggled her rear end, and pounced. She almost never caught anything, but I winced anyway, half expecting her to crawl out from underneath the bush with a protesting June bug in her mouth.

She didn't come out.

I parted the branches and peeked at her. Rump still raised, she toyed with something that looked like a stone. "A stone, Dep?" I asked her. "Are you so lacking in toys that you have to lower yourself to playing with stones?"

As if I'd requested a better look, she backed away from the stone.

I glanced over my shoulder. The corner of the house hid the garage from me. No one on the garage roof would be able to see my next, rather undignified move. On all fours, I crawled toward the forsythia's trunk.

The stone was dark, greenish-gray, round on top, and splotched with dirt. It was the size and shape of one of our larger, puffy raised donuts, complete with a hole in the middle. Unlike the hole of a donut, though, this one was smooth inside. I blew at the stone and dislodged bits of dirt. "What did you find, Dep? This looks like someone carved it." Despite my gardening through the years, I'd never found anything remotely like a carved stone.

And this one had been near one of the new holes. Walking along the garden's edge, I counted them. Four, all near where someone had knocked dew off the grass earlier that morning. A person—thinking back, the trail in the grass appeared to have been made by only one person—must have made that scalloped path by swerving several times to the bare earth border to dig.

Now I was certain that a prowler had been in my yard the night before. He or she had opened my mailbox and removed the new keys to my garage's back door and then had done some digging. Maybe he or she had dropped the map with my address circled on it. And the thump I'd heard could have been this heavy stone donut landing on the ground. And then they'd left the door unlocked and deposited the keys where I could easily find them in the garage.

Why?

None of it seemed like I needed to involve the police, especially since I hadn't called them when I heard the noises. I wouldn't report the incident now, either. I could tell Brent about it the next time I talked to him.

Taking Dep, the scrap of paper, and the peculiar stone with me, I went inside. I put the map segment and the carved stone on the living room hearth. The stone donut was like a sculpture representing Tom's and my shop.

In the kitchen, I made a batch of the tomato, onion, garlic, and ginger sauce that I used as a base for many Indian recipes. I froze most of the sauce in single portions but reserved a cup of it. I made a salad, started cooking enough rice for one person, and cut a boneless, skinless chicken breast into one-inch cubes. I sautéed the chicken pieces in clarified butter until the chicken was almost cooked through, and then I added the sauce plus additional spices and salt. The chicken finished cooking in the sauce. I added a pinch of dried fenugreek leaves and stirred until they softened slightly. I spooned the chicken and its sauce over the rice and drizzled cream over it all in a pretty pattern.

With Dep nearby, probably investigating the strange holes in our garden, I ate dinner at the patio table. The butter chicken was just spicy enough, delicious Indian comfort food. I didn't need or want dessert. I took the dishes inside, cleaned up the kitchen, and went outside again with Dep.

The construction noises ended. People shouted their good-byes. Truck doors slammed.

All was quiet except for an insistent cardinal chirping high in the oak tree and children laughing on the next block. Dep and I were alone again in our own private garden. I stretched out with a book on a chaise longue.

Through my home's open windows, I heard my doorbell.

Chapter 18

❧

Enjoying my lazy solitude, I was tempted not to answer.

I had to know who was at my door.

I closed the book and clambered off the chaise longue. "C'mon, Dep."

She stopped in the sunroom and poked her nose underneath the love seat. I continued to the living room.

I checked the peephole in the front door. The man who had rung my doorbell must have given up. He was heading down the porch steps. After a second, I recognized my new neighbor. This time, he was wearing jeans, a red plaid shirt, running shoes, and no socks.

I opened the door. "Hi!"

He turned to face me, came back onto the porch, and pointed with one thumb over his shoulder. "I just moved in across the street. Daniel Suthlow." The skin on his face was pale and freckled. He probably hated blushing so easily, which, along with the thick, sandy-blond hair made him look about fifteen.

I gave him a friendly smile. "Emily Westhill. Welcome to the neighborhood."

"Thank you. I just got off work, and I hoped you were home." His gaze drifted away from me, not like someone making up stories, but like a shy introvert. Bracing his shoulders, he looked into my eyes again, and his frown made him look closer to what I suspected was his actual age, probably mid twenties. "There was unusual activity around your house last night."

Shocked but not surprised, I asked, "What?" Dep attempted to sneak past my feet and run out onto the porch. "Just a second." I made certain she stayed inside, shut the door, and gestured to the two white wicker armchairs flanking a glass-topped wicker table. "Have a seat."

Daniel hesitated. "Am I interrupting? I could come back later."

"You're not interrupting. Can I get you a cup of coffee or something?"

"I'm fine." As if he feared that the puffy yellow and white cushions might swallow him, he edged down onto one of the chairs.

I sat in the other. "What do you mean, 'unusual activity'?"

"Last night, a big burly man came up onto your porch and went to your front door. I don't know if he knocked or rang the bell, but no one answered. You had lights on, both downstairs and upstairs, and your porch light was on."

By the time I'd arrived home around two, the timer had switched off all of my lights. Daniel had seen this man earlier than the prowler I'd heard in my walled garden at three in the morning. I didn't know which might be worse—two prowlers, or only one who was brazen enough to come twice during one night. I asked, probably too abruptly, "What time was this?"

"A little after ten. It stays light late at this time of year, and it was fully dark." Daniel pointed over his shoulder at my living room window. "He walked over here, and I think he peered through your window for a few seconds. Then he went back to your front door and waited."

Despite the warm June evening, I was getting chills. "How long?"

"A minute or two. He went down your porch steps, but he was turning his head, looking around like he was checking to see if anyone was nearby. That made me even more suspicious, so I kept watching. He went into your partly built garage but came out almost immediately. Then he stared at that side of your house for a few seconds as if checking for more lights or anyone at your windows. I thought he might leave, but he came back up here onto your porch. He opened your mailbox and looked inside, and I'm sure he put his hand into it. Then he turned around and hurried back into your garage, and then there was a screeching noise, and I didn't see him for about ten minutes. I kept watching. I heard another screech, and then he came out of your garage. He kind of hunched his head down between his shoulders and walked up the street." Daniel pointed east.

"Did you see a vehicle?"

"No. I waited. Nothing passed. I wondered if I should call the police, but I thought maybe he was your father or an uncle or someone you'd asked to come and do something for you."

"My father was with me. We were at a wedding. I got home around two. Maybe the man you saw was the contractor who's building my garage. He's big and burly." I should have asked the contractor when he put those keys into my mailbox. Coming back after ten at night seemed odd, but maybe he'd forgotten earlier.

Daniel gazed toward his pickup truck in the driveway across the street. "I heard another screeching noise around three. Did you make it?" Blushing again, he resembled an earnest little boy. "Not with your voice, a screech like metal against metal."

I laughed. "If you ever heard me sing, you might think I did it with my voice. I didn't, but I heard it, too."

"It woke me up. I came outside. The only thing I saw that might have been out of place was a light-colored pickup truck parked beside the fire hydrant on the next block, like some-one was in the truck or planned to move it soon. I went back to bed. The pickup was gone when I left for work this morn-ing, which doesn't prove anything."

"Most of the people working on my garage drive pickup trucks. A couple of gray ones, a tan one, and the others black. The contractor's is white."

"I couldn't say for sure what color it was, and I wouldn't recognize your workers' vehicles. I usually leave in the morn-ings before they arrive and . . ." He bit his lip and stared toward one of the baskets of yellow and purple pansies at-tached to my porch railing. He looked back at me. ". . . and this time of year with it being light so late, I come home after they leave." I wondered why color climbed from his neck to his cheeks and slightly furrowed forehead. "It was probably a coincidence. There are lots of pickups in this part of Wis-consin, and not all of them are as recognizable as the one I drive." His blush became fiercer. Did he know I might have seen his truck near the murder scene? I hadn't seen the driver, but he could have thought that I did—and recognized him.

I prompted, "Your company probably has more than one truck like that."

The blush receded. "Several. Don't tell them, but I'm only working for them long enough to save up and go to college to learn more about history."

"'History' covers a lot."

His frown disappeared. "And more every second!"

"Do you have a particular time period in mind? Choosing between so many must be hard."

"My biggest interest is Victorian history, specifically Wis-consin in the late 1800s. This perfectly kept Victorian neigh-borhood intrigues me, and almost the first thing I became curious about after I was lucky enough to rent my place and move in was the high wall on your property and the one be-hind it on Walnut. Your house has an interesting story."

I smiled, guessing what was coming next, but wanting to hear what Daniel had learned.

He knew about the two sisters and correctly told me their names. He corroborated what my father had thought, that Hattie and Esther were originally from Cleveland. Daniel added, "The sisters were going to live together, but they had a fight and built identical houses back to back, separated by that wall."

"Do you know what they fought about?"

He rested his hands on his knees. "I wish I did. Maybe it had something to do with their father's death. Renniegrove is an unusual name, so I was easily able to find information about their father, Ernest Renniegrove. He was mostly known for his unusual death."

This was news to me. I asked with genuine interest, "How did he die?"

"He fell off a cliff in Newfoundland."

I blinked. "Newfoundland?"

I thought I saw a glint of pleased pride at surprising me. "Yes, in 1887. Newfoundland was still a British colony."

I explained that my late husband and I had read Harriet's obituary. "I remember that she was born in 1867, so she was only twenty-two when her house was finished."

"Esther was even younger. She was born in 1869. Their mother died that year."

"Young, unmarried women building homes and living alone was unusual for those days, wasn't it?"

"I think so. I'm guessing they used their inheritance after their father's death to build the houses, but neither Harriet nor Esther married or had children, and the inheritance must not have been enough to live on. Harriet taught school, and Esther was a secretary for a mining company."

"Do you know what their father was doing in Newfoundland?"

"Not specifically, but he was an archaeologist, so maybe he traveled a lot."

"Archaeologist! Wait here. My cat found a couple of things in my yard."

I brought out the piece of map and the stone that resembled a raised donut. Still standing, I held them where Daniel could see them.

Daniel took one look at the stone in my hand and stood up. "That looks like a . . ." He took a deep breath as if to steady himself.

He let me set it on his palm.

He turned that hand and craned his neck to inspect the stone without touching it with his other hand. When he finally spoke, his voice was quiet with reverence. "This is soapstone. It's heavy, but easily carved, and I think that if you washed off the dirt, you might find designs carved into the stone. I think this is a Viking relic, one that's known as a 'whorl.'" He spelled the word for me and explained, "Whorls were made of materials like antler, bone, and stone, and were used to weight the spindle and control the speed while spinning fibers into yarn. Heavier whorls like this were used for heavier yarns." He raised his head. His eyes, although a light shade of blue, seemed to be almost on fire with excitement. "The Viking settlement at a place called L'Anse aux Meadows in Newfoundland wasn't discovered until the 1960s, after Newfoundland became part of Canada. Researchers believed long before then that the Vikings had landed in North America and might have stayed awhile. I don't know why Ernest Renniegrove was in Newfoundland in 1887. Maybe he was trying to find out if the rumors about a Viking settlement were correct. Maybe he found this whorl and became certain that the Vikings had spent time in Newfoundland. Renniegrove might have been one of the first archaeologists to pick up a relic from the settlement."

Sensibly, I asked, "If he fell off a cliff, how did the whorl get here?"

"He could have sent it to Harriet, or he could have brought

it back from earlier explorations." Daniel looked off into the distance, and then gave me a rueful smile. "It would be fun to believe that he was one of the first to find a Viking relic in Newfoundland, but maybe he picked it up in Greenland or Iceland. Or the UK. The Vikings traveled far."

"Aren't archaeologists supposed to turn over relics to the country where they find them?"

"They didn't always. I found more articles to read about him and his death. I'll let you know what I find."

"I'd love that. I know very little about Hattie and about the early days of my house, and I'd like to know more." I wanted to tell Daniel about the letter and photo that Chief Agnew had shown me, but I didn't think they would add much to Daniel's historical studies. Besides, Daniel had been one of the people outside Deputy Donut when Pamela became agitated, and I believed, based on his blush several moments before, that he had probably been driving the Ever Green Forestry truck I'd seen shortly before I'd found Pamela's body. Daniel seemed too shy and innocent to be a murderer, but appearances could be deceiving. Possibly, Pamela had owned other original materials about my house or our neighborhood besides the photo and letter, and my new neighbor had murdered Pamela in the process of stealing them. Maybe those were the articles he planned to read and tell me about. Not about to ask him, I showed him the scrap of map. "I found this in my yard today, too, but it wasn't dirty like the stone. I don't think it had been buried."

"Was the whorl?"

"I'm not sure where my cat found it." I wasn't about to tell Daniel that whoever he'd heard or seen around my house the previous night might have dug holes and might also have thrown that stone donut into the border underneath a forsythia bush. I wasn't sure that Daniel hadn't been the one to borrow the keys, unlock the door, and prowl around my yard. He could have made up the big man and the light-colored pickup truck to cover for himself. However, based on his excitement about the whorl, I was almost positive that he had not left it in my yard.

He studied the scrap of map. "This looks like it was torn from an atlas of the Fallingbrook area that was originally printed in 1891. I have a reproduction copy, but the paper in mine isn't as heavy. Someone ruined an original." He looked from the map to me, and his expression was one of bewilderment. "Why do people do that?"

I didn't have an answer.

With the purr of a massive but well maintained engine, a large black SUV pulled up in front of Daniel's house. In his dress uniform, Chief Agnew walked to Daniel's driveway.

Beside me, Daniel stiffened. "That's him," he murmured out the side of his mouth. "The burly man."

"Are you sure?"

He muttered, "Yes, by the way he walks, like his knees are pinned together and his big toes might trip each other."

"That's Chief Agnew, Fallingbrook's new police chief." I hadn't noticed the man's distinctive gait before.

Agnew stood near the back of Daniel's Ever Green Forestry truck for a couple of seconds. I couldn't see what he was doing, but I didn't think he touched the truck. Maybe he took a photo. Thrusting his phone into a jacket pocket, he started toward Daniel's house.

"I'd better go see what he wants." Daniel ran down my porch steps.

Some instinct, maybe the desire to protect this young and possibly too-trusting person, or maybe simple curiosity, kicked in.

I followed him.

Chapter 19

❧

Crossing the street with Daniel, I heard a shrill old-fashioned doorbell ring inside Daniel's house. Without waiting even a second, Chief Agnew raised a hammy fist and pounded on Daniel's front door.

"What's he trying to do," I muttered, "break down the door?" If so, he didn't succeed. Instead he seemed to almost press his face against the window in the door.

Daniel threw me a grin, reached the sidewalk near his house, and called out, "Can I help you?" He sounded confident and in control. Some of the tenseness went out of my shoulders.

Agnew whirled around and glared at Daniel. "Who are you?"

"Daniel Suthlow. I live here. I was across the street and saw you." Daniel climbed up the steps and joined Agnew on the porch.

I followed.

Agnew looked beyond Daniel to me. "And what are you doing here?"

That was a good question. I wasn't about to explain that Daniel seemed young, and I felt the need to protect him from this police chief whom I did not trust, especially now that

Daniel had identified Agnew as the burly man who had been prowling around my house and garage around ten the night before. I managed, "Daniel was with me on my porch when you drove up. I thought I'd introduce you. Daniel, this is Chief Agnew."

Agnew scowled at me. "I don't need civilians introducing me."

Neither man offered to shake hands.

Daniel probably didn't realize he was still carrying the soapstone whorl. It was flat on his palm, but since I'd last looked at the donut-shaped stone, his fingers had closed around it.

Agnew must have noticed the whorl, too. "What's that in your hand?"

Daniel opened his hand and stared at the whorl lying on his palm as if he had never seen it before. "It's not mine. It's hers."

I added, "I found it in my yard this afternoon. Daniel's interested in history. He thinks it might be from a Viking settlement."

Agnew scoffed, "Here?"

I thought of another reason how the whorl might have ended up in my yard. "Early Scandinavian settlers might have brought it."

Agnew pointed at Daniel's front window's yellow brick sill. "Put it there and back away from it."

Did Agnew think the stone was about to explode? Or that Daniel might hit him with it?

Daniel did as Agnew asked and then stood beside me at the edge of the porch. One misstep, and we could tumble backward down the stairs.

Apparently, Agnew didn't fear explosions or other trouble from the stone donut. He took a small but powerful flashlight from his pocket and slowly shined it over nearly every surface of the whorl.

Daniel and I waited in silence. I thought I remained outwardly calm, but Daniel's breathing sounded harsh and uneven.

Finally, Agnew shut off his flashlight. "Tell me again where you got this. You first, Mr. Suthlow."

I wondered how valuable a Viking-era spinning tool could be.

Daniel stood straight with his hands behind his back like a schoolboy trying to appear brave while the principal interrogated him. "Emily showed it to me. It was in her house, but she said it had been in her yard." His voice wavered as if our police chief frightened him.

I braced my own shoulders and raised my chin. "That's where I found it before I took it inside. I wouldn't have noticed it, but my cat uncovered it. Someone came in through my new garage sometime during the past twenty-four hours and did some digging. I heard a thump around three this morning. Maybe whoever dug it up decided it was worthless and threw it down."

Agnew demanded, "And where did the blood come from?"

That stunned me. "Blood?" Now my voice was the one trembling.

Agnew pointed his flashlight. "There's dried blood on it. Ms. Westhill, you were at the scene of a crime recently. Did you perhaps bring this stone from there?"

"I never saw it before my cat found it." This time I managed to sound sure of myself. Which probably didn't help my case with Agnew, who seemed determined to disbelieve everything I said.

His dark eyes became beadier than ever. "I'm going to have the blood analyzed. You two, go stand beside Suthlow's truck and wait there until I say you can leave."

I started down the steps. "Are we under arrest?"

I doubted that Agnew heard Daniel's sudden intake of breath. Daniel reached the sidewalk first.

Agnew followed us. "Ms. Westhill, you're mighty friendly

with one of our detectives. You should know we don't arrest people without informing them of the situation." He was obviously pleased with himself for the snarky put-down. Heading away from us toward his SUV, he called over his shoulder, "But don't press your luck."

Daniel and I stood near the driver's door of the Ever Green Forestry truck. Agnew opened the hatch of his SUV and shuffled things around as if he were looking for something.

I muttered to Daniel, "Don't worry."

He whispered back, "I don't understand. Nothing like this has ever happened to me before."

"It'll be okay. I think he just wants to show how tough he is."

"Were you really at the scene of a crime recently?"

"Unfortunately. I discovered the body."

"That woman who died out near Fallingbrook Falls?"

"Yes. Do you know the area?"

"The guys at work were talking about her."

I didn't point out that he hadn't answered my question. Maybe one of Daniel's co-workers, not Daniel, had been driving the Ever Green Forestry truck that I'd noticed Sunday evening shortly before I found Pamela. I tilted my head toward him. "Did the guys at work have any idea who did it?"

"Just the usual guesses, you know, like her boyfriend or husband or an ex."

Agnew slammed the hatch of his SUV. Carrying a brown paper evidence bag, he walked toward us.

My phone rang. Before I could pull it out of my pocket, Agnew ordered, "Whoever's phone's ringing, don't answer it."

Agnew reached us and stood so close that I guessed he'd eaten more garlic for dinner than I had. My phone stopped ringing. Agnew asked for our full names, addresses, and phone numbers and wrote them on the evidence bag. We had to recite our phone numbers slowly and repeat them several times before he managed to write them down. He didn't have us spell out our addresses.

My phone beeped a notification that someone had left a message. Brent, I hoped, but I kept the phone in my pocket. Reminding Agnew that Brent and I were staying in touch might make Agnew even more suspicious than he already seemed to be.

He ordered, "Stay there." He returned to Daniel's porch and slipped the stone whorl into the evidence bag. Without dismissing us or speaking to us standing there waiting for him, he went back to his SUV, put the filled evidence bag in the back, and then slipped into the driver's seat. He didn't drive away. From the little I could see of him, he seemed to be fiddling with the cruiser's computer.

Daniel and I stayed where we were.

Daniel said, "I'm sorry, Emily. It's my fault he took that whorl. It didn't occur to me to set it down before I came over here from your place. Will they give it back to you? It's probably not terribly valuable, but it's interesting, and you should be able to keep it."

"Probably, eventually. Sooner, when they discover that there's no blood on it or that there is blood and it doesn't match the type of the woman who died. Pamela Firston. But even if it does match, they can check the DNA and get a better answer than blood type, but that might take a long time."

"What if it's hers?"

"The whorl will probably end up in the evidence room in the basement of the police station until after a suspect is tried. But unless the killer brought the murder weapon into my yard, I really can't see how that whorl could have Pamela's blood on it. The chief is really reaching to solve his case. Maybe he didn't see dried blood and is merely hoping to frighten us into confessing to something we didn't do."

I accidentally slumped back against the cold, hard metal of Daniel's truck and straightened quickly, as if I'd received an electrical shock.

Daniel asked me, "Could your cat have bled onto the stone?"

"She might have. She was playing with that torn map before she found the stone. Maybe she got a paper cut. I didn't notice blood on the map, though."

"I didn't either, but don't paper cuts usually take a few seconds to bleed, if they bleed?"

I turned to look at him. Those light blue eyes showed no guile. His desire to look for answers was endearing.

I reminded myself not to trust him or believe everything he said. "I'll have to check her toe pads and mouth when I get home." I heaved a loud pretend sigh. "If I get home."

Agnew came back and stood, legs apart and knees for once not close together, in front of us. "Ms. Westhill, show me where you found that stone. Suthlow, you come along."

Luckily, my key ring was in my pocket. I didn't know what Agnew would have done if I'd needed to run inside for the key to the door into my yard. Insisted on going with me, probably. I was glad that Daniel was coming along, even though it was probably only because Agnew wanted to watch Daniel's reactions. I didn't want to be alone with Agnew in a walled yard where no one could see us and hardly anyone might hear me, even if I yelled.

And there I was, trusting Daniel only seconds after reminding myself not to. I didn't want to be alone in my yard with either of the men. I hoped that each of them would keep me safe from the other.

I unlocked the garage's rear door and opened it slowly. *Screech.* Although expecting the noise, I tensed, halfway between a wince and a shudder. Leaving the door open, I led Agnew and Daniel to the forsythia bush. I pushed the branches aside and pointed at the ground near the bush's base. "The stone was back in there, and four holes appeared in my yard in the past twenty-four hours. The stone wasn't in one of them, though."

Together, the three of us found the four straight-sided holes I'd counted before.

I told Agnew, "I heard someone in my yard last night. The door screeched, and then there were scraping noises that could have been shoes on my flagstone patio or a trowel touching stone. The ground here is stony. Rocks, including that soapstone relic I found, could have been added when my property was first landscaped, back in 1889. I also heard the thump of something heavy, probably that whorl, hitting the ground. Maybe someone dug up the whorl, but decided it was worthless and tossed it. I don't think it's been under that forsythia bush very long. I raked the winter's accumulation of dead leaves out of there recently."

Agnew's dark eyes bored into me. "What time did you hear someone in your yard?"

"Around three."

"Did you call us?"

"No."

"Why not?" He didn't add, "gotcha," but I heard it in his tone.

I hid my anxiety. "I guess I was tired and not thinking clearly, but there didn't seem to be much to report—only unusual noises and a trail in the dewy grass that might have been from someone walking past this flower border. I didn't realize until this evening that the prowler must have dug holes while he was here."

Agnew asked, "Do either of you own a trowel?"

Daniel said, "I don't."

Agnew glared at him as if trying to force him to change his mind.

I nodded toward the garden shed in the back corner of my yard, on the same side as the new garage. Alec had designed and built the shed. It resembled a storybook cottage, complete with window boxes and a roof that looked thatched. "I do. It should be in that shed. I'll go see if anyone appears to have tampered with the door or windows." The shed was still locked. I returned to the other side of the yard and the two men.

Agnew got out his notebook. Other detectives would have been taking notes long before this. "Westhill, just now you had to unlock the door from your garage into your yard. If you keep that door locked all the time, how did someone get in?"

"When I came outside at three, it wasn't locked. The door is new, and I didn't yet have the key. I was lucky enough to find the keys inside the garage, so I locked it after the prowler had gone. As far as I know, it stayed locked until just now."

Grunting, Agnew lowered his head and wrote in his notebook.

Daniel offered, "I heard that door screech at three, too, from inside my house. The windows were open. A pale pickup was parked farther up the block, beside the fire hydrant. It was gone by the time I left for work this morning."

Without looking up, Agnew asked, "How can you see a pickup parked farther up the block from inside your house?"

Daniel blushed. "I went for a walk."

Agnew pounced. "What were you doing walking around at three in the morning?"

Daniel's face got redder. "I'd heard that screech and came out to investigate. By the way, Chief Agnew, I can see the front of Emily's house and her new garage from inside my house. You were on Emily's porch last night, much earlier than three this morning."

No, Daniel, no, I thought. *Don't accuse him. Don't rile him. We'll figure this out together. Later. With Brent's help.*

Despite my warnings to myself, I seemed to have landed firmly on Team Daniel.

Chapter 20

✻

Naturally, Daniel couldn't hear my thoughts. Standing still beside us in the middle of my yard, he went on, accusing Chief Agnew. "You disappeared into her garage, and I heard that same screech. You didn't come out of her garage for, I think, about ten minutes."

Trying to dampen the anger I saw flashing in Agnew's eyes, I suggested, "Daniel, if it was after ten, it was dark. Maybe it was someone else, not Chief Agnew."

Daniel didn't take the hint to back down. "There are streetlights," he said, "and your porch light was on. A ball cap partially hid his face, but it was him." It was no wonder I had landed on Team Daniel. He told the truth, or the truth as he saw it, even when staying silent probably would have been safer for him.

Agnew stuffed his notebook into his pocket. "Suthlow, did it never occur to you that I might have been on police business?"

Daniel took a half step backward, almost lost his balance on the uneven grass, caught himself, and stood straight, shoulders back, again in his schoolboy posture. "I didn't know who the person was or that he, you, were a police officer."

"You didn't know who I was, and you still don't know who you saw last night."

I asked politely, "Chief Agnew, did you have a search warrant?"

Agnew kept his voice low. "As you should know, buddy-buddy as you are with police officers, we don't need a search warrant to enter premises if we believe a crime is being committed."

"A crime?" I repeated. "You didn't tell me."

"You weren't here. You were with a detective who took time off from the job I assigned him. Apparently, he needed to go to the wedding of another of our officers. And in case you don't know, the homes of people attending weddings and funerals are often targeted by thieves. I made sure that wasn't happening to you, here. So, there was no crime, thanks to me."

Not that we know of at that moment, except for your trespassing, I thought, but I asked, "Wasn't the door from the garage into my yard locked?" I carefully did not look at Daniel. I'd found the keys to the garage doors in the garage, but the contractor had said he'd left them in the mailbox. Daniel had said he'd seen Chief Agnew doing something with that mailbox before he went into my garage.

Agnew's face reddened again. "You said yourself it wasn't locked when you came out at three."

Although I was certain he was going to remind me that he was supposed to be doing the questioning, I asked, "And was it unlocked when you left?"

"Locking it requires a key."

I let Agnew's evasion pass. I had a different important question for him. "While you were here, did you notice these holes in my yard?"

"I had a flashlight. I didn't see any holes. You say someone came in here around three?"

Daniel and I both nodded.

Agnew concluded too easily, "Three this morning was

when the digging was done. Nothing to do with me, but you should have called. Next time you hear noises back here in the night, call the police. Unless you're certain you're only hearing an animal." He pulled out his notebook, wrote something and then underlined it or crossed it out, and turned to Daniel. "Suthlow, did you know Pamela Firston?"

I interrupted. "Wait. Are you questioning Daniel? Does he need a lawyer?"

Chief Agnew retorted, "No, he doesn't, but he can have one if he wants, or you can stay here and advocate for him."

Despite his youthful appearance, Daniel seemed to have a strong core. He stayed calm. "It's okay, Emily. I have nothing to hide. And . . . and if I can help catch the person who harmed the poor woman, I'd like to." He stared straight at Agnew. "I didn't know her or know of her until today when some of the guys at Ever Green Forestry were talking about the murder."

With a satisfied nod, Agnew made notes. "Mr. Suthlow, where were you Sunday evening between about four when Ms. Westhill saw you near her coffee shop, and about six?"

If Daniel felt I'd betrayed him by reporting his whereabouts before I'd officially met him, he didn't show it. "I went from the center of town to my truck, and then I was . . . just driving around."

"'Just driving around,'" Agnew repeated. "In your employer's truck. On a Sunday."

Red crept up Daniel's neck. "One of the perks of my job is having the use of that truck to get to and from wherever we're working. So, I have it on weekends. On Sunday my boss would have appreciated my driving around." Daniel licked his lips. "This is embarrassing. I'd left a door ajar. Interior lights stayed on, and I was afraid I'd come close to running down the battery." He glanced at his feet and added, speaking quickly but so softly he mumbled, "So I drove around to charge the battery."

I was almost certain that he was lying. And upset about lying. Watching a flush spread over his face, I wondered what he was hiding. Murder?

Agnew obviously wondered, too. He demanded, "Where'd you go?"

Daniel pointed over his shoulder toward the street. "I headed south to see what was there. I'm new to Fallingbrook. Mainly, I just drove around."

Agnew stabbed his pen at his notebook, threatening to poke holes in the paper. "When did you get back?"

As if he could see the late Esther Renniegrove out enjoying her yard, Daniel seemed to stare through my garden's rear wall. "I'm not sure. Around six or seven."

Agnew's pen ground into the notebook page. "That's a long time to charge a battery."

Daniel scuffed at the grass with a toe. "I couldn't help sightseeing. It . . . it's beautiful around here."

Agnew scoffed, "Sightseeing in the company truck—that's something else your employer would appreciate."

"Probably not." Daniel's shoulders still looked tense, and his slight sniff of a laugh did not sound the least bit cheerful.

Agnew closed his notebook. "See, Ms. Westhill? My interview of your protégé wasn't so bad."

Not certain that I agreed, I gave Agnew a wan smile. He headed toward the still-open door in the wall. All three of us went into the garage. I turned the dead bolt with the key, keeping my yard safe from intruders again. I hoped.

Daniel crossed the street, but Agnew waited for me. As soon as Daniel closed himself inside his house, Chief Agnew demanded, "What's Suthlow to you?"

"I met him for the first time this evening. We discovered that we share an interest in the history of this neighborhood."

A shared interest in history—or probably anything else—did not seem to impress Agnew. "Why are you protecting him?"

"I'm not. I mean, I don't think he has ever had to deal with police officers before, and he seems young. He might not know his rights." I didn't admit it, but I wondered if I might have, at first, underestimated Daniel Suthlow's abilities and knowledge.

"He has no rights to go around murdering innocent women."

"Of course not."

Agnew became conciliating. "Did you really find that stone in your yard or did Suthlow have it all along? He seemed anxious to tell me that it was your stone."

"I found it, but it probably belongs to the people of Newfoundland."

"What?"

"It could have come from there. Or anywhere the Vikings or their descendants lived—Scandinavia, Great Britain . . ."

"But you're saying that you found it in your garden, underneath a bush."

"Definitely."

"Suthlow admitted he was wandering around at three this morning about the time you heard someone. Suthlow could have brought that murder weapon into your yard and attempted to bury it. But you almost caught him, so he made up seeing a pale pickup truck down the block."

Based on Agnew's questions and his confiscating the whorl, I shouldn't have been surprised, but I squeaked, "Murder weapon?"

"Very likely."

I doubted it, but was too stunned to say so.

Agnew asked me, "Did you yourself come out to the street at three in the morning and look for vehicles?"

"No."

"There you go. Don't trust your neighbor, as choirboy innocent as he looks."

And, I thought, *don't trust your police chief, as smugly confident as he looks.* I reminded Agnew, "Don't forget that Pamela told Summer Peabody-Smith that she, Pamela that is, had moved to Fallingbrook to escape an ex who, as she put it, 'knew all about medicines.' And when Pamela was in Deputy Donut, one of the people outside who might have frightened her was a man named Gregory who told me he was a pharmaceutical sales rep." I wanted to ask Agnew if he'd investigated Gregory, but I only suggested, "Maybe Gregory was Pamela's ex."

"You said that your new neighbor was also outside your shop at the time. This Daniel Suthlow is that same neighbor, right? Or did I somehow get that wrong?"

"You got it right." I didn't remind Agnew that he himself had also been driving past our shop, slowly. "But Pamela seemed most frightened when she was in our office in the back of Deputy Donut and the pharmaceutical sales rep started in through our front door. She asked to be let out the back rather than through the dining area."

"You spotted someone in an Ever Green Forestry truck like Suthlow's in the vicinity of the Peabody-Smith cabin around the time of her murder." Agnew showed his teeth in something between a smile and a snarl. "If you want to protect your young friend from across the street, you could admit that you yourself killed Pamela Firston."

Now I was the one offering the closed-teeth, open-lipped smile. "I'd be lying if I said that."

Agnew snapped his fingers. "Maybe you two worked together. I'll dig up the truth." He turned and strode, knees nearly knocking into each other, across the street.

Chapter 21

✿

My forehead in knots, I climbed up to my porch and watched until Chief Agnew drove out of sight.

Dep meowed at me from inside the window. Muttering in frustration at the impossible police chief and his unwillingness to suspect anyone besides Daniel and me, I grabbed the scrap of map from the glass-topped wicker table, went inside, and locked the door.

I sat in the wing chair and put the scrap of map down on a side table. Dep jumped into my lap. Examining a cat, even one as docile as Dep, for paper cuts, isn't easy, but I saw no evidence of blood on her anywhere. She settled down and purred. I pulled my phone out of my pocket.

Brent had left a message. He would try again later.

I called him. After a quick greeting, I blurted, "Chief Agnew came into my yard uninvited last night while we were at the wedding and stayed about ten minutes. I don't know what he was doing, but I don't trust that man, and maybe you should check your security cameras."

"Okay," he said, "but you don't live way out in the country like I do, and you don't have security cameras. How do you know about his visit?"

"A neighbor." I explained the whole thing, finding the

donut-shaped stone, Daniel's visit, and then everything Agnew had said and done.

Brent remained silent for a second, and then he whistled. "The Fallingbrook police don't routinely check on the homes of people attending weddings or funerals. I'll check the feeds from my cameras and call you back."

A few minutes later, my phone rang. "He came to my place, too, around nine when it was still light." I could hear the restrained annoyance in Brent's voice. "He must not have noticed the camera at the end of the driveway. He parked in view of that camera and walked to the house from there." Brent owned acres of hilly, wooded lakefront, and his driveway was long. "He was wearing jeans, a hoodie with the hood up, and a baseball cap pulled low, but I recognized him by his size, the way he walks, and that jutting chin. Also, when he came into view of the house, he looked up. He must have been searching for cameras because as soon as he looked at one of them, he lowered his head and hurried away. He drove out soon afterward, so he didn't have time to do much exploring. Now, tell me about the guy across the street. Should I be jealous?"

"I go for older men."

"I'm old?"

"Older than Daniel. But don't stay away too long. He seems sweet and interesting."

"I wish I could come back this weekend."

"So do I. If Agnew clears this up quickly, maybe he can go do the teaching he signed up for, and you can come back, but I don't see how he can solve the crime without you here guiding him away from innocent people. Like me, for instance."

"Has a DCI agent shown up?"

"I don't know. Agnew came by himself this evening."

"Why did he come?"

"Actually, he went to Daniel's, but Daniel and I were on my front porch, so we went across the street. I think Agnew was finally getting around to questioning Daniel about the Ever Green Forestry truck I saw near Peabody Lane on Sunday evening. Maybe there's a DCI agent looking into other facets of the case."

"You'll keep that new door into your yard locked, won't you?"

"Yes, and I won't store the keys in the mailbox."

He laughed. "I didn't think you would. Interesting that Agnew would look there. Did Daniel say what Agnew was wearing?"

"He only mentioned the ball cap pulled low. He didn't realize that Agnew was a police officer until he saw him in his dress uniform this evening. He recognized him by his size and walk."

Brent warned, "Don't trust Daniel. And don't trust Agnew, either."

"I won't. Agnew was so certain that the whorl was the murder weapon and had blood on it that I can't help wondering if he knew it was the weapon because he was the one who wielded it and then tossed it under my forsythia. Maybe he planned to get a warrant to search for the stone on my property, and then he could mysteriously 'find' it. Case closed. I go to prison, and he goes free."

Brent had me describe the stone donut. He concluded, "It sounds like the size and shape of the object that slammed into Firston's head, so I can understand Agnew's interest, but if the first owner of your home was an archaeologist's daughter, that relic has probably been in your yard since before she wrote that letter in 1949, and the investigators won't find Firston's blood on it. I wish I was there, Em."

"So do I." We spent the next half hour discussing the really important things, like how much we missed each other. Finally, acknowledging that we both needed to work early the next morning, we disconnected. Dep and I went out into the garden in back. The door in the wall was still locked. In case someone needed evidence about the prowler, like fitting a trowel to the sides of the holes, I didn't fill in the holes. Maybe someone was going around the neighborhood digging up flower borders. But why? None of my plants or bulbs seemed to have been disturbed. Dep and I went inside, made certain that doors and windows downstairs were locked, and wandered off to bed.

If anyone came into my yard to do weird things during the night, I slept through it, and when I took breakfast outside to eat in the dewy post-dawn, the door in the wall was still locked, the holes in the garden were still there, and no more had appeared.

I loved the long days of June when I could walk to work after sunrise and still make it to Deputy Donut by six thirty. Although restrained only slightly by her harness and leash, Dep wasn't rambunctious, and we didn't have to stop often.

It was Thursday. Tom had Thursdays and Fridays off. I did the frying while Olivia formed the dough and frosted and decorated the donuts, and Jocelyn waited on customers. Olivia and I helped Jocelyn when the shop got busy.

By midafternoon, we'd made enough donuts for the rest of the day. I turned off the deep fryers and had time to socialize with customers, which was perfect—wearing his police uniform, Hooligan came in.

I asked him, "Where's your temporary partner?"

"Tyler's at the station. Our new chief brought in boxes of supermarket donuts and suggested that we shouldn't leave the premises for breaks because we have coffee and donuts right there in the office." He clutched at his throat. "The donuts aren't horrible, but they aren't yours, and our uniforms end up splattered in gobs of powdered sugar. The chief himself choked on some of it. And what he calls coffee! It's undrinkable." Hooligan winked. "I snuck out for some decent coffee and donuts. What's your special coffee today?"

"A medium roast from Burundi with notes of chocolate, citrus, and cloves."

"Sounds good."

"Come to the display case and tell me which donuts you'd like while I pour your coffee."

He chose a sour cream blueberry-filled donut. I dolloped whipped cream on it and suggested, "Let's go into the office. I want to talk to you."

He was as always, agreeable. Equipment jingling from his belt, he carried his plate and opened the office door for me. I brought his mug and handed him a spoon and a fork. "You can't eat this donut with your fingers without making a worse mess than you might with Chief Agnew's powdered sugar." We sat on the couch. Hooligan set his plate on the coffee table but had to pick it up almost immediately. Dep dashed down one of her staircases to greet him. And, probably, hoping for an introduction to his whipped cream.

Hooligan gazed at me. "I wanted to talk to you, too. You go first."

I described Chief Agnew's visit of the night before and his surreptitious trips to both Brent's and my homes during the wedding reception. Twisting my fingers together, I baldly stated, "I know this sounds silly, but I can't help wondering if our new chief is suspecting innocent people to protect the actual murderer, which, considering how quickly he decided that the stone donut was the murder weapon, could be him."

"You're not being silly. And I agree with Brent. Don't trust him, and if he wants to talk to you, meet him at the police station."

"I'll try." My smile twisted. "But he knows where I live. And here's another thing—it seemed to me that Agnew arrived at the murder scene too quickly to have come all the way from downtown Fallingbrook."

"When your call came in, he wasn't at police headquarters. I was there that afternoon, writing up reports. He left after four and didn't come back. The next time I saw him was around six thirty when he was in his SUV parked on Peabody Lane, showing the rest of us where the driveway was."

"Had he come there from another call, one that was close to the Peabody-Smith cabin?"

Hooligan loaded donut, thick blueberry filling, and whipped cream onto his fork. "No. The first scene he attended since he took over in Fallingbrook was the Firston case. He'd been in meetings and—I don't know—shuffling paperwork. He didn't tell anyone he was leaving early Sunday afternoon or where he was going." Frowning, Hooligan set down his mug. "Here's what I came to tell you, Emily. Agnew seems almost gleeful about working on this homicide. Most of the time, he's keeping himself shut in his office, but when I was walking past his office this morning, he happened to open the door, and I saw the whiteboard where he's listed his suspects. Your name is first."

I wasn't surprised, but hearing it made me feel like my heart nearly dropped into my left knee. "What?" My gasped word came out barely above a whisper. "Why?"

Hooligan's answer didn't surprise me, either. "These are some of the things I saw below your name: 'First on scene. No good reason for being on scene. Prior contact with deceased.' When Agnew saw me looking, he closed the door. He probably guesses that since I took time off for the wedding Brent was attending that you and I know each other."

"You need to watch your back, too."

He nodded soberly. "I do. And Tyler and I have each other's backs. No one says it aloud, but our new chief hasn't been making a lot of friends in the department."

"Did you notice other names on the list?"

"There was someone with a hyphenated last name, maybe the owner of the place where Firston died."

I suggested, "Summer Peabody-Smith?"

"That sounds right."

"I know her. It's her parents' cabin. She's been looking after it while they're away. There was no evidence of a break-in. Agnew suspects her because she has keys. Of course she has keys! Besides, why would she kill someone who was a source of income for her parents, at least for the rest of the summer? Or did Pamela pay for the entire season up front?"

"As far as I know, she was paying month to month."

"Did you see names like Gregory or Diana?"

"I didn't see the whiteboard long enough to read it all, but I think that one possible suspect's name began with a D, but I think it was a man's name, not Diana."

"Daniel Suthlow?"

Hooligan set his fork down. "That could be it."

"So, you're not on the team combing through evidence and clues with Chief Agnew?"

"He's doing it by himself."

I sighed. This didn't sound good, especially for me. And maybe for Daniel and Summer, also. I asked, "No DCI agent?"

"Not unless he or she is hiding. I wish Brent was here. And Misty."

"I agree with you about Brent, but I wouldn't want Misty to miss her honeymoon."

"You've got a point. Listen, Emily, don't worry too much about being Suspect Number One."

"Easy for you to say! Chief Agnew thinks that Daniel or I killed Pamela and put the murder weapon in my flower garden. Or we worked together."

"He can't go around making accusations and arrests based on hunches and wishes. He'll end up with a case that won't stand up in court even if it makes it there. Except for appearing to possess a stone object that might be the murder weapon but probably isn't, his so-called evidence against you and Daniel is circumstantial. Even if the stone turns out to have Pamela Firston's blood on it, you have a witness stating that Agnew was in your yard before the stone donut showed up there. Judges would find that interesting."

"I hope you're right. But the witness is Daniel."

"Brent will be back next Friday night. He'll straighten things out."

"If Agnew lets him. This is only Wednesday. Nine more days!" I made it into a dramatic wail.

"Want to stay with Samantha and me? I don't like you being there when people are prowling in your yard at night, and I know Samantha would agree. Bring Dep."

"Thanks. It's tempting, but as long as no one else has a key to that door into my yard, I should be fine."

Hooligan looked skeptical.

"I always keep the front door of my house locked, too."

"Whenever we can, Tyler and I will swing by your house on our patrols, but think about my offer." He dabbed at his chin with his napkin. "Did I get all the whipped cream off? I wouldn't want to return to the station wearing donuts that are obviously not the ones Chief Agnew provided."

"I can give you some powdered sugar to dribble over your uniform."

Grinning, he stood up. "No, thanks."

He helped me carry his dishes to the serving counter, paid for his snack, and told us all goodbye. Outside, he walked quickly toward the police station. I hoped his long break wouldn't get him into trouble with Chief Agnew, especially if Agnew guessed where Hooligan had been and that Hooligan had told me I was Agnew's primary suspect.

After our last customer left, Jocelyn, Olivia, and I tidied up.

Jocelyn demanded, "What's wrong, Emily?"

I didn't want to worry my assistants, or worse, involve them in something that might endanger them. "Not much."

Olivia accused, "Your face is like a thundercloud, and you keep sighing."

Jocelyn asked, "Did Hooligan upset you? He's usually so nice."

That gave me an answer that mollified them. "He is, but talking to him reminded me of how much I miss Brent."

Walking Dep home, my mood darkened again. Chief Agnew had left his office on Sunday while Pamela was still in Deputy Donut, and he'd shown up near the cabin where she'd been killed suspiciously quickly. Detectives usually asked themselves who had the means, the motive, and the opportunity to commit the crime.

Chief Agnew had had the opportunity to kill Pamela. And if the stone donut or a random rock was the murder weapon, he'd had the means. But what had his motive been? Would a police officer murder someone in order to "solve" a case so he could go on to a more powerful position in a bigger police department? That seemed much too risky.

All of the builders' vehicles were gone from in front of my house, but a tan pickup that might have been Kayla's was parked near the fire hydrant farther up the street, and I wondered if someone on that block owned a truck like hers, and if that person's pickup had been the one that Daniel saw after he and I heard that screech around three Wednesday morning. The wall of the garage facing me was now covered with siding, the window on that side had been installed, and plywood sheathing covered part of the roof, but the front opening still gaped with no overhead door.

Dep and I went inside. Dep dashed toward the back of the house. I went up to my bedroom and changed into jeans and a T-shirt.

Through sheer curtains at my back window, I caught a glimpse of movement.

Someone was in the walled garden behind my house.

Chapter 22

I tiptoed down the stairs and into the sunroom.

Kayla swept a long-handled tool over the grass near the flower border where I'd found the stone donut. As if she'd just come down from working on the garage roof, she was wearing her leather tool apron and safety harness over her jeans and T-shirt.

Preventing Dep from escaping outside, I opened the back door. The screen door squeaked.

Kayla jumped and whirled to face me. "Oh, it's you, Emily."

Who else might she have expected? I reminded myself that she was my parents' friend. Also, like the other builders, she could have had a good reason for being farther from the garage than expected. I walked to her.

Kayla flushed from heat or embarrassment. "Sorry for intruding, Emily. I lost an expensive drill bit."

Below the handgrip of her tool, a curved shaft held a digital screen angled for the operator to see. A flat thing shaped sort of like the paddles for our industrial electric mixers at Deputy Donut was at the tool's base. I asked, "What's that, a metal detector?"

"Yes."

"Any luck?" Maybe I should have been more specific and asked if she'd found anything. I'd dug up pennies and marbles while planting bulbs. The most valuable treasure, besides the Viking relic, if the soapstone donut actually was one, might have been the 1936 silver quarter containing more than twenty-five cents' worth of silver.

"No." Kayla waved toward the new garage. An aluminum ladder was propped against the wall. "I started over there. The bit, um, flew out of my hand, so I kept searching and ended up over here."

"Did you hunt for it on Tuesday, too?" I pointed at the dirt surrounding my flowers and shrubs. "Those holes appeared, and I didn't dig them. I don't think my cat did, either."

"No. I lost the bit this afternoon when we were finishing up." She prodded at dirt near one of the holes. "I figured you'd been getting ready to put in some plants. I did wave the metal detector over the holes, but it didn't find anything. I guess I'll have to give up."

"Keep trying if you like. And I'll watch for it. Did you use that ladder to get over my wall?"

"I climbed the ladder to your garage roof, pulled the ladder up after me, and then lowered it into your yard. There were keys for that door, but I guess you have them now, and I didn't know you'd be home this soon, or I would have waited and asked. I should have. Sorry I didn't." She started toward the ladder. "I'll buy a new bit. Maybe that one was reaching the end of its useful life, anyway."

I followed her. "How about if I let you out through the door in the wall? Pulling that ladder up onto the roof can't be easy." I was strong, but she must have been really strong. She was also taller than I was, which probably helped.

"I'm used to it, but it would be easier to go out through the garage."

I unlocked the door and opened it quickly. It didn't screech.

While Kayla shortened the ladder, I closed the door and then opened it again, more slowly. It screeched.

Kayla frowned at it. "We'd better do something about that."

"It doesn't do that when it's opened quickly."

"Yeah, but it could be annoying for you."

I took one end of the ladder. Together, we maneuvered it into the garage. She chained it to other ladders and the stands of power tools and padlocked the chain. Unless they had a powerful chain-cutter, no one else was going to climb over the wall using any of those ladders.

I pointed at the opening at the front of the garage. "When do you think the overhead door will be installed?"

She picked up her metal detector. "Soon, I hope. We're almost done."

"Do you have another job lined up?"

"Yes, a good one, a new build out in the country. It's like a mansion, so we'll be working on it for a nice, long time. And thank you again. If you hadn't told me about this job, I might not have been offered that one."

"You're welcome." I walked out through the wide opening and peered over the hedge. "Is that your truck down there?"

"Yes."

"You parked far away."

She shrugged. "It was the best spot I could find this morning."

"I wondered if it was yours or a neighbor's. A similar one was near there at three yesterday morning." I didn't tell her that I wasn't the one who had spotted it.

"Three? I can't imagine being awake then. That truck must have been a neighbor's." She said goodbye, strode up the street, put the metal detector into the passenger side of the tan pickup truck, and drove away.

I returned to my garden through the garage. I locked the door and went into the sunroom.

Dep hopped off one of the windowsills and looked up at me.

"That was strange," I told her. "How far would a drill bit fly from a garage roof?"

"Meow."

"Not all the way to the other side of the yard, right?"

"Meow."

"But I suppose if the drill bit was expensive, Kayla thought it was worth it."

"Merow."

"Do carpenters usually take metal detectors to work?"

Dep sat down, stretched out one back leg, and gave it a vigorous licking.

I suggested, "I suppose, if they often drop expensive metal things off roofs, they might."

Dep set her foot down beside the other three, lining up all four of them in a perfect row. She blinked at me.

"Let's be careful," I suggested, "not to be nearby if Kayla is on a roof with heavy objects."

"Mew."

"I felt like she might have been lying about the drill bit, but she seemed honestly surprised that anyone would think she was driving around at three a.m."

Dep walked to her empty food dish and stared down into it.

I fed her and made myself a cheeseburger with all the fixings and some oven fries that I made from scratch by cutting up a potato, spraying the fries with a light coating of oil, and roasting them in a hot oven with the convection fan running to crisp them. I ate outside while Dep frolicked in the grass. If anyone could find the missing drill bit, if there was one, it might be Dep. She didn't, though, and after I ate, we went inside.

Sitting on the half wall between the kitchen and the sunroom, Dep watched me fill and start the dishwasher. I asked her, "Who dug the holes if Kayla didn't? Could Daniel be lying about the light-colored pickup truck? Could he have dug those holes?"

She jumped off the wall onto the love seat behind it. "Mew."

"I didn't think so, either, Dep."

The doorbell rang.

I walked quietly into the living room and checked the peephole in the door.

Holding sheets of paper in one hand, Daniel was on my front porch, with his back to the door as if he were watching for Chief Agnew to cruise into our neighborhood. I slipped outside without Dep and joined Daniel on the porch. His eyes reflected the enthusiasm of his smile. "I read more articles and found more cool stuff about the father of Hattie and Esther Renniegrove."

We sat in the wicker chairs. He handed me a copy of a newspaper article from August 1887.

The headline was: "Archaeologist's Assistant Also Presumed Dead."

The article stated that when Ernest Renniegrove fell to his death, his assistant, Otto Nobbuth, must have also fallen. Although Ernest Renniegrove's body was found on a rocky beach, Nobbuth's body was assumed to have been washed out to sea. No one was sure why either man had been in Newfoundland or why they were close to the edge of cliffs. Inhabitants of the nearest outport suggested that their visit had something to do with archaeology. One fisherman claimed, *"There's been strange doings up there since before the first whale swam out of the ark."*

The reporter wrote, *Renniegrove was nearing sixty years old, and perhaps not steady on his feet. Did he stumble, and did the younger man attempt to save him, and in the process, compound the tragedy and sadly lose his own life?*

When I finished reading, Daniel handed me another article. This one was dated a month later. The headline was: "Mystery Surrounding Archaeologist's Death."

Two weeks after Ernest Renniegrove's body was found, several people reported seeing someone resembling Otto Nobbuth on the *SS Plover*, a steamer leaving St. John's, Newfoundland, and bound for Halifax, Nova Scotia. *No one*, the reporter sternly reminded the reader, *can be certain that the young man they saw was the archaeology student, Otto Nobbuth*. The article pointed out that the *SS Plover* was the steamer involved in a collision with the fishing schooner, the *Trixie H*, in which five souls were lost, only a couple of months before.

Daniel told me, "The *Plover* was nicknamed the 'jinx ship.' It sank in 1890."

"Presumably Otto Nobbuth, if he was ever on that ship, had disembarked by then."

Daniel grinned. "You'd think. And here's some possible background on both Renniegrove and Nobbuth. Look at this 1886 article in an archaeological journal." He handed it to me.

This headline read: "Treasures Missing?"

According to the article, several gold objects were thought to have disappeared from a site in Norfolk, England, where archaeologists had been searching for King John's treasure, lost in 1216 in a tidal estuary known as "The Wash." The article listed the staff at the dig. The staff included Ernest Renniegrove and his student assistant, Otto Nobbuth. No one had been able to prove that the objects in question had ever existed. The wife of a different archaeologist claimed that she herself had found the objects, but they quickly vanished. She was subsequently chastised for mischief and her husband was relieved of his duties.

"Well," I said, "that proves exactly nothing."

"But it does make you wonder about Renniegrove's fall and Nobbuth's disappearance. It was too bad that they disappeared before they could confirm that the Vikings had settled for a time in Newfoundland. That discovery could have made them more famous than being part of a dig where treasure might have gone missing or an unusual death and a mysterious disappearance."

I suggested, "Maybe Renniegrove and Nobbuth hoped to find gold in a Viking settlement in Newfoundland, if they found a Viking settlement."

"As far as we know, the Vikings didn't use gold. No gold has been found in their settlements. Yet."

I joked, "Unless Renniegrove or Nobbuth found it and caused it to vanish."

Daniel laughed. "That's a possibility."

I gazed at the tops of trees behind Daniel's house. "I wonder what really happened on that cliff in Newfoundland, and whether Otto Nobbuth also fell, or if he left Newfoundland on a jinxed ship."

"Then you'll want to see this obituary." He handed me another page he'd printed.

A man named Otto Nobbuth had died in California in 1940 at the age of seventy-four. He was predeceased by his wife Susan and had left behind a son and a granddaughter whose names did not appear in the obituary. I did some quick math. "So, this Otto Nobbuth would have been born in 1866. He'd have been twenty-one when Ernest Renniegrove died, and only twenty when the gold did or didn't go missing from Norfolk. He could be the same Otto Nobbuth. Why do some obituaries leave out careers? Was this Otto Nobbuth associated with archaeology, or did he have nothing to do with it?"

"If he truly stole gold and pushed his boss off a cliff, he probably left the archaeological world, but it would be nice to know. I stayed up too late last night, looking things up. I had to force myself to stop. After I come back from, um, an errand I have to run, I'm going to go see what else I can find about anyone named Nobbuth from around that time." He stood.

I offered him the sheets of paper.

He waved them aside. "Those copies are for you. Keep them, if you're interested."

"I am. I'll look for Renniegrove obituaries. It's lucky they all have unusual names."

"It is!" He gave me a dazzling smile, blushed, and trotted down my porch steps and across the street.

Chapter 23

I went upstairs. With Dep purring in my lap, I turned on the computer and looked up Hattie's obituary again. Alec and I had been disappointed because it didn't say much about the woman and had given no information about our house besides the address, which we already knew. Maybe new information had mysteriously appeared.

Harriet (Hattie) Renniegrove of Happy Times Nursing Home, Fallingbrook, formerly of 1212 Maple Street and originally from Cleveland, departed this life peacefully on Thursday in her eighty-second year. Beloved daughter of the late Mabel Renniegrove and the late Ernest Renniegrove, beloved sister of the late Esther Renniegrove.

I'd forgotten that Hattie spent her last days at Happy Times Nursing Home.

Pamela Firston had received a severance check from Happy Times Home Health Care. I searched online. The two companies were connected. The original Happy Times Nursing Home had been opened in Fallingbrook in 1930 by Dr. Frank Aimes. Since then, other homes with the same name and owned by the Aimes family had sprung up in small towns across northern Wisconsin. The home care agency began in 1990. The brief Happy Times history did not mention any delightful young ladies named Teller who might have prevented residents of one of the homes from coming into Hattie Renniegrove's room or coveting her gold-headed cane.

I wondered what had become of the gold-headed cane and if some of its gold might have once belonged to King John before he lost his jewelry in The Wash.

Next, I looked up Esther Renniegrove's obituary. Hattie, who had outlived her younger sister, might have written it. Even more succinct than Hattie's, this obituary did not include the word "beloved." Esther died in 1943 at the age of seventy-four.

At the Happy Times Nursing Home in Fallingbrook.

Neither of the Renniegrove sisters had offspring, and no cousins, aunts, or uncles were mentioned in their obituaries. If Pamela Firston was related to the Renniegrove sisters, I wasn't going to find the connection through Renniegrove obituaries.

An obituary for Pamela Firston did not seem to have been published. In a short article, our local newspaper merely mentioned her possibly suspicious death at a cabin on Deepwish Lake. The reporter quoted Chief Agnew. "We are looking into it."

I did find obituaries for a couple with the last name of Firston who were survived by their infant daughter and by the man's mother, Matilda Firston, née Aimes. Armed with that information, it was easy to find an obituary for Matilda Firston. She'd been known as Tillie and had worked in Happy Times Nursing Home, in Fallingbrook, Wisconsin, from 1946 to 1949. Matilda had been predeceased by her son and daughter-in-law and survived by a granddaughter. The names of those three relatives weren't given, but the obituary mentioned that the nursing home had been owned by Tillie Firston's late grandfather, Dr. Frank Aimes.

I strongly suspected that the name I'd guessed might be Teller was actually Tillie, that Tillie was Matilda Firston, Pamela's grandmother, and that Pamela had obtained the letter from her grandmother. I felt especially sad because Pamela had not been given time to share the letter with me. She had probably looked forward to surprising me with information that she might have guessed, correctly, would fascinate me.

It had gotten late. Wondering if Daniel had returned from his errand, I stood, put Dep on the floor, stretched, and leaned forward to peer through my guest room window. A light was on inside Daniel's house and his truck was in the driveway.

Down on the street, a large black SUV stopped beside my front walk. Chief Agnew got out and slammed the driver's door. I considered pretending I wasn't home, but he looked up.

The overhead light in my guest room was on. I was sure that Agnew saw me silhouetted in the window.

With a sigh, I started down the stairs. Dep and I reached the foot as the doorbell rang. The timer had already turned on the living room lights.

Remembering Brent's and Hooligan's advice not to trust Chief Agnew, I scooped Dep into my arms and opened the door just enough for me to slip out clutching the cat.

That was a mistake. With only one hand free, and not very free because Dep wriggled, I couldn't control the door and couldn't prevent Chief Agnew from opening it wider and striding into the middle of my living room.

I stifled a complaint. Still clutching Dep to my chest, I bumped the door shut with one hip and followed Agnew inside. The door didn't latch. That was fine. I would hang on to Dep and not let her run outside. And if I had to make a quick getaway, I could, with Dep in my arms.

I mentally rehearsed running across the street and pounding on Daniel's door.

Meanwhile, what was I supposed to do, offer our police chief a cup of coffee and a plate of cookies? Ask what he wanted?

I hugged Dep and stared at Agnew.

He turned around, seeming to take in the stained glass above the front window, the shelves of jewel-toned vases beside the window, the fireplace decorated with its summertime bouquet of pretty leaves, the wide doorway into the dining room, my couch and chairs, the coffee table and end tables, the glass-doored bookcase next to the stairs, and the stairs themselves. "You own this place by yourself." It wasn't a question.

"The bank owns most of it."

Focusing on the shelves beside the window, he pointed one stubby index finger. "Where'd you get that vase? The green and blue one."

"It was my grandmother's. I inherited my antiques from her."

"It's identical to one reported missing from a home where Pamela Firston worked. You didn't happen to pick it up when you were visiting the woman, did you?"

I felt like the roots of my hair were beginning to smolder. "Of course not. I saw a similar but not identical one at the cabin Pamela rented. Did it disappear after I was there, like the severance check I saw?"

He widened his stance and crossed his arms, not an easy position since he again seemed to be wearing an armored vest underneath his dress uniform jacket. "That check turned up."

I opened my mouth, didn't know what to say, and closed it.

He went on the offensive. "You spent time snooping around inside that cabin, didn't you?"

That, as he had undoubtedly planned, put me on the defensive. "I was looking for Pamela. It seemed like she'd been interrupted while cooking. I thought she might be injured or sick." I told myself to calm down and speak more slowly. Dep's feet scrambled as if she were trying to leap out of my arms. Tightening them around her probably didn't help.

Agnew only grunted and then turned toward the glass-doored bookcase. "Where'd you get that gold watch?" An old-fashioned pocket watch and chain were displayed inside a glass dome.

"It was my great-grandfather's." The doors to the bookcase were locked. I was glad I hadn't left the key in the lock but had stowed it upstairs in the safe that Alec had installed inside the bedroom closet. "Why? Did one of those disappear from a home where Pamela worked?"

The ruddy face turned redder. "An identical one. Did you see one like it at the scene?"

"No. There was a pile of what looked like costume jewelry along with the Art Deco vase similar to mine. I didn't touch any of it, so maybe a watch could have been buried in that heap."

"It wasn't."

It was my turn to go on the offensive. "Can you tell me what, if anything, was engraved inside the stolen watch?"

Agnew cleared his throat. "I'd have to check the incident report." From the stubborn look on his face, it wasn't something he planned to do.

"Because I might be able to find the key and unlock that cabinet to show you the inscription, but I won't do that until I hear a description of what's engraved in the watch you're looking for. Initials, perhaps?" Agnew could probably find out the initials of all four of my great-grandfathers, and then he would have a twenty-five percent chance of guessing correctly which great-grandfather had owned the watch. But he wouldn't know how those initials were arranged or that my great-grandmother had paid the jeweler to add a love note and her own initials, so unless he obtained my watch, he wouldn't be able to correctly describe it. He could get a search warrant and examine it that way, I supposed.

I missed Brent. And agents from the Wisconsin Division of Criminal Investigation.

Agnew must have realized he might have trouble proving that the watch in my bookcase was one that had supposedly gone missing from a home where Pamela Firston worked. He grumbled, "I don't have that information."

Knowing I could get myself into even more trouble, I returned his glare. "And I don't have the key."

It was the wrong thing to say. Agnew perked up. "Key. I suspect you do have the key. That letter you left in Firston's home appeared to be missing a key." He cocked his head toward the bookcase. "And judging by the rust stains on the letter, the key that had been folded inside that letter for a long time would have been about the size of a key that would fit those doors. You left the letter behind but kept the key."

Where to start? I took a deep breath. "First of all, I never possessed that letter."

"It was addressed to you."

"But it was never sealed or stamped or sent." But I felt like stamping. My foot. Preferably onto his, not that my sneakers could do more than scuff his shiny black policeman shoes.

He continued being obstinate. "It could have been hand-delivered. You yourself confessed that the deceased visited your place of business shortly before her murder."

"She didn't give me the letter. Maybe she meant to, but in her rush to leave, she forgot. The first time I saw that letter was when you showed it to me."

"And I'm supposed to take your word for that."

Shrugging with a wiggly cat in my arms wasn't easy. "Only if you're interested in the truth."

The narrowing of Agnew's already beady eyes showed that he recognized the insult.

I added, "And whether I ever possessed that letter, which I didn't, if there was a key in it, the key would not have been for this bookcase. That letter was signed by Hattie Renniegrove. When she wrote it, this bookcase was in my grandmother's or great-grandmother's home. That bookcase never belonged to Hattie Renniegrove, so she couldn't have given the key to the mysterious Teller."

Agnew didn't correct me about the name Teller. Maybe he had not discovered that Pamela's grandmother Matilda had worked at Happy Times when Hattie was a resident there. Or maybe he hadn't realized that the name I'd interpreted as "Teller" could have been Tillie. Or maybe he knew but wasn't about to give me any information.

He demanded, "What was the key for, then? The woman's handwriting ran off the edge of the letter, and words are missing. What did Harriet Renniegrove possess that this Teller woman would have owned if she had the key?"

"I don't know, but whatever it was, Teller must have long since used it up or disposed of it. She's probably no longer alive." If she was Matilda Firston née Aimes, she wasn't alive. But I didn't tell Agnew I'd been searching obituaries for connections between Hattie and Pamela. If Brent or a DCI agent were here, I'd have shared what I'd found.

Suddenly, the word *TREASURE* leaped into my mind. Was "treasure" one of the words missing from the letter? Maybe the gold in the head of Hattie's cane was only part of what Ernest Renniegrove had hidden away during his archaeological explorations. Hattie might have buried more than the whorl in my yard. Had Agnew gone back there Tuesday night searching for a treasure chest? He could have unearthed a small one and taken it with him.

What had Kayla been trying to find with her metal detector? It didn't make sense that both she and Agnew could be hunting for buried treasure in my yard.

I tried to keep all thoughts of gold and jewels off my face.

Agnew stared at me. Suspicion burned in his eyes.

It must have been too much for Dep. "MEROUW!" With a mighty thrust of all four legs, she flung herself out of my arms and ran for the front door. She dabbed at the edge of the door, wedged a claw into the gap, widened it enough to squeeze through, and scooted outside.

Chapter 24

✣

I shouted, "Dep! Come back!" Leaving Chief Agnew alone in my house to gape at my treasures and perhaps search for more, I dashed out onto the porch.

Daniel was coming up the walk. Tail up, Dep wound herself around his ankles. Daniel picked her up. She didn't complain. Halfway up my front walk, I met them. My would-be runaway was purring.

Instead of handing her to me, Daniel whispered, "Are you okay?"

I whispered back, "Yes. No. Chief Agnew is here, and I don't want to be alone with him."

"I saw him arrive." Daniel gripped Dep more tightly and said in a normal, and possibly louder than normal, tone of voice, "I'll bring her in for you."

"Thank you." I also spoke loudly. Relieved, I led Daniel up the stairs and into the house.

Agnew was peering through the glass at the gold pocket watch. Or maybe he was studying the lock on the antique bookcase. He could probably open it with a paperclip.

Luckily, he wasn't trying. Yet.

He turned and watched us come into the living room. This time, I latched the door. I didn't want to be alone with Daniel, either, but I would again have to hope that each of them would protect me from the other one.

And I felt much safer with Daniel than with Chief Agnew.

Daniel set Dep down. She raced out of the living room and into the dining room.

Chief Agnew studied my face and Daniel's. A small but malicious smile played around the chief's mouth while his dark eyes seemed to bore into Daniel. "Daniel Suthlow," he pronounced slowly. "Just the person I wanted to see. Daniel Suthlow, I'm placing you under arrest for the murder of Pamela Firston." Mumbling the Miranda warning, Chief Agnew gestured for Daniel to turn around. Daniel obeyed. Without being told to and as if he'd done this before, Daniel put his hands behind his back and let Agnew handcuff him.

Although fearing that if I wasn't already next on Agnew's to-be-arrested list, I was putting myself there, I croaked out a question. "Based on what evidence?"

Agnew concentrated on snapping the handcuffs shut. "The blood type on the stone that was in Suthlow's possession is the same as the blood type of the deceased."

I couldn't help sounding skeptical. "Was there really blood on that stone?"

Agnew growled, "Don't question me."

"I was merely surprised." And despite his demand, I needed to correct him. "That stone was in my possession, not Daniel's. And it was in my possession only because my cat found it in my garden." I didn't add, *And that was after Daniel saw you, Chief Agnew, going into my yard and staying there for about ten minutes.*

But it didn't matter what I said or didn't say. Chief Agnew announced, "And Suthlow could have made up seeing that pickup truck down the street."

Daniel finally spoke, in a small voice. "I did see one, but I can't say for sure what make, model, or color it was."

I said slowly, "Chief Agnew, I should have mentioned this

earlier. A carpenter who owns a tan pickup truck was in my yard when I got home this evening. I'm sorry I forgot to tell you."

Grasping Daniel's forearm, Agnew turned toward me. "If he works here, being in your yard makes sense."

"She. Her name's Kayla. I don't know her last name, but my contractor could tell you. It didn't make sense for her to be in my yard after the others left, and it didn't make sense for her to get in by climbing to the garage roof, pulling the ladder up after herself, and then lowering it on the other side of the wall instead of merely ringing my doorbell and asking to be let in. Anyway, she's supposed to be working on the garage, not exploring my garden with a metal detector."

That seemed to catch Agnew's attention. Maybe I shouldn't have mentioned the metal detector. Agnew might return at three in the morning with picks and shovels to dig for treasure.

Not if I could help it. Which I might not be able to do if he threw me in jail . . . Maybe that was his plan.

"Musta been looking for stray roofing nails," Agnew concluded. "It's what good roofers do. They clean up thoroughly. Wouldn't want people or pets stepping on nails and suing for damage. And your roof is done, right?"

"Yes, but my point is that your evidence against Daniel is circumstantial, and there's as much circumstantial evidence against other people, like a carpenter in my yard when she doesn't need to be, and the deceased woman moving here to get away from her ex."

Agnew walked Daniel toward my front door. "People saw Suthlow's pickup truck near the scene of the crime around the right time."

"'People,'" I repeated. "Only me, and I didn't see who was driving the truck. That pickup might not have been the one that Daniel drives."

Agnew yanked my front door open. "It wasn't only you,

Ms. Westhill. A security camera captured the license number perfectly."

Daniel finally spoke. "It's okay, Emily. I was driving around, and it was just bad luck that I was near where someone was killed. I didn't kill anyone. I didn't know the woman who died."

Agnew nudged Daniel onto the front porch. "You don't have to know—"

I interrupted with an urgent question. "Daniel, do you have an alibi? Did anyone else see you Sunday evening? Did you have an appointment with someone or an errand you had to run that night, like you did last night and this evening?"

With Agnew hanging on to his upper arm and wrist, Daniel started down my porch steps. He didn't answer until he reached the walkway in front of the steps, and then, despite Agnew's grip on him, Daniel turned halfway toward me. I couldn't see his entire face. "No. No, Emily, I don't have an alibi. Like I said, I was just driving around. No one saw me, except accidentally, at the wrong place and time."

I followed the two men. "Do you need a lawyer, Daniel?"

Daniel was again facing away from me. The back of his neck was bright red. "Don't worry about it, Emily. I can handle this."

But I was going to worry, especially after Agnew put Daniel into the back of his SUV, slammed the door, and turned around, hands on hips. "He's right, Ms. Westhill. You don't need to concern yourself with Mr. Suthlow. If we discover he had a co-conspirator, we won't hesitate to arrest her, and then she can worry about getting herself a lawyer." He stomped to the driver's door, got in, and drove away. With, I was nearly certain, an innocent man.

Chapter 25

❧

Grumbling, I went back inside. Dep met me at the door and meowed. I picked her up. "I wonder," I murmured, "why Daniel hesitated when I asked him if he had an alibi. Maybe he was with someone Sunday evening, someone he's trying to protect."

"Meow?"

"No, not the murderer. Or Pamela, either. But . . . maybe he was with a woman Sunday evening, and maybe last night and tonight, too, and he can't tell anyone. Maybe she's married."

"Meow!"

I put Dep down. She ran to the front window, jumped onto the windowsill, and stared out toward where Chief Agnew's SUV had been. "Mrrrp."

I burst out laughing. "Are you saying that Agnew is married, and Daniel was with Agnew's wife?"

Dep didn't answer.

I stared out at Daniel's house. The light I'd seen earlier was still on. Had he locked his front door before coming over to—he thought—rescue me from Chief Agnew?

I told Dep, "I'll be right back."

I ran across the street and tried Daniel's front door. He

hadn't locked it. Feeling like an intruder, I reached around the edge of the door and turned the locking mechanism. I shut the door. I'd succeeded in locking it. I hoped that when they set him free, he'd have no trouble getting inside his house, and I hoped they would let him go soon.

I crossed the street to my house and took Dep out to our walled yard. Hugging the warm cat, I wondered what else I could do to help prove Daniel's innocence.

I thought back to Sunday evening, and seeing that Ever Green Forestry pickup truck. Shortly after I'd passed it, I'd wanted to turn around in a driveway, but the driveway had been blocked by branches of a tree that, judging by the green leaves, had recently been trimmed.

On Tuesday, when Samantha was driving the donut car past that driveway, she commented that she could have squeezed an ambulance past the pile, but a fire truck wouldn't have fit.

That pile had shrunk between Sunday and Tuesday.

Had Daniel been cutting down trees? Illegally? And on such a great scale that admitting to it could be worse than being arrested for murder?

I wanted to investigate, but it was already too late to try visiting whoever lived in the white house at the far end of that driveway.

Still holding Dep, I sat down in the wing chair, called Brent, and asked how his course was going.

"It's fun, but I can hardly wait for next Saturday. Let's get together as soon as we're both off work."

"Okay! I'll have dinner ready for you here. What are your students like?"

"Eager and enthusiastic. They seem like a good group of thoughtful and caring young people who will be capable of making good decisions even when stressed."

"Despite missing you, I guess I'm happy that you're teaching the course, not Chief Agnew. If anyone could teach them how to make the worst decisions, it would be him."

Brent must have heard the anger and bitterness twining through my voice. He became instantly serious. "What's he done, Emily?"

I explained.

Brent began to sound almost as worked up as I was. "Are you saying that Agnew came to your house by himself and barged in without an invitation, and then arrested your neighbor? Didn't Agnew bring backup?"

"I probably should be glad he didn't, or I might be cuffed and trying to call a lawyer right this very minute. But Agnew's probably afraid of falsely arresting the girlfriend of the best detective in his police department."

"Don't count on it. But you can relax about your grand-parents' watch and vase. I can testify that you've owned both the watch and the vase for years, and I'm certain your other friends can, too. And your parents."

"I hadn't thought of that. Thanks! Besides, Agnew's not going to be able to guess the inscription on the watch and pretend I stole it from Pamela Firston, who, he claimed, stole it from a client."

"No, and if he does get a warrant to view the inside of that watch, don't open it in his presence unless at least one other officer is there."

"Easier said than done, the way he just walks into my house as if he owns it."

"Probably. But you're strong."

"Not strong enough to pick him up and heave him out the door and over the porch railing!"

Knowing I would never attempt such a thing, Brent laughed.

Talking to him on the phone was fun and comforting, which made me miss him even more after we disconnected.

Dep was purring in my lap. I asked her, "Should I have told him about Daniel's hesitation when I asked about the alibi?"

"Mrrrp?"

"Maybe I imagined it. Besides, Daniel was probably distracted, and that's why he was slow to answer. But I can't do anything about it until tomorrow evening after work."

Dep seemed to agree.

The next day, Friday, was Tom's second day off in a row. Shortly before lunchtime, I was again doing the frying. Out in our dining room, the Knitpickers had been knitting and chatting ever since they'd finished their sweet treats around nine thirty. They were now at the stage of turning down refills of coffee and tea. They and the group of retired men were contentedly teasing one another at their regular tables and preparing to leave when they always did, before the lunch crowd arrived. Olivia appeared at my shoulder. "Your parents are coming in. I'll take over so you can go talk to them."

Jocelyn signaled to me that she could look after everyone in the shop and on our patio.

I went to my parents' table. The kitchen of their RV had no room for an espresso machine, and they loved to treat themselves to cappuccinos. "With cinnamon sprinkled on top," my mother said. "And what exotic donut are you making today, Emily?"

"Olivia concocted raised donuts filled with chocolate cream and covered with double-thick butterscotch frosting."

"They sound nice and gooey. I'd like one." She winked. "With a fork, please. Or maybe a spoon if you think it would prevent me from dribbling goo on my blouse." She'd worn that floral-print peasant blouse off and on for years, and it still looked great. So did she.

My father tossed her one of his loving looks. "Steamed, foamy milk will be enough on my coffee. I'll splurge on a chocolate-glazed peanut butter donut and a glazed donut with sprinkles."

I brought them their order and a cappuccino for myself, and then I sat where I could watch the dining room and patio in case customers needed me.

My mother spooned up donut and frosting. "How's your garage coming, Emily?"

"It's almost done."

My mother tasted the donut. "Yum. I'm glad that Kayla got that job, but now we hardly ever see her. When we were in Florida, she came to our campfire nearly every night, and she and Logan do that sometimes now, but most often, they go off somewhere for the evening."

The night of the murder, Kayla and Logan had arrived in separate vehicles at their campsite and had joined us and other neighbors for cinnamon twists, s'mores, and a sing-along. I set my cup down carefully on the glass tabletop and stayed silent, hoping to hear more.

My father licked milk foam off his upper lip. "It's our fault. We told Kayla about Fallingbrook Falls and the trails around it. We have only ourselves to blame if they're off hiking every evening."

Hoping they wouldn't notice that I slid the subject a little away, I asked, "How did you two get to know them?"

My mother looked off into the distance. "Kayla set up camp next to us in Florida and came over and introduced herself. We didn't meet Logan until he joined her here."

My father added, "They're both from California, but Kayla doesn't like staying in one place. She worked her way from California to Florida. She told us they planned to go somewhere cooler where neither of them had ever been as soon as Logan finished the school year. He finished, and they came here."

My mother leaned toward me. "We asked if they'd ever been to Wisconsin, and Kayla said they hadn't, so we told her about northern Wisconsin in general and Fallingbrook in particular. Since Kayla was hauling a camping trailer behind that pickup of hers, we told her about the Fallingbrook Falls Campground. We were thrilled when she rented the site next to us."

I turned my cup around and around on the table. "Kayla must have trusted you." The cup warmed my fingers, a contrast with the chill spreading between my shoulder blades.

My mother flung her long, curly hair over one shoulder. "Why wouldn't she? By the time she decided to come here, she'd spent many evenings with us. She knew we had a daughter and that you live in Fallingbrook." My mother gave me a mischievous grin. "For some reason, that must have made her feel safe being near us."

I tried to make my next question sound like normal small talk. "How did she know about me?"

My mother stared at me over the rim of her cup. "I guess we told her. You know how it is, chatting with new acquaintances. Like people do, being polite, she asked if we had children. We must look like parents, because she didn't seem surprised when we said we had one daughter. And then when we said you were having a garage built, she commented that Fallingbrook might be a good place to find work for the summer, or part of it. And, thanks to your recommendation, she did!"

"How did she learn that I live in Fallingbrook?" I tried not to make the question sound as pointed as it actually was.

"We must have told her. I don't remember. She's very friendly and nice." My mother believed the best of everyone. I wasn't about to tell her and my father about Kayla's peculiar exploration of my property or that she, or someone driving a truck similar to hers, might have helped herself to the keys in my mailbox and come into my yard around three in the morning after I got home from Misty and Scott's wedding.

Still attempting to seem merely chatty, I asked, "Did Kayla work while she was camping in Florida?"

My father drained his cup. "She didn't find a job while we

were there, and she must not have stayed in Cypress Knee for very many days after we left. We came almost straight here—"

My mother winked. "For us!"

I couldn't help smiling back at them. On their trips to and from Florida, they meandered wherever their whims took them.

My father finished his sentence. "And she showed up a few days later. And Logan came the next day, right, Annie?"

My mother nodded. My parents finished their snack and said they should do their shopping and get back to their campsite. Who could blame them for wanting to spend as much time as possible in that peaceful campground in the shade of towering pines and maples? They would relax and enjoy themselves.

I followed Jocelyn into the kitchen, helped fill the orders she'd taken, and asked if she remembered Kayla and Logan from my parents' campfire Sunday night.

"Sure. I see them often, exploring the trails around the falls while I'm jogging."

"You were jogging at the campground earlier that evening. Did you see them then?"

"What's this about? Have they done something to your parents?"

"No, just wondering."

"That's the night that woman was killed, wasn't it?"

"Yes, but . . ."

Her contagious grin showed off a dimple on one side of her mouth. "Don't worry. I wouldn't stop you from sleuthing."

"I'm not investigating, and I don't want you to, either."

"But solving crimes is satisfying. And I have ways of escaping danger."

"I've noticed." Her gymnastic skills had occasionally come in handy.

"Anyway, I don't think you have to worry about those two.

I did see them Sunday evening. They were near the top of the falls, hiking and taking pictures."

"Do you remember what time it was?"

"No, but the next time I passed your parents' site, Brent was there, but you weren't. Later, you were there, and he wasn't. Does that help?"

"Sort of."

We ended our conversation and went out into the dining room to give our customers plates of donuts and mugs of coffee and to receive praise that was almost embarrassingly hearty.

We were busy during the remainder of the day, and I couldn't allow myself to think about the murder or Daniel's arrest, but at home after enjoying a quick bowl of cheddar-cauliflower soup, I told Dep, "I'm leaving without you again. I shouldn't be long."

Chapter 26

I drove quickly toward Fallingbrook Falls. I passed the sign for Peabody Lane, and then, cautioning myself not to confront a gang of timber pirates, I slowed down.

The pile of branches was still in the driveway. It had shrunk since Samantha commented on it, and the leaves dangling limply from twigs had shriveled, their spring green faded to brown-spotted lemon.

And someone was in the driveway.

The woman did not fit my image of a timber pirate. She was tiny with pure white hair, neatly cut and permed. Wearing a dress, thick stockings, and sensible shoes, she bent and pulled at a branch. It had obviously snagged another one, and they were threatening to bring the entire pile down on her.

I swerved into the driveway.

I wasn't sure how to begin my questions, but I didn't need to worry. I stepped out of my car, and the tiny woman asked, "Are you from the church?"

"Um, no."

"Because I called the pastor just now, and he said he'd come and bring some other church members. He tried to reach Daniel, but Daniel didn't answer. Daniel was supposed to finish hauling this stuff away for me last night, but he never showed. I mean, he's a nice young man, and maybe he's found himself a sweet girl and forgot, but he was worried about emergency vehicles not being able to come up the driveway. I told him not to worry, now that he took those trees down, I'm not about to be pinned inside my house."

She stopped for a breath, so I asked quickly, "When did he take down the trees?"

"It was, oh, let's see . . . he did it over several weeks, you know, just working evenings like he did. That boy knew what he was doing! Scrambled up those trees like a lumberjack and lopped off the branches one by one, then the trunks. They went crashing down onto the lawn with big *thumps*! Not a single twig or branch landed on my roof. That Daniel—he's a real professional. Those trunks are still back there, and he's going to have someone take them away and pay me for the wood! And I don't have to give Daniel a cent—actually, he said to give it to the church instead—until after I get the money for the lumber. Do you know where he is and when he's coming back?"

"Sorry, I wish I did. Do you remember if he worked here last Sunday evening?"

She tapped her lips with an index finger. "Let me think. Yes, of course, now I remember. He worked all afternoon. I said it wasn't right to make him work on a Sunday, but he said that was his best day for working, and it was a lovely day, a little breezy, but he loved being up there in the branches with all the leaves, and I said, it's like being close to heaven, and he agreed, so yes, I do remember that he worked here the past two Sundays. But I wouldn't let him work all evening, too. I made him stop and have something to eat, and then I told him to go home."

She had to catch her breath again.

I asked, "Do you remember when he left your place Sunday evening?"

"Yes. Both Sundays, he left around six. You see, Sundays

at six fifteen is when I start calling the people on my shut-ins list."

"Did he come in his own car or his company's pickup truck?"

"His company's truck. As I said, he was a real professional. Do you think he'll be back soon?"

I tried not to show my excitement. I'd seen the Ever Green Forestry pickup around six. Daniel had probably been driving it, and he had probably come straight from this woman's house, which meant that he couldn't have found time to drive down the Peabody-Smiths' treacherous driveway and return up it, let alone run into the cabin, clobber Pamela, and search the place. This sweet little woman probably held the key to Daniel's release, if I could get the police to interview her. I said quickly, "I hope he'll be back soon. Meanwhile, why don't you sit at the pretty bistro set over there, and I'll work on this until someone comes or it gets dark?"

"I might be ninety-four, but I'm strong as an ox. We can work on it together."

There was no arguing with her. Fortunately, cars, vans, and pickups pulled into the driveway, and about fifteen men got out and cheerfully greeted the woman.

As I headed toward my own car, I heard her agree to let them do all the work. She headed toward the table and chairs under a young and healthy-looking tree and called to the men, "Do you know where Daniel is?"

The man wearing the clerical collar answered, "He's still not answering his phone. Won't he be surprised when he discovers we took care of this?"

I got into my car, maneuvered around the other vehicles, and made a mental note of her address. On the way home, I decided not to tell Chief Agnew about Daniel's alibi. He would probably dismiss it.

At home, I phoned Brent and was disappointed. He didn't answer. I left him a message to call me. "It doesn't matter how late." I carried Dep upstairs and turned on my computer. With my warm cat curled in my lap, I searched for articles about Happy Times Home Health Care.

The most recent one was from only three weeks ago. A woman had complained that a Happy Times Home Health Care employee had stolen from the woman's late grandmother when the older woman was an invalid living in her own home near Rhinelander. Items that had disappeared included jewelry and a valuable Art Deco vase. Also, the granddaughter had alleged that the caregiver must have stolen her grandmother's grocery money, too, and that a diet of cheap carbs had contributed to the frail senior's death. The woman who had made the complaint wasn't named, but the article mentioned that she worked in a Fallingbrook clothing shop.

Fallingbrook had a menswear shop, a women's shop, and a consignment shop for children's clothes and toys.

And Fallingbrook also had the bridal shop where Diana worked. . . .

When Pamela was in Deputy Donut Sunday afternoon, Pamela must have recognized Diana out on the street. Had Pamela rushed away from Diana only to have Diana spot her in the parking lot? The next day, Madame Monique and I discussed the murder. Diana hadn't admitted to knowing who Pamela was, but Diana had become suddenly almost as expressionless as a police officer.

The article said that Happy Times had not admitted to any wrongdoing, but considering that this was the second time in the past year that allegations had been made about the employee in question, Happy Times had accepted the employee's resignation. The reporter quipped, *The employee has left Happy Times behind.* Ouch. If the employee had been Pamela, she certainly had left happy times behind.

I dug up an article about the earlier set of allegations. A caregiver from Happy Times Home Health Care had supposedly neglected a man's grandfather and had stolen an antique gold pocket watch. This time the complainant was named. He was Irving Agnew, who, when the article was published, was a detective in the Green Bay police department. Irving Agnew's grandfather had died in his own home in Rhinelander.

Both Tom and Brent had mentioned that Chief Agnew had come to Fallingbrook from Green Bay. . . .

Even though the article did not include photos, I was certain that the man whose grandfather's pocket watch had been stolen was now heading our police department.

I double-checked Fallingbrook's recent announcement about hiring a new chief.

Chief Agnew's first name was Irving.

Chapter 27

✻

Now I knew Agnew's possible motive—revenge for the way his late grandfather had been treated.

There was additional circumstantial evidence against him. He had sent the department's other detective away. He had been in my walled garden around the time the stone whorl could have been thrown there. He had immediately recognized the whorl as the murder weapon. He had avoided asking for help from the Wisconsin Division of Criminal Investigation, even though he was supposed to. And he had, all by himself, quickly built a case against Daniel on flimsier circumstantial evidence.

Chief Irving Agnew was, I suspected, a dangerous man.

Which meant that I didn't dare do anything that could give him an inkling that I suspected him.

Luckily, Brent phoned before I could work myself into what my grandmother might have called a tizzy. I told him about Agnew and the connection between his grandfather and, I was almost certain, Pamela Firston, and I linked it to his earlier claims that the watch in my house might have been stolen. Finally, I added, "And I think I discovered that Daniel has an alibi."

I told Brent about the woman waiting for someone named Daniel to remove the brush from her driveway.

Brent asked, "Did she mention the last name of the Daniel she was talking about?"

Uh-oh. Why hadn't I asked her? "No, but it has to be him."

"Did she describe him?"

"Not physically, but what she said about his personality and attitudes matched what I noticed about him. But I can't tell Chief Agnew what I learned from the woman. If Agnew murdered Pamela, what might he do to a sweet little old lady?"

"Don't contact him, okay? Let me handle it."

Brent was, as always, reliable. Late the next afternoon, I was sliding covered bowls of freshly kneaded dough into our proofing cabinet when Jocelyn called to me from near the front door, "Look who's here, Emily!"

I turned around. Jocelyn was beaming up at a distinguished man in a black suit, white shirt, and dark gray tie.

A couple of years before, Jocelyn and I had gotten to know DCI Agent Rex Clobar. He had proven himself to be fair and competent. Heading toward him, I couldn't help a broad smile. The tall, muscular man was still slim and hadn't aged except for more gray flecking his dark hair.

I shook his hand. "Am I ever glad to see you!"

His smile crinkled the skin beside his eyes. "I don't always get that reaction. Except for the circumstances, it's good to see both you and Jocelyn again. Can I talk to you, Emily?" He was carrying a briefcase.

Jocelyn made a shooing motion with her hands. "The rest of us can handle everything. I'll bring you a mug of today's special blend of Hawaiian coffees, Detective Clobar."

"Please call me Rex, Jocelyn."

"Okay. Want to try our raised coconut-covered pineapple donuts, Rex?"

"How can I resist?"

"You can't. I'll bring your coffee and donuts in a minute."

I thanked her, led Rex into the office, and picked up Dep. "Have a seat. The desk chair might have less cat hair than the couch."

"I'm fine." He sat on the couch and opened his briefcase. "I hear you've had some trouble around here."

I tried to restrain a less-than-polite face. "Did Chief Agnew finally call you in?"

"It might not have been his idea, but he had to. You have friends who have friends in state agencies."

I sat on the other end of the couch and stated, "Brent."

His smile was kind and appreciative. "Yes. Detective Fyne."

Automatically, I rubbed my right thumb and forefinger around my bare left ring finger, a leftover habit from the years, including long after Alec's death, that I'd worn a wedding ring. "Brent and I are . . ." It was always hard to know how to word it. "Close. Dating now."

Those smile wrinkles deepened. "Glad to hear it. I saw it coming, or thought I did. I'm glad my detection skills were still keen."

Jocelyn brought a steaming mug of coffee and a plate with two pineapple donuts on it and placed them on the coffee table in front of Rex. She left, quietly closing the door behind her.

Rex bit into a donut. "I'm glad she talked me into this."

"It didn't take a lot of talking."

"True. Brent said you had something specific to tell me, information you weren't willing to give to Chief Agnew."

"Sorry, but I don't trust him. He arrested Daniel Suthlow based on almost no evidence. I think Daniel has an alibi, but for some reason he told us he didn't." I gave Rex the address of the woman whose trees Daniel had cut down and admitted that I hadn't asked for the woman's name.

"I'll go talk to her." He removed papers from his briefcase and fingered the top set of stapled-together pages. "Chief Agnew had you come in and give a statement. It was typed up, but you never came back to sign it."

"He . . . no one told me it was ready, and I didn't think of it. Sorry."

"No need to apologize. They should have called you." He grinned over his shoulder at the cheerful dining room behind him. "Or brought it over and enjoyed a coffee and donut. Speaking of which . . ." He picked up his mug and took a sip. "Mmm. I haven't had such good coffee since the last time I was here."

We went over the statement that Chief Agnew had produced from our interview. "That's strange," I said. "He left out a lot of what I said. For instance, I told him that Pamela seemed to drop part of an earring, and one of the reasons I went to her cabin was to return it to her, but I panicked when the smoke alarm started screeching, and I lost track of what I did with that earring. Also, Chief Agnew didn't mention my having seen a check made out to Pamela Firston. His version of my statement will have to include all of what I said, which he recorded, before I can sign it."

Rex's eyebrows lifted in apparent surprise. "Of course."

"I wrote a statement, printed it, signed it, and gave it to him. It was complete. The original is at home on my computer. I can print and sign it again if that would help."

"I have it." He removed it from his briefcase, and we read both statements together. He tapped a finger on the pages I'd taken to Agnew. "I'll attach your statement to the one Irv produced and add that the two statements together constitute your statement. Will you be able to sign that?"

"Yes, after I see what you add."

His mouth twitched.

Petting Dep, I glanced up toward her tunnels and catwalks. "Is Irv short for Irving?"

"I believe so."

"I want you to see two articles I found about possible thefts by an employee of Happy Times Home Health Care. That's the company that wrote Pamela's final severance check." I put Dep down, led Rex to the computer on the office desk, and opened the newspaper articles.

Rex skimmed through them. "I see." I couldn't read his expression. He handed me his business card. "Can you email me the links?"

While I was doing that, I suggested that the clothing store clerk could have been Diana. "She was one of the people I described in my statement."

We went back and sat on the couch. Rex ate donuts and drank coffee. I told him everything that Chief Agnew had said and done that had made me think his main purpose was arresting anyone besides himself for the murder.

Again, Rex said nothing about Chief Agnew's possible guilt, but I could tell that the idea startled him and that he would mull it over and look into it before discarding it. Or agreeing with it.

I again thanked him for coming to Fallingbrook even after an arrest had been made.

"It's my job, but I don't know why Agnew didn't call us. Tell me more about this Diana and about the other people, besides Agnew and Suthlow, who you thought might have frightened the deceased when she was here."

I told Rex about Diana's tale of a tooth extraction. "She said she was home alone that evening. So, she doesn't have an alibi, either. However, Pamela told my friend Summer Peabody-Smith that she, Pamela that is, had moved to Fallingbrook to get away from an ex, a man who, she said, 'knew all about medicines.' The person who appeared to cause Pamela to flee out the back door when he appeared at the front door told me his name was Gregory and that he had also recently moved to Fallingbrook. He claimed to be a pharmaceutical sales rep, with appointments that evening. I heard from the hospital administrator that he did have an appointment with the head pharmacist, but he canceled at the last minute."

Rex rustled papers inside his briefcase and pulled out three snapshots. "Did Gregory the sales rep resemble any of these men?"

I pointed at the middle photo. "That's the man who was in here."

"Are you sure?"

"Positive."

Rex tucked the photos into his briefcase. "Ms. Firston's former landlady gave us the ex's name. He's the man in the photo you chose. His name is Gregory Tinsletter. He and Pamela broke up recently, and he is a pharmaceutical sales rep. You probably won't be surprised to hear that when we investigate a murder, almost the first people we talk to are the people closest to the deceased. The last call on Ms. Firston's phone was a voice message from Mr. Tinsletter. That message could be interpreted as a threat."

I tilted my head questioningly. "Could be?"

"Or not. Tinsletter said, 'Don't do it unless you want real trouble.' He could have been threatening her. But maybe you'll agree that there's another way of looking at it. He could have been warning her to stay out of trouble."

"Could you tell from his tone of voice?"

"It was somewhere between stern, scolding, and angry. Possibly frustrated. Or some combination."

Dep was on my lap again. I stroked her. "So, because Gregory Tinsletter dated Pamela and left that voice message on her phone, would you have looked into him before arresting Daniel?"

"Maybe. Suthlow was near the scene, Agnew saw what he thought was the murder weapon in Daniel's hand, the blood type on it matched the victim's, and Suthlow did not offer an alibi. Maybe the lady you just told me about will confirm that he was with her."

"Is a bail hearing scheduled for him?"

"It's to be on Monday afternoon. Agnew is hoping the judge will set insurmountably high bail."

"And this is only Saturday."

"Don't fret about your young neighbor, Emily. I'll be looking into other things. Has Tinsletter been back here?"

"Not that I know of, but I wasn't here on Tuesday and Wednesday except for a few minutes. You'll have to ask Jocelyn, Tom, and Olivia."

"Olivia?"

"We hired her since you were last here."

"I'll talk to them. Can you keep my business card and call me if you see Gregory Tinsletter?"

"Sure. Does that mean you don't know where he is?"

Rex twisted one side of his mouth up in a rueful smile. "You are the last person I know about who saw him. He's renting a cabin close to the one the deceased was renting."

"Aha!" Dep tucked her paws underneath her and purred.

"I've called him, and I drove out there this morning. There's uncollected mail in the mailbox out on the road, the place is locked up tight, and there were no vehicles nearby." He must have seen the question on my face. "And I didn't go inside the cabin to check." He teased, "There was no smoke, no burnt burger, and no smoke alarm." Serious again, he added, "We'll get a search warrant or help from the landlord to enter the premises. Also, I'll talk to the hospital and see if he's been in touch with them, and I'll ask his employer for his appointment schedule." Rex looked through his notes. "Do you have any guesses about why an envelope addressed to you was in the deceased's cabin?"

I spread my hands in an I-don't-know gesture, nearly causing Dep to slide off my shorts. I grabbed her before she could slow herself by digging in with her claws. "The letter in that envelope was from Hattie Renniegrove, the first owner of my home. She had it built for her. The letter mentions a key and something that will belong to the addressee, which I first thought was someone named Teller, but now I think is probably Tillie, short for Matilda."

Rex tilted his head.

"I've been looking into the history of my house. Hattie died in Fallingbrook's Happy Times Nursing Home in 1950. At the time, one of the nursing home's founder's granddaughters worked there. Her name was Matilda Aimes. She later married a man named Firston. I'm almost certain that Matilda was Pamela's grandmother. Pamela must have gotten the letter from Matilda. Hattie's words ran off the edge of the letter, but I wonder if the missing words include 'treasure.' Maybe Pamela was planning to give me the letter, but I wonder if she wrote the address on the envelope as a way of keeping track of my address and never intended to give me the letter. She could have been planning to break into my house or dig in my yard for whatever she thought Hattie Renniegrove had said would belong to Matilda. Could that have been what Gregory Tinsletter's threatening message referred to?" I shuddered. "Gregory could have been warning Pamela about the consequences of breaking into my place or doing her own 'archaeological' dig."

"Possibly."

"I told you about someone, maybe Chief Agnew, digging in my yard. Yesterday when I got home from work, one of the carpenters building my new garage was running a metal detector over my lawn and garden, including over the holes that someone dug. The carpenter claimed she was looking for a drill bit that had flown out of her hand when she was on my new garage roof, but if so, it had wings. The carpenter was on the other side of my yard. Not that it's huge."

"What's her name?"

"Kayla. I don't know her last name. She and her boyfriend, Logan, are camping next to my parents out at Fallingbrook Falls Campground."

Rex smiled. During a previous investigation, he'd been to that campground and had met my parents. "I can't say that I blame them."

I added, "And I can't help wondering if Kayla somehow believes there's buried treasure in my yard. It's all very weird!"

"It is. I'll have a talk with her. If nothing else, maybe she can be persuaded not to wander around your place at three in the morning."

I had to admit that I wasn't sure that Kayla had been there around three on Wednesday morning. "It could have been Daniel Suthlow or Chief Agnew. Or just about anybody."

Rex finished writing his notes about our conversation and asked me to send the other Deputy Donut staff, one by one, to talk to him.

After Rex questioned them, I walked with him through the dining room. He told me that Tom, Olivia, and Jocelyn all remembered Gregory from the photo Rex showed them, and they were certain that he had not been inside Deputy Donut since Sunday.

At the front door, Rex gave me a nice smile. "I'll be in touch."

If he suspected me of murder, he was hiding it. Which, I knew from experience, detectives could do, often quite well.

Chapter 28

Our final customers of the day left shortly after four thirty, and then Jocelyn, Olivia, Tom, and I prepared the shop for the Jolly Cops Cleaning Crew. Tom went out, got into his SUV, waved, and drove off. I left Dep in the office for only a few minutes—I hoped—and started walking south with Olivia and Jocelyn, who was wheeling her bike beside us. I stayed with them only as far as Thrills and Frills.

Inside the lavender-scented bridal boutique, Madame Monique was pinching purple satin together to tighten the waist of a future bridesmaid's dress. "See? We take this in just a wee bit, and ooh-la-la! Perfection."

Diana rushed to greet me.

I held up my phone. "I brought snapshots from Misty's wedding."

Madame Monique must have heard me. She called out, "One minute, Mademoiselle Emily! Here, Diana, you help this lovely young lady remove the gown. I know just how to take it in."

Diana winked at me and then ushered the future bridesmaid into the changing room.

I showed Madame Monique how to view the pictures on my phone. She gushed, first with only words, but then also tears over the "oh, so beautiful Misty" and Samantha and me in our gowns. We went through the photos a second time, more slowly, so I could send Madame Monique the ones she wanted.

She exclaimed, "I must have this one! You know, the poor petite Diana is still suffering from her tooth. Oh, and send me that picture, too. I told her she didn't have to, but she brought me a note from her dentist. This one is divine! He wrote that he'd told her to go directly home and rest. I must have a copy of this one, too! He also wrote that she argued that her profession was not strenuous, and she could go to work, but he said, no—Samantha's gown is lovely from that angle, don't you think?—he told her she had to go home and rest. I'm so glad I found that gown for Misty. So elegant. The poor petite Diana, how she must have suffered. If only I had known, I could have closed the shop and driven her home, me."

Diana showed the customer out and then joined us. Commenting rapturously, Madame Monique showed Diana all of the photos. "And did I ask for this one, Mademoiselle Emily? I must, simply must, have it!"

I might have sent her some of the photos more than once. . . .

Madame Monique excused herself and hurried back to her office to download and print the pictures. Misty, Samantha, and I would join brides and attendants in Madame Monique's ever-growing scrapbook.

A mother and her dewy-eyed daughter came in to look at wedding gowns. I waved goodbye and went back to our office. Dep voiced her disapproval at being left behind, but she was willing to wear her harness and leash and walk home with me in the fragrant warmth of the early June evening. The sun was still high in the sky.

No one was working on my garage. The big overhead door had not been installed, and the opening gaped, showing ladders and tools chained inside it.

As soon as we went into our house and I unfastened Dep's harness, she scampered to the kitchen. I opened windows to let in fresh air, and then I put a serving of my homemade Swedish meatballs into the oven. I fed Dep, made a tomato, cucumber, and fresh dill salad, and ambled out into my walled garden. The rear door to the garage was still firmly shut and locked. Back inside again, the meatballs and gravy smelled mouthwatering. I heated water. When it reached a rolling boil, I dropped broad, flat egg noodles into it. Stirring, I lowered the heat a little. The noodles cooked quickly. I drained them, tossed them in buttered breadcrumbs, and ladled the meatballs and their gravy onto the noodles. I topped the dish with a dollop of sour cream, a sprinkling of freshly grated nutmeg, and a sliced green onion. With Dep leading the way, I carried my dinner outside. It was delicious.

I missed Brent.

Dep crept around underneath bushes and behind peonies.

After I washed dishes and cleaned the kitchen, I took Dep outside again. She had disturbed some of the dirt piled around the holes. Watching ants crawling purposely over peony buds, I wondered if I should dig more holes to try to find whatever it was that someone else—or maybe several someone elses—had been searching for.

Maybe the whorl was not the murder weapon. Maybe someone whose blood type was the same as Pamela's had dug it up, scratching or cutting themselves in the process, and when they heard me inside the house, they threw the whorl down and ran off.

Or maybe it was the murder weapon, and someone had brought it into my yard to implicate me.

Someone. Like Police Chief Irving Agnew, for instance.

But Daniel had seen a pale pickup truck parked down the street. Kayla drove a tan pickup. And I'd found Kayla wielding a metal detector strangely far from where a drill bit might have landed if it had been on the garage roof.

Rex Clobar called me. "I just talked to your carpenter and her boyfriend. The evening that Ms. Firston was killed, those two were together, hiking along the river above the falls. They snapped photos of each other there, and the time stamps show they didn't have time to drive over to Peabody Lane."

"Good to know. I took wedding photos to Thrills and Frills today, and Diana's boss told me that Diana's dentist had written a note explaining Diana's absence from the shop Sunday afternoon. So, unless Madam Monique is lying or the note was forged or Diana went out instead of resting as she was supposed to, Diana's in the clear, too."

"I haven't talked to her. I will, and I'll check with her dentist about the note."

"And what about the ex, Gregory Tinsletter?"

"We haven't been able to locate him."

"Aha."

Rex laughed. "Have a good evening, Emily." I heard a big smile, like he had a private joke, in his voice.

We disconnected.

A few minutes later, the doorbell inside my house rang.

I muttered to Dep, "If that's Chief Agnew, I don't want to go inside and answer the door. Maybe he'll decide I'm not home, and he'll go away."

"Meow." Tail straight up, Dep started toward the house.

What if the smile in Rex's voice meant that my evening might be especially good because Rex knew that, for some reason, Brent was in Fallingbrook? "Okay, Dep," I said, "Let's go see."

I peeked out the peephole and let out a gasp.

Daniel was on my front porch.

Chapter 29

I threw open the door. "Daniel! How did you get here?" I slipped out onto the porch and shut Dep inside.

Daniel's clothes were rumpled as if he'd slept in them. He grinned. "I didn't break out of jail, if that's what you're thinking."

Suspiciously, I peered past him toward the street. No vehicles were sliding away from the curb, but while I was coming inside from the garden and tiptoeing through the house, a vehicle could have made a clean getaway. Across the street, Daniel's Ever Green truck was in his driveway, where it had been since before Agnew arrested him. I planted my fists on my hips. "Did they make you walk home?"

"A nice detective from the Wisconsin Division of Criminal Investigation dropped me off."

I waved toward the wicker chairs. "Have a seat. Was Detective Clobar on the phone with me while he was driving you here?"

"It seemed that way."

I sat down. "No wonder he sounded like he was enjoying a private joke when he told me to have a nice evening. It has suddenly become a very good evening. Did he break you out of jail?"

Daniel sat in the other chair. "The charges were dropped, thanks to you for discovering my alibi and telling Detective Clobar about it."

"Why didn't you tell Chief Agnew where you'd been Sunday afternoon and evening?"

Daniel leaned forward, rested his forearms on his thighs, and stared down at his clasped hands. "I thought I could keep my moonlighting a secret, and I didn't believe anyone would seriously suspect I'd murdered anyone. Obviously, I was going to need to confess to moonlighting, since being arrested was worse than losing my job. I don't even like my job. I love being outside and up in the forest canopy, but I hate cutting down healthy trees for reasons that don't make sense to me. I have this skill, so I use it, but I hope to earn enough to quit and go back to school."

"I hope you can. Why did you moonlight?" I had some good guesses, but waited for his answer.

"One of the first people to befriend me in Fallingbrook was this woman at church. She's a tiny little thing who likes to brag that she's ninety-four years old. Sweet and grandmotherly. She told me she lives alone and is quite capable of it and likes it. She loves her home, but she was afraid she would have to move because three huge trees were looming over it, and she thought they might fall on her house and hurt her. She invited me over. I hoped I could reassure her that the trees were no danger to her, but she was right. The trees weren't healthy, and they were a threat to her house and to her. I suspected that if she knew how much some companies would charge to remove those trees, she'd have a heart attack, so I cut them down." He gazed across the street, but I didn't think he was registering what he was seeing. He continued, "I said I was just driving around on Sunday, but I was actually piling branches in her driveway. Around six, she told me I'd done enough for a Sunday. You saw me about the time I was starting for home. I went back other nights with a woodchipper, but I didn't manage to clear her driveway before I was arrested. She wouldn't let me cut down those trees for free, so I told her to put the money—I gave her a very low figure—in the collection plate for the next year of Sundays instead. I hope she never finds out how much it would have actually cost, or she'll badger me about undercharging her or want me to take some of the payment she gets for the timber."

"That was very nice of you."

He blushed. "Not really. It's how I was brought up, to help people who need it."

"How could helping her make you lose your job?"

"I used company equipment. And our contract stipulates that we're not allowed to moonlight."

I gave him what I hoped was a reassuring smile. "I won't tell."

His answering smile was small. "Yes, well, I'm going to have to, after missing work on Friday due to being incarcerated."

I guessed, "And you were also brought up to tell the truth?"

"Of course."

I had been, too, but I sometimes stretched it. Maybe more than stretched it . . . "Also, I bet you don't want people to know that you did a good deed."

His forearms still rested on his thighs. He turned his palms up and spread his hands apart in a hands-only shrug. "It's not much of a good deed if we profit from it by going around bragging about it."

"I suppose not."

He threw me a quick glance. "It's just how I was raised. I bet you were, too."

"My parents tried. When I was talking to the lady with the trees, I mean without the trees, people from your church arrived and started clearing the brush out of her driveway. They said they were going to clear it all, and they weren't going to let her help."

He let out a sigh that sounded like it had been pent up ever since Agnew arrested him. "That's a relief. I've been worrying about her."

"Did the police feed you? Can I get you anything?"

"I'm good. Before I did anything else, I wanted to thank you and tell you I was free. Now I just want to go home, clean up, and call to apologize for not clearing that brush. I also need to thank the people who pitched in. If I don't need to go right out and finish the job, I'll get on the internet and try to find connections between Pamela Firston and the ladies who built your house and the one behind it."

I quickly summarized what I'd learned. Thinking about Hattie and Esther Renniegrove seemed to help Daniel forget his forty-eight-hour ordeal. Already looking less stressed, he stood up to leave.

I rose from my chair, too. "Will you be okay?"

He smiled. "I'm fine. Knowing I'm innocent helped."

"Do you have your house key? After Agnew arrested you, I went over and locked your door."

He patted one of his front pockets. "I have my keys. Thank you for thinking of that. It was very kind of you."

I grinned. "It was how I was brought up."

He smiled back. "I figured."

I watched him cross the street and shut himself into his house. He walked like a person with no heavy burdens.

With a powerful thrum of its engine, a large black SUV eased to the curb in front of my house. Chief Agnew got out. Standing so that his SUV was between him and the sidewalk, he stared up at my house. The charges had been dropped against Daniel. That could only mean one thing—Chief Agnew was on the prowl for a new suspect.

Hoping that the pillar supporting the porch roof was hiding me, I stood still.

Naturally, since I could see him past the pillar, he spotted me. He closed his car door quietly and started toward the house, walking in that peculiar knees-together and toes-pointing-inward way, but putting his police-issue boots down softly as if afraid of making noises that would alert neighbors to peer through windows or come out onto their own porches.

I threw a hopeful glance toward Daniel's house. His front door remained closed.

Agnew carried a small plastic sandwich bag in one hand. Something in the bag glinted. Gold. He came up onto my porch. "Ms. Westhill, can we go inside?"

"I . . . no. The cat might get out." It was a weak excuse. I restrained myself from glancing again toward Daniel's house.

"You might prefer not to have your neighbors watch us."

And I might prefer them to. I folded my arms. "It's okay." I didn't want to be alone with him where no one could see or hear us. Anyway, if Agnew handcuffed me and perp-walked me to his unmarked police SUV, I wasn't going to be able to hide.

He held the plastic bag almost in front of my face. "Do you recognize the object in this bag?"

"It looks like the dangly part of one of the earrings Pamela Firston was wearing in Deputy Donut, but her earrings didn't have black fingerprint powder on them."

He seemed startled, as if he had expected me to lie. Although I'd already told him about that earring, I was almost certain I knew what was coming next.

He accused, "There are partial fingerprints on this. Some are the deceased's. Others are on top of them, and they are yours."

"That makes perfect sense. As I told you in my statement, when she ran out of Deputy Donut, she must have dropped it. I picked it up."

Still holding the bag so close to me that I could barely focus on it, he gave it a little shake. "We found the earring in the cabin the deceased was renting."

"Both earrings should have been there—the one she was wearing when I last saw her alive, and the one I found. In my hurry when the smoke alarm went off, I think I tossed that one onto the love seat beside the front door." I didn't point out that those facts had also been in my statement.

"Are you certain that you didn't grab it off her when you were struggling with her?"

I said forcefully, "I never struggled with her. Ask Diana, the clerk from Thrills and Frills. As I told you before, I think she saw Pamela drop the earring. Diana pointed at her and would have called out, but she had a mouth full of gauze. Also, you can ask my business partner at Deputy Donut, Tom Westhill. I told him that if Pamela came in asking about a lost earring, I had it."

"But you didn't show Westhill the earring." As far as I knew, Agnew had never talked to Tom. Agnew was doing everything in his power to convince himself that I had killed Pamela.

I couldn't help correcting him. "Chief Westhill. He retired a few years ago from the position you currently hold." I hoped that Agnew hadn't interpreted my use of the word "currently" correctly—I wanted him to move on to a new position. Even better, maybe he should leave policing entirely.

"You seem to be in the habit of being buddy-buddy with law enforcement and retired law enforcement."

"Tom's the father of my late husband." *Why had Agnew come alone again? Where was Rex?*

Agnew tucked the earring, still in its plastic bag, into a pocket, and pulled out a sheaf of folded papers. "I brought your statement. You never signed it. Here. Let's go inside and you can sign it."

"I can sign it out here if you lend me a pen."

With a sigh, he pulled a pen from his chest pocket. "Here."

"Have a seat." I indicated one of the wicker chairs and sat in the other one. I unfolded the papers. There weren't as many pages as I expected. Sure enough, the statement Agnew brought me was the incomplete one from my interview at the police station, the one that left out much of what I'd said and he'd recorded. I asked him, "Where's the rest of it?"

"That's it, in its entirety." His face reddened.

"I talked to DCI Agent Clobar today. He was going to add a clause saying that the statement I wrote formed part of my statement. This is incomplete." I shoved it and the pen across the glass tabletop toward him.

"You have to sign this."

I stood. "You know that's not true."

"I'll add the other pages and the extra wording you want put on it after I go back. Just sign it now and save yourself another trip to the police station after the additions are made."

"I absolutely will not do that. I don't know how an upstanding police chief can ask such a thing." I'd gone too far. He would handcuff me any minute . . . I backtracked a tiny bit, in a way that I knew was aggressive and might annoy him even more, but I had to protect myself. "If you like I can take it to my lawyer and see what he says."

"That won't be necessary." He folded the pages again and stuck them in his jacket pocket. "I'll be back, and next time, I might have a search warrant for the watch you took from the cabin of the deceased."

I stood as tall as I could. "Ask Detective Brent Fyne if he's ever seen a gold pocket watch in my house. He'll be able to describe it perfectly, plus he can tell you who else might have seen it in my house for years, including Chief Tom Westhill, the father of my late husband. My mother will vouch for it."

He scoffed. "Your mother! Like she'd be unbiased."

"Bias doesn't come into it. The watch you saw inside my house originally belonged to her grandfather."

"We're done." He stomped down the steps.

Shaken by anger, I watched him get into his SUV and drive away.

Chapter 30

I went inside, locked the door, and took Dep out into our walled garden. Maybe looking at flowers would help me relax enough to phone Brent and speak rationally.

Brent called me.

Heading back into the house, I asked him about his day.

"This is a nice change, but I can hardly wait to come back. I understand that a DCI agent has now arrived in Fallingbrook and taken over the investigation."

I held the door open for Dep. She bounded into the sunroom, and I shut the door, making certain that none of my neighbors could eavesdrop on my side of the conversation. "Rex Clobar. He got Daniel released, and he's trying to locate the victim's ex. Rex seems to be trying to prevent Agnew from focusing on me."

"What motive could Agnew possibly think you have?"

I plunked onto the love seat facing the windows into the garden. "I don't know, but he must think he's going to find one. Maybe he's not interested in motive." Forgetting my resolve to be calm and not run to Brent with every little problem, I told him about Agnew's allegations about the earring, his attempts to force me to sign an incomplete statement, and his threats to return with a search warrant. I added, "But I can't go around accusing a police chief of murder when that police chief seems intent on accusing me of the same murder."

Brent was silent for a moment. I thought I heard his fingers drumming on the desk in his hotel room. Finally he said, "Agnew didn't kill Firston."

I stared through my sunroom windows but was only barely aware of the beauty of the greenery and the colorful splashes of late springtime flowers. "He's been acting guilty. I mean he's been doing things that make me suspicious."

Brent answered calmly, "I know, and it's easy to understand why you suspect him. What time did you see him drive past Deputy Donut on Sunday afternoon?"

I was clutching my phone so tightly that my hand hurt. "Shortly after four."

"He was on his way home. He lives about fifteen minutes south of Fallingbrook. He changed into civilian clothes and switched from the department SUV to his personal car. Then he drove to a cemetery near Rhinelander where his grandfather is buried. At the speed limit, that cemetery should be almost an hour from Agnew's home. Agnew speeds. He made it to the cemetery by five, when a married couple also visiting the cemetery talked to him there. They saw him drive away about five thirty. You made your 911 call at six fifteen. The dispatcher contacted Agnew while he was pulling into his driveway. He switched vehicles, didn't take time to change into his uniform, and drove his department SUV to Peabody Lane. He arrived right after I got there around six twenty."

I thought of a possible flaw in Agnew's alibi. "Was he the one who contacted the couple to verify his own alibi?"

"A DCI agent did. She followed up on relatives of people buried near Agnew's grandfather."

"Is the couple related to Chief Agnew?"

"No, and they had never met Agnew or anyone from his family before Sunday. The DCI agent showed them photos of several men. They correctly identified the one of Agnew as the person they talked to at the grave."

Dep sat up straight on my lap and peered toward the sunroom windows. A robin hopped around on the grass. I suggested, "Maybe Agnew did not go to the cemetery on Sunday. Maybe the couple was wrong about the day."

"They were positive that it was Sunday, not Saturday or Friday. Besides, I saw Agnew in the office both of those afternoons."

I conceded, "It's good to know that our police chief—your boss—is probably not a murderer. Not this time."

Brent laughed. "Oh, Em! You're good for me."

"And you're good for me. But I'll be glad when Rex locates Gregory Tinsletter."

"There could be other suspects—"

I completed the sentence for him. "That I don't know about. Don't worry. I'm not about to go searching for them."

"That's reassuring. But you were right about Agnew suspecting that Pamela stole from and neglected his grandfather and some of her other clients. After Pamela moved into Agnew's new jurisdiction, he was planning to talk to her about his suspicions. When you found her, he was about to change into his uniform and drive the departmental SUV to that cabin to question her."

I burrowed fingers into Dep's comforting fur. "That sounds like an interview that might not have ended well."

"Possibly not, but if he'd been there when Pamela's killer arrived, he might have prevented the murder, at least temporarily."

"How do you know about all of Agnew's movements on Sunday?"

"Even though I'm not officially on the case, I will be coming back, and I need to know about new developments. Rex and I talk to each other."

I could say things to Brent that I might never say to anyone else. "I still feel like Agnew's looking for evidence against me."

"Rex won't let him continue arresting people based on little or no evidence. And I'll be back a week from today." The warmth in Brent's voice wrapped around me.

Dep mewed and rubbed her face against the phone. Brent and I let her join the conversation, which was mostly about counting the days until we three were together again. At least, I thought that was what Dep was saying. I wondered how long a cat might think a day was.

About ten the next morning, Rex Clobar showed up in Deputy Donut. I ushered him into the office. Tom brought him a maple and pecan donut and the day's special coffee, a rich, medium roast from Costa Rica, and then Tom shut us into the office and went back to the kitchen.

Dep must have been hiding up in her playground. She didn't show herself or make a noise.

Rex and I seated ourselves on opposite ends of the couch. I teased, "Last night, you knew I was going to have a good evening when you told me to have one and then dropped Daniel off at my house."

"He should have told the truth in the beginning even though he risked losing his job."

I gazed up toward one of Dep's tunnels. "Yes, but I'm not sure it would have helped. Chief Agnew was determined to arrest someone that very minute, alibi or no alibi."

Rex took a sip of his coffee and closed his eyes for a second. "Now, that's coffee." To my disappointment, Rex didn't say anything, pro or con, about Agnew. I would have liked Rex's agreement that Agnew was racing to unwarranted conclusions, and I would have liked to hear Rex's speculations about why Agnew had been in a hurry to solve the case by himself. But maybe Rex understood my concerns. He gave me a half-apologetic glance and then pulled a sheaf of papers out of his briefcase. "I had them make the additions to your statement for you to sign."

He ate his donut, and I read the statement. It was complete. Signing it, I told Rex about Agnew's bringing me the wrong statement to sign.

Rex's only comment was, "That was a strange mistake to make."

"Maybe not, since that statement didn't include my description of finding Pamela's earring and then leaving it in the cabin. He showed me the earring and tried to get me to say I'd torn it off her while fighting with her. All he had to do was go next door"—I pointed across the alley to Thrills and Frills—"and talk to Diana. She saw Pamela drop something."

"I've confirmed that with Diana. And you were right that she is the woman who complained to a reporter that Pamela was neglecting an elderly relative. Diana was almost positive that Pamela had stolen jewelry, a vase, and money from her grandmother. Diana also showed me the note from her dentist. I checked with the dentist. He wrote the note. He had pulled a tooth and told her to go home and rest."

I counted on my fingers. "Chief Agnew, Daniel, Diana . . . If Diana truly did go home and rest, the only one of the four people who I thought might have scared Pamela that day who hasn't been cleared is Pamela's ex, Gregory Tinsletter."

Rex shook his head. "Gregory Tinsletter did not kill Pamela Firston."

Chapter 31

I liked and trusted Rex. I tried not to let my face show my disbelief. "Does that mean you found Gregory Tinsletter, and you're sure he didn't kill his ex?"

"Yes. As he was leaving here Sunday afternoon, he received a phone call he'd been hoping for, an invitation to present a sales pitch in Duluth early Monday morning. He was excited to get on the road right away, so he canceled his appointment at the hospital and headed for Duluth."

"Without packing first?" Sarcasm crept into my voice.

"He had packed, just in case he got the call."

"So he says." This was more than sarcasm. It was out-and-out doubt.

Rex didn't comment on my tone. He carefully set his cup down. "He checked in at a hotel earlier than he could have if he'd detoured to Pamela's cabin."

I couldn't easily let go of suspecting Gregory Tinsletter. "Maybe he drove really fast."

"He did. An hour after he left here, he bought gas at a station that should have taken him nearly an hour and a half to reach. He couldn't have detoured to Deepwish Lake on his way."

This was getting repetitive. Two suspects turned out to be

fast drivers who ended up too far away to have committed the crime. Why couldn't they have stuck around so I wouldn't have to keep developing new theories in my attempts to prove that I was not the guilty one? I apologized to Rex. "Sorry for having sounded skeptical."

"It's understandable, since he seemed to have disappeared. His presentation on Monday morning netted him more sales opportunities, which I've verified. He stayed in the Duluth area and arrived at the cabin he's renting near Pamela's late last night. I found him there early this morning. He didn't answer my calls because he didn't recognize the number."

I folded my arms. "Wouldn't a sales rep answer anyway, in case it was a lead?"

"Apparently this one doesn't. He did try calling Pamela when he was about halfway from here to Duluth. She didn't answer. He left that message I told you about, the one that could have been interpreted as a threat."

"Was she already dead?"

"We think so."

I winced. "Were you the one who had to tell him about her?"

"He'd seen it on the news."

"Who made the positive identification? My recognition of her nail polish and her being in the cabin she was renting couldn't have been enough."

"She had no close relatives or friends, it seems, besides Tinsletter. We had to get her former landlady to ID her. The landlady didn't like her, but the landlady was preparing and serving a fundraising dinner Sunday afternoon and evening. Several people have attested to that."

"What about Pamela's former boss, or the owners of Happy Times?"

"So far, they all have good alibis."

I looked up into Rex's face. "That means you don't have any really good suspects."

"I'm not saying that."

"Maybe she neglected and stole from other clients besides Diana's grandmother and Chief Agnew's grandfather."

"We're following all leads." He pulled a page of printed photos out of his briefcase and laid the sheet of paper on the coffee table where I could see it. "You also wondered about the carpenter who was wielding a metal detector in your yard. Some of the Fallingbrook police officers verified that these pictures were taken at Fallingbrook Falls, but as I recall, you know almost every inch of those trails, and you and your friends Misty and Samantha made up names for them. Would you mind looking at these photos that Kayla and Logan took with their phones on Sunday evening and telling me whether or not you agree that they were taken at Fallingbrook Falls?"

"I don't mind, and I didn't really suspect her, but after finding her exploring my yard, I couldn't help wondering if her pickup truck was the one that Daniel saw near my place early Wednesday morning." I leaned over the photos. Some were obvious selfies of the two of them, usually with the longer-armed Kayla holding the camera. Some of them showed only Kayla, and some showed only Logan. The series of pictures started at the base of the falls and followed the trail to the top of the falls, along the river, and back, ending at the base of the falls. In some of the pictures, Kayla and Logan were solemn or pensive, and in others, they were obviously having fun. Kayla must have sat or knelt on the ground for some of them, pointing the camera up and capturing Logan against the sky. In one of them a pine leaned toward his head. In other photos, the view of the river or the falls upstaged the couple. Both Kayla and Logan were good photographers. "These all look like they were taken at Fallingbrook Falls to me, too."

"Can you account for the variations in color and lighting?"

"It was a sunny evening, but breezy, so shadows of trees would have shifted."

Rex pointed at the captions showing the model numbers of their phones and the times the photos were taken. "They apparently started this hike on Sunday around five and ended it around seven along that main trail. What did you and your friends call it? Something to do with a crow?"

"The Noisy Cawing Crow Trail."

He laughed. "You three must have had a lot of fun there."

"We still do. Misty's wedding was in the chapel at the other side of the campground, and some of the wedding photos were taken beside the pool at the base of the falls."

"I knew I should have been called here sooner! But I'd have been too busy to join Misty's fun. She's a good officer." He put the sheet of photos into his briefcase. "And I guess I'd better get back to it. I thought I should tell you about Tinsletter so if he shows up here, you won't freak out."

I made a face that was just short of sticking out my tongue. "Thanks."

He grinned and set down his empty coffee mug. "Besides, I wanted some decent coffee, and that was more than decent. And your donuts are the best."

"Anytime."

He winked. "It makes me want to move to Fallingbrook."

"How would you like to be police chief here?"

He merely laughed.

I let him out the back. He got into a gray unmarked police car and drove down the alley between our building and Thrills and Frills. I stood looking out through the glass door and wondering who could have killed Pamela.

As I'd said to Rex, Pamela could have had enemies I didn't know about, and now that Daniel had been freed, I didn't need to know about them or even think about them.

Still, I couldn't help wondering about Diana, whose alibi was weak. But if the murder weapon really was the soapstone whorl, where had she gotten it, and why had she hidden it in my garden? Besides, I felt guilty for not trusting Diana, whose statement to Rex helped prove that I hadn't pulled the earring off Pamela's ear during an unexplainable battle.

And we still didn't know if the whorl truly was the murder weapon. Maybe whoever had been digging in my garden hadn't put it there. Maybe they'd uncovered it and thrown it down.

Up near the ceiling, Dep rustled around on a catwalk. Something small but sharp bounced off my head and landed with a clink on the floor. I looked down. The stuffed donut that had been up among Dep's ramps and tunnels ever since Dep snatched it from Gregory's hand was beside my feet.

I rubbed my head. A stuffed toy shouldn't have hurt my head when it bounced off it. And it wouldn't have clinked when it landed.

I picked up the catnip-filled donut.

The thing that had banged into my scalp was underneath it. A small key, rusted with age.

Crouching on a catwalk up near the ceiling, Dep grinned down at me.

I picked up the key, stood, and rubbed my head. "Thanks for your concern, Dep. I don't think my injuries are serious."

"Mew." She trotted down a kitty stairway.

I stared at the key on my palm. Because of the rust, I couldn't make out the entire insignia stamped into the metal, but it looked familiar.

Pamela had asked Summer if the donut's seam was easy to rip open so she could add catnip. Had she also added a key?

This key was approximately the right size and shape to have made the marks in the letter Hattie Renniegrove had written to Tillie.

Had Pamela meant for me to have the key, and that's why she'd given the toy donut to Dep? And had she meant to give me the letter, but in her hurry, she'd forgotten?

That didn't make sense.

If she'd wanted me to have the key and the letter, why

hadn't she simply handed them to me? Why had she gone to the trouble of buying a stuffed toy, ripping open a seam, and inserting the key into the toy along with the catnip and then giving it to my cat, who might—or might not ever—let me have it?

Gregory had reached for the donut. Had he known that the key was inside it? Had he and Pamela arranged a hand-off? And neither of them had guessed that the cat might disrupt their plans. The cat, and a murderer . . .

But maybe I had it wrong. Maybe Pamela had hidden the key inside the donut to keep Gregory from getting it. Gregory . . . or someone else? Someone had searched Pamela's tote bag and the Peabody-Smiths' closet. Could they have been hunting for this small, rusty key?

I again pictured the cinnamon twists crumbled over the cabin's dining table. Maybe Pamela hadn't been planning to make a piecrust, bread pudding, or rum balls from donut crumbs. Maybe her murderer had torn up the cinnamon twists in the strange hope of maybe finding the key inside one.

What had that letter said? Something about giving Tillie a key that would unlock a chest, and then something would be Tillie's. Something valuable, perhaps, so valuable that someone killed Pamela to—he or she hoped—obtain the key that was now lying on my palm.

Dep pussyfooted her way to me and stretched upward, placing her front paws on my bare leg. Luckily for me, she didn't extend her claws. "Mew?"

The stuffed donut was in my other hand. I asked Dep, "Is this what you want?"

"Meow."

A partially dried leaf stuck out of the rip in the seam. I pulled it out and straightened it. Pamela had stuffed at least one whole fresh catnip leaf into the donut. I poked it back into the hole and gave the donut to Dep. She batted the toy underneath the couch, flopped down onto her side, and scooted in after her prize.

I looked up. Staring toward me, Gregory Tinsletter opened the shop's front door. I thrust the key into my pocket, re-arranged my face into the most non-suspecting expression I could muster, and went out from the office to the dining room.

Chapter 32

✖

Gregory sat at the same table as before, which was also the one where Pamela had spent hours observing everyone in Deputy Donut. Goose bumps formed on the back of my neck, but I put on a friendly smile and went to that table. "Hi, Gregory, welcome back to Deputy Donut."

"You remembered me."

I waved my hand toward the rest of our dining room. "It's kind of my job to remember people. But I won't bring you the same thing you ordered before. I'll make you ask for it again."

He lifted one corner of his mouth. "Do you remember what I ordered?"

I had to admit that I didn't.

"I'm in sales, too, and I remember you. It's Emily, right?"

"Right. What can I get you?"

He asked for an espresso and a raised donut filled with black raspberry jam and dusted with powdered sugar.

I brought them to him. "How have you been? You were excited about a phone call when you left here."

"I was then, but other parts of my life went downhill. Can you talk?"

I glanced around the dining room. Olivia and Jocelyn had

everything under control, and Tom was unlikely to require help in the kitchen. "Sure." I sat in the other chair at Gregory's table. Instead of asking what was wrong, I quietly waited.

He picked up his espresso and sat there holding the tiny cup like it was a warm and comforting kitten. Finally, without meeting my gaze, he spoke. "I lost somebody. We were no longer dating, and I guess you could say that in several ways, I'd already lost her. Basically, she wasn't the person I thought she was. I was drawn to her at first because, well, I guess I have a type: women who look, I don't know, like all they need is love, and maybe I could be the one who would make them happy. Put like that, it sounds arrogant. I guess I also thought she might be the one who could make my life all I ever hoped it could be. Like together, we'd live a long, happy life." He looked up at me with sad puppy eyes. "I guess I'm not a great judge of character."

"It can be easy to like something about someone, assume you're going to like everything, and later, realize that you misjudged." I was speaking from observation, not experience. I'd married Alec when I was young, and if he'd had faults, I didn't discover them in the short time we'd been together. And Brent was the only other man I'd loved that strongly. I'd known Brent for years, and he was also nearly perfect.

Gregory set down the cup. "You're right. She had some of the good qualities I thought she'd have, just from the way she looked and talked, and she was a caregiver, so I thought she was caring, but as I got to know her, I didn't like some of what I was learning. Her parents died when she was a baby, and her grandmother raised her, but that grandmother must have been cold and distant. If the woman loved her granddaughter, she probably didn't show it, and I couldn't help trying to make up for some of the things my friend had lost, some of the attention she'd probably never had." He pointed his spoon toward the office. "The last time I saw her, she was in here, in your office with you and your cat."

"Pamela," I said.

"Yes."

If he didn't already know that I was the person who had come upon her body, he might learn about it later. I had to tell him. "That evening, I went to see her at the cabin she was renting. I was the one who . . . found her. I was too late to save her. I'm sorry."

Before I could be certain that I saw tears welling in his eyes, he lowered his head and mumbled, "In a way, it could be my fault." He looked up at me again, and his eyes seemed dry. "I never harmed her, but she was planning to do something that was illegal and just plain wrong."

I managed not to gasp or question him, but I couldn't keep my head from jerking backward in surprise.

Gregory went on. "We argued. Well, fought, some people would say, although I never touched her. There was a lot of yelling, and I threatened to turn her in to the police. I thought the threat would make her understand how wrong she was, and she'd change. I was living in Wausau, and she was from near Rhinelander. After our argument, she pulled up stakes and left. I guess I'm a slow learner, but I still thought I could persuade her not to do the illegal thing—a crime, really—if I kept talking to her. I knew that the scheme she'd hatched involved Fallingbrook and that she'd always dreamed of living in the northern Wisconsin woods beside a lake, so I wasn't surprised when she posted online that she'd moved to Deepwish Lake. The only Deepwish Lake I could find is near Fallingbrook. I looked up lakeside rental homes near Deepwish and called the owners of the three I found listed. One was already booked for the summer. Figuring that if all else failed, I might be able to make contacts that could lead to sales, I arranged to rent a cabin on the other side of the lake. I drove up here. Pamela's car was outside the cabin I'd suspected she might be renting. Our relationship was broken, but I still cared enough that I hoped I could, I don't know, persuade her to change her plans." His lips twisted into something like a rueful grin. "I'm not only arrogant, but optimistic."

I thought he could use encouragement. "You wanted to keep her out of trouble, which should have helped make her happier. What did you want to prevent her from doing?" I had a few guesses.

His shoulders drooped. "She'd been fired because someone believed she was stealing from clients she was caring for. And maybe she was stealing. She hardly owned anything except a carton of jewelry and stuff like that, all jumbled together."

I sat on my hands and kept my mouth firmly shut, waiting for more.

He must have felt the need to explain. "I wouldn't have seen inside it, but it was open. She became unreasonably angry when she saw me glance into the box. I suggested that if she was robbing people, she ought to stop. She said she couldn't rob her clients because she no longer had any, and then she pretended she hadn't been angry. Her expression got sadder than ever, almost too dramatically sad, you know?"

I nodded.

"She told me her clients had given her the jewelry and it was all she had to remember them by." He shook his head as if clearing water from his ears. "And who's to prove they didn't? People sometimes do things like that, especially when they have no one else. She said she wasn't supposed to accept gifts from clients, but she didn't want to hurt their feelings, so she did. She said she'd been planning to return everything to the clients' families." He glared down at his still-untouched donut. "But she seemed to change her mind and decide that losing her job over the jewelry entitled her to sell it so she could get by until she found another job. Or . . ." This time his smile lacked any semblance of humor. "Or until she found a treasure chest of gold that supposedly belonged to her."

I realized I was leaning forward and breathing quickly. I sat up straighter and tried to take deep breaths.

Gregory must have noticed. His eyes narrowed, but he continued his story. "Pamela claimed that a letter an old lady gave to Pamela's grandmother when the grandmother was young and working in the family's nursing home said that the old lady meant for Pamela's grandmother to have a hoard of gold. The old lady died before Pamela's grandmother got the gold, but Pamela had a cane with a gold head that the old lady had given Pamela's grandmother."

Maybe if I held my breath I wouldn't hyperventilate.

I must have managed to look almost normal. Gregory went on, "The letter even contained a key to the treasure chest. Pamela was going to break into someone's home and look for the gold she was convinced belonged to her. I told her she was delusional about long-gone treasure, and she shouldn't break into anyone's house. We fought about it, and she moved away."

I tried to exhale calmly. "Did she show you the letter?"

He scrunched his napkin into a ball. "I'm not sure it even existed."

"It did. Does. The police found it in the cabin Pamela was renting. They showed it to me because the envelope was addressed to me, and they thought I might have lost the letter in that cabin. I didn't, but the woman who wrote the letter was the first owner of my house. I guess that Pamela meant to give or mail the letter to me."

Gregory gave his head a firm, negative shake. "No way. Pamela would never have given up that letter. She thought it proved her claim to treasure that would keep her in riches for the rest of her life. If Pamela wrote your name and address on the envelope, it was her way of keeping your address handy so she could break into your house and search for gold."

"That letter was written in 1949. If there was a hoard of gold in my house, it has long since disappeared. Between then and when my late husband and I bought the house, there were other owners. If those homeowners found gold in the house, I never heard about it, which makes sense. People don't publicize that sort of thing. Alec and I restored and renovated the house. We didn't find any gold."

"Poor Pamela. I didn't want her breaking the law, but her dream of treasure sustained her through bad times, I guess. She should have just kept dreaming instead of acting on it."

The sudden widening of his eyes worried me. Was he speculating that Pamela threatened me when she was here in Deputy Donut, and that I killed her before she could break into my house?

Or was he wondering if he should try breaking into my house to search for treasure?

I answered with only a slight hiccup in my breath, "As far as I know, she didn't act on it. To me, the house itself is a treasure. It was built in 1889." I looked toward the office. Sitting alertly on the back of the couch, Dep stared back at me, giving me courage to think aloud about grief, sorrow, and loss. "Hattie, the lady who wrote the letter, died in 1950." The key in my pocket felt like it was burning a hole through the fabric and into my leg, but I wasn't about to tell Gregory that I'd found the key or that it had been inside the toy donut that Dep had snatched from him during his first visit to Deputy Donut. According to Rex, Gregory could not have killed Pamela, but it seemed to me that Pamela could have tried to keep that key hidden from him. And I did not want him considering visiting my house in the middle of the night to hunt for a treasure chest or the key to it.

Gregory said, "Detective Clobar asked me about a key."

I didn't say anything. I couldn't. A shock that was almost electric jolted through me.

If Gregory noticed my mini-flinch, he didn't show it. "Detective Clobar said the letter appeared to have once contained a key that left a rust stain, but the key was missing. I told him everything I knew about Pamela claiming she had a key to the treasure chest, and that I had tried to get her to give me the key so I could prevent her from breaking into the house where she thought the gold was—your house, but I didn't know that until you told me just now." Again, that look of planning or plotting flickered through his eyes, and then he was telling me more, maybe tossing me some bait in the hope that I would divulge more than I already had. "She claimed she'd hidden the key where no one would find it. From the look on her face, I was certain the key was in her car or in the cabin she was renting, but of course there was no way she was going to let me search either of those places. She told me to go away and never come back. She acted like I was a physical threat to her, but I wasn't." Barely opening his mouth, he spoke between tensed lips. "That afternoon, I followed her here. I saw her leave a toy donut in your office. I'd spotted that toy near her cabin's front door." He rolled his shoulders as if to relax, and his words became clearer. "That was when I guessed that she'd hidden the key inside the toy, and to make doubly certain that I couldn't find the key, she was going to leave the toy with the key inside it in your shop. Later, when no one was around, she must have been planning to break into your shop to retrieve the key. It was convoluted, but that's what she was like."

Attempting to imitate his calm demeanor, I asked in a friendly way, "Is that why you asked to pet Dep?"

"Yes, and I didn't lie about loving cats. I wasn't going to take the donut, not without your permission, of course, but I wanted to get a really good look at it. If I found that key, I was going to tell Pamela that I'd figured out she was planning to break into your office to retrieve the key and then break into your house and try to find whatever it unlocks. I was going to tell her that you were moving the key offsite and I was calling the cops if she didn't change her mind, but Dep ran off with the donut before I could examine it."

I said softly, "And Pamela didn't live long enough to break into either place." *But Chief Agnew and possibly someone else barged into my yard after her death, while Gregory was in Duluth. Was the supposed "treasure chest" common knowledge, except to me?*

Gregory slid forward in his chair and asked a little too eagerly, "What did Dep do with the donut?"

I pointed toward the office and gave a truthful but not complete answer. "She has a maze of catwalks, tunnels, and ramps up near the ceiling."

"I saw her carrying the donut up there on Sunday, but when I came in just now, didn't you have that donut in your hand?"

"Those donuts come from The Craft Croft down the street." That part was true. With his determination to be honest, my neighbor Daniel had been a good example. However, if Gregory believed that the key would unlock a hoard of gold somewhere inside my home, I was only going to skirt around the truth. "Pamela wasn't the first person to give Dep a stuffed toy from The Craft Croft." I could assuage my guilty conscience about not being forthright with Gregory by confessing to Rex Clobar that I'd found a key that might have been folded into that letter way back in 1950.

Gregory looked skeptical.

I said, "I'm sure there's no key in the donut I was holding when you came in. But every time Dep brings one of them down from her catwalks and tunnels, I'll check." That was mostly true, since I was almost certain that Dep did not have any other faux fur donuts in her lofty playground. I just had to hope that Dep didn't choose that moment to pop up onto the back of the office couch with the donut trailing almost-fresh catnip leaves from its torn-open seam.

Gregory held up both hands, palms toward me. "I don't want to know about that key if you do find it. This has all been painful. I feel terrible about not answering the detective's calls. I couldn't have saved Pamela, but it's still tough."

I murmured a sympathetic agreement.

Gregory scrunched up his napkin. "Since breaking into people's places didn't seem to daunt Pamela, I checked the back of your building while I was leaving and answering my phone call. I saw your camera and realized that if Pamela broke in here, she would probably be caught. I didn't want her getting into trouble." He quickly added, "Plus I didn't want her to harm you or your business."

I pretended I hadn't noticed that his remark seemed like an afterthought.

He blushed and edged into a slightly different subject. "My phone call was from someone in Duluth, asking me to give a presentation the next morning. I was already packed, just in case, so I took off. An hour or so later, I stopped and called Pamela. She didn't pick up." His mouth worked, and his Adam's apple bobbed. "I left her a message, warning her to give up her plans. I don't remember what I said, but the police thought I was threatening her. I wasn't."

"Do you know who might have wanted to harm her? Did she have enemies?"

"She could have. If she was robbing clients or even if they were just giving her valuable objects, their relatives might have wanted revenge or maybe they harmed her while they were trying to take back their things. Or maybe someone from the Happy Times network of companies wanted to get back at her for giving them a bad name. That company was owned by some of her family, once. I don't know if they're still involved, but if they are, they might have been angry about the distant cousin who was harming their company's reputation and maybe causing them to lose revenue."

"Do you know the names of any of Pamela's clients whose relatives might want revenge?"

"Detective Clobar asked me that, too. I don't." Gregory had finished his donut and coffee. He put bills on the table and stood. "I came to say goodbye. I still have my apartment in Wausau, so I'm going back. I'll stop by whenever I'm in this neck of the woods again."

My encouraging smile was probably not very genuine. I felt too sorry for him to give him a huge smile, and besides, I didn't want to encourage him to stick around or return in case he had notions of ransacking my sweet little home in search of nonexistent treasure. "Do that."

He held out his hand. "Thanks for listening."

We shook hands, and he left.

Chapter 33

Rex Clobar had believed Gregory's alibi, which must have been confirmed by several people, and Gregory's sadness about Pamela's death seemed genuine.

According to Brent, Chief Agnew's alibi was also solid. I doubted that Agnew would have risked forcing people to lie for him.

We believed that Diana had followed her dentist's instructions and had gone home and stayed there Sunday night after her emergency tooth extraction. But had she?

Photos showed Kayla at Fallingbrook Falls at the time of the murder.

Were other relatives of Pamela's clients besides Diana and Agnew disgruntled at Pamela's uncaring "caregiving" of their loved ones?

Serving our customers and helping make and decorate donuts, I reminded myself that Rex Clobar was investigating the case. I didn't have to concern myself with any of it. Brent would be home in a week, and my life would be fun, warm, comfy, and safe again.

Putting Dep's harness and leash on her after work, however, I remembered that Agnew might still suspect me of killing Pamela. I didn't think he would be able to convince

Rex, but I had exactly zero alibis for the time when she was killed.

Who else might Rex be investigating?

Summer Peabody-Smith, because she had keys to her parents' cabin?

The Craft Croft was only a block out of our way. I asked Dep, "Would you like to take a side trip?"

She didn't answer, but she also didn't resist when instead of turning onto Maple, I headed farther south on Wisconsin Street.

At The Craft Croft, I picked Dep up, opened the door, and asked the artist working at the reception desk if Summer was in. "I don't want to bring my cat inside in case someone has allergies."

The woman smiled. "Thank you. I love kitties. I'll go get Summer."

Seconds later, Summer, in one of her cool linen dresses, this one in navy blue with white piping, and matching heels that accentuated her height, was cooing to Dep, scratching the orange-striped patch between Dep's cute little ears, and telling me, "You can bring her into my office."

Summer sat at her desk. Her red curls were again piled on top of her head, with a few stragglers touching her cheeks, ears, and white hoop earrings. I edged down onto one of Summer's visitor's chairs, hugged my wiggly cat, and asked, "Are you still afraid that Chief Agnew suspects you of murdering Pamela Firston?"

She toyed with a pen. "Our new police chief scares me, but that detective from the Wisconsin Division of Criminal Investigation doesn't seem to find it suspicious that the daughter of property owners has keys to their summer home, and he doesn't seem to automatically conclude that her having the keys proves she's a murderer." She fanned her face with a hand. "He's hot."

"Rex Clobar? I guess he is."

Her mouth fell open, and she dropped the pen. "You only guess? You don't notice anyone besides your handsome detective."

Picturing Brent, I couldn't help a smile. "True, but I have noticed that Rex is a good detective, and I do like him."

She caught the pen before it rolled off her gleaming white desk. "Agnew told me they've cleared what he called the 'scene of the crime.' Ugh! I've had our handyman replace the broken closet door, and professional cleaners gave the place a good cleaning, but I need to go inside and make certain the cabin is ready for the next tenants or my parents when they get home. I love the place, but after what happened there, it's going to give me a severe case of the creeps. But putting it off will only make it worse."

"I don't blame you! Would you like me to come along? I'll get the creeps, too, but it will be a lot less icky if two of us are there. Or three. Or ten!"

Summer tucked a wayward curl behind an ear. "Would you?"

"Sure. When would you like to go?"

"Are you available this evening?"

I intoned with heart-stopping drama, "Brent's out of town. I'm available."

"Can you make it there by six thirty?"

"Sure."

"You don't have to rush. I'll wait for you before I go inside." She grinned at my squirming cat. "Do you still keep your kayak on your car? We could paddle around on the lake after we're done checking the cabin. It doesn't get dark these days until after nine."

"I'd love to." I let the corners of my mouth droop. "My kayak is out at my handsome detective's place, off in the wrong direction." Referring to Brent as "my handsome detective," after so many years of denying that he was mine, ended the pretend-sad grimace.

"You can use one of ours. We have paddles and life jackets that should fit you."

"I can hardly wait." Dep and I hurried home. I would try to see the Peabody-Smiths' cabin as a lovely place where Summer's family would spend many more happy and relaxing days, and not think about the way it had looked the first time I'd been there. I could try, anyway.

It appeared that my garage was finished. A lovely new overhead door covered the entry. The ivory doors and trim and the brownish siding were almost perfect matches to the ivory trim and the brownish yellow bricks of my house. The workers had cleaned up and gone home, and Dep and I would again have the place to ourselves.

On the porch, I felt inside the mailbox. The contractor had left me a garage door opener that I could keep in my car, the code to unlock the keypad beside the garage door, and instructions for resetting the code. Not wanting to take any chances, I reset the code before taking Dep into the house. I fed her, ate a quick sandwich, and changed into stretchy shorts and a T-shirt. Dep must have figured out that I was planning a car trip. Warily perched on the couch, she watched me head toward the front door with my new garage door opener, a jacket, and a pair of water shoes. I pictured her wearing a kitty life jacket and sitting on the prow of a kayak. And possibly being splashed . . . I told her, "I don't think you'd like kayaking."

"Mew."

Apologizing, I locked her inside and left.

In the grassy space at the foot of the Peabody-Smiths' nerve-racking driveway, Summer was waiting for me beside a silver pickup truck parked next to the lettuce patch. I'd never seen her when she wasn't working at The Craft Croft and wearing a dress and heels. Like me, she was in shorts—hers were denim cutoffs—with a T-shirt and sneakers. Her hair was braided in one long queue with curls at the end. The outfit and hairstyle made her look younger than she did at The Craft Croft, but her forehead wrinkled as if she dreaded going into her family's cherished cabin.

I thinned my lips. I would do my best to dispel Summer's and my negative emotions.

As I had guessed, Summer's long legs made it easy for her to reach the widely separated flagstones on the path up to the cabin. Needing to step on grass between the stones, I trotted up the hill behind her.

On the front stoop, the faded beach towel was gone from the railing. Summer looked down at me and chanted, softly, "I love this place, I love this place."

"I can see why." Sun slanted through trees, bathing the cabin in a warm glow. Ripples murmured against the base of the rocky point jutting into the lake. Beyond that, the water shimmered, silvery blue, underneath the still-bright sky. The far shore was a fuzz of dark evergreens and lighter deciduous trees.

Summer unlocked the door but stood unmoving on the threshold. "Everything looks okay." Hesitation sounded in her voice, and then a semblance of her usual easy confidence returned. "But don't mind me. The first thing I do when I get here if the weather is decent is open all the windows and air out the place." Maybe the confidence was an act, but she strode toward the living area of the main room.

I headed the other direction, toward the dining area and the kitchen.

The cinnamon twist crumbs were gone from the table, and there was no sign of the overheated skillet or the charred burger or the bun with its ketchup and wilting leaf lettuce. Everything was neat and clean.

We opened windows and then met at the four steps leading up toward the short balcony-like hallway, the bathroom, and the bedrooms. The handwoven blankets on the railing had been straightened, their wrinkles apparently smoothed by caring hands.

Summer took a deep breath. "Let's do this."

The linens and toiletries were gone from the bathroom, which was sparkling. Summer opened the linen closet. "The cleaners washed the towels and put them away." She tapped packages of toilet paper, tissues, and paper towels. "We're still well stocked."

The jewelry and vase had been collected from the first bedroom, and the bed had been stripped. Summer opened that closet door. "The sheets, blankets, pillows, and bedspread are here where the cleaners always put them." She closed the closet door and turned toward the hallway. "She was in the front bedroom, wasn't she?"

I pointed toward the slightly larger bedroom. "Yes." I led the way and bravely stepped inside. Like the other bed, this one had been stripped. A new door was on the closet. The floor between the closet and the bed was clean and clear. Outside the window, sunshine glinted on the lake. I called over my shoulder, "It all looks fine, now."

Blushing, Summer stepped out of the hallway and into the bedroom. "Thanks for looking first, Emily." She checked the closet door. It was locked. "Before we rent the place again, I'll print another sign about this closet being out of bounds and tape it to this door." A second closet that I hadn't noticed before was unlocked. Summer opened it, shut the door, and gave the jamb a pat. "The linens for this bed have been cleaned and put away, too. Let's go kayaking."

But after we'd gone down to the lower level, Summer bit her lip and looked toward the kitchen end of the room. "Sometimes the cleaners leave more food behind than they should. I guess we should check." She went into the kitchen and pushed things around on a shelf in a cabinet. "Three tins of cinnamon. They'll keep."

The inside of the fridge was spotless and empty except for condiments arranged on a shelf in the door.

I found ice cubes and a half gallon of butter pecan ice

cream in the freezer. The plastic tub looked like it had been around for awhile. I nudged it with one finger. "Oh."

Summer turned toward me. "I didn't like the sound of that. Did the cleaners miss something?"

"Maybe." I pulled the tub out and set it on the counter. The weight felt approximately right, but the sides of the plastic tub squished too easily for ice cream. "I don't think this is really ice cream."

She opened the container. "This looks like . . . rice?"

"It does." I looked up at her. "Do your parents store rice in the freezer?"

"I've never known them to. Maybe Pamela did."

What if the tub of rice held the key that Hattie had folded into Tillie's letter, and the key that I'd found, which was still at home in the pocket of the shorts I'd worn to work, was a decoy meant to fool Gregory? I opened the drawer underneath the oven. As I'd hoped, it contained baking pans. I pulled the largest one out, making a racket that clashed in the otherwise peaceful woods. "Sorry about the noise, Summer. I have a hunch. May I use this?"

"Yes, but you're being mysterious."

Flashing her a grin, I held the pan up like a gong and bopped it with my free hand.

Something fluttered off the bottom of the pan and landed at my feet.

Summer pointed at it. "What's that?"

I gulped. "An envelope. We shouldn't touch it." It was ecru, spotted with age and rust. With the pan still dangling from my hand, I twisted my upper body so I could read the front of the envelope. "This is not surprising," I told Summer. I read aloud, "To Miss Tillie Aimes. From Miss Harriet Renniegrove." Across the lower right corner of the envelope, someone had written in red, "Save for Pammie" and had circled the words.

Chapter 34

I told Summer about the letter and photo that Agnew had found in this cabin. "They were in a new envelope addressed to me. I can't help wondering if Chief Agnew took them out of this envelope and put them into a different one. I'll have to call your hot detective about it, not Agnew."

"Why would Agnew make that switch?"

I could think of only one reason. "As a way of implicating me? Brent told me that Agnew's alibi is solid. I'm not sure about that, but maybe Agnew knows who the murderer is and is trying to protect him or her."

"Is Agnew married?"

I glanced up at Summer. "Could he be?"

We both burst out laughing.

I had to admit, "Pamela's probably the one who put the letter and the photo in the newer pink envelope. The writing in the address was loopy and feminine like Pamela Firston's signature on her driver's license, not that I took time to study her signature."

"I wouldn't have, either." Summer pointed at the pan I'd nearly forgotten I was holding. "You still haven't told me why you wanted that. Did you know the envelope was stuck to the bottom?"

"That was just luck, and I doubt that anyone put it there. Maybe the pan was damp on the bottom, and Pamela set it on the envelope and didn't notice that the envelope came with the pan when she picked it up."

I set the pan on the table and slowly tipped the plastic tub over the pan. Grains clicked against metal and bounced. With a whoosh, more rice slid out, and then something else.

Not a key.

An antique gold pocket watch.

The watch had fallen facedown in the rice. Summer and I bent over and read the initials on the back of the case aloud. "*E S A.*"

Neither of us touched the watch.

I asked Summer, "May I borrow a dinner fork?"

She stepped around the fallen envelope, found a fork, and handed it to me. I ran the tines through the rice. I saw no other pieces of jewelry, and no keys, either, though I didn't mention keys to Summer.

She opened a cabinet next to the short wall beneath the balcony railing and pulled out a magnifying glass. "I've kept this here ever since I got it for my sixth birthday. I've used it a lot, for things like rocks and butterflies, not rice."

I shined my phone's light on the rice, and we took turns peering through her magnifying glass into the mass of white grains. I described Chief Agnew's allegations of Pamela's theft of a pocket watch. We were careful not to touch the watch, not even with the fork.

Finally, Summer set the magnifying glass down and slapped the back of one hand dramatically against her forehead. "I was hoping for a diamond or a ruby, but if any loose gems are in here, they're skinny and look exactly like grains of rice."

I called Rex Clobar and told him about finding the envelope and the watch.

He asked, "Can you two stay there? I'll come right away."

I winked at Summer. "We'll wait for you, Rex." We disconnected.

Summer and I went outside and down the hill. Afraid that Rex might block us in, we turned our vehicles to face the driveway and parked them as far to one side as possible, with Summer's pickup behind my SUV and closer to the cabin. We figured that Rex would probably leave before Summer would. She'd need to lock up. "But," she said, "if we're lucky, Rex will leave in time for you and me to go out in the kayaks."

I teased, "Maybe you should invite him kayaking instead of me."

She placed a hand over her heart. "Maybe sometime when he's not on duty. Meanwhile, we can wait for him on the beach. We'll hear him coming."

We followed the short path down a rocky but gentle slope to the crescent of sand beach in the cove. Optimistically, we removed the two kayaks from the sawhorses that had been holding them up off the weed-choked ground and carried the kayaks to the water's edge. Summer pointed at the yellow one. "You can use that, Emily. It's smaller."

Back at the cabin, we found paddles and life jackets. On the beach again, we adjusted the life jackets and put them and the paddles beside the kayaks, and then we sat in Adirondack chairs and watched the water. It was just after seven thirty. The sun hung low above trees lining the far side of the lake.

Summer patted the broad arm of her chair. "Ordinarily, we would go out in boats, and then come back here and relax with adult beverages and watch the sun set."

"I'll take a rain check for a time when we can actually relax."

Her laugh chimed out over the water and echoed back to us. "You've got it."

The sun lowered, warming my face and forcing me to look away from the water. We heard a vehicle up on Peabody

Lane and then the jolting of springs and the pinging of stones against metal on that steep, gullied driveway.

Summer and I scooted out of the comfy wooden chairs, stretched, and strolled up the pathway between trees and rocks. Probably appearing less tense than we felt, we waited in the grassy area where we'd left space for Rex to park.

A huge black unmarked SUV bumped slowly toward us and stopped. A dark gray unmarked cruiser followed it.

Wearing his dress uniform over an armored vest again, Chief Agnew got out of the SUV.

"Wonderful." Summer's and my realization that we had breathed the word in unison and sarcastically made us laugh, which allowed us to greet the chief with smiles that might have looked genuine.

Wearing a dark suit, white shirt, and a green tie that matched some of the new leaves in the forest around us, Rex stepped out of the cruiser.

The way that Agnew had parked forced Rex to walk farther down the hill, but he strode with a spring in his step. He smiled up into the trees, and I realized I'd been hearing the sporadic tapping of a woodpecker.

Chief Agnew, however, was not smiling at woodpeckers or anything else. Frowning, he marched into my personal space. I had to force myself not to back away. He barked—there was no better word for it—at me, "What are *you* doing here?"

Rex stopped smiling and hurried toward us.

Summer moved closer to me. "I asked her to come."

"Why?" Another bark.

Standing slightly uphill from Agnew, Summer appeared taller than he was. Probably on purpose, she straightened her spine, lifted her chin, and looked even taller. "We're friends."

Rex stopped beside her and gave her one of his penetrating looks.

Summer shrank a little and added more quietly, "And I

didn't want to come here by myself the first time after . . . after what happened."

Agnew stomped up toward the cabin.

Rex gestured for Summer and me to precede him up the hill.

Agnew called back, "What did you two touch?"

Summer was right behind him. "I understood that the scene was clear and we could touch anything."

He accused, "So, you touched everything."

I was having trouble keeping up. "Not everything. We did not touch the envelope or the watch."

Climbing behind me, Rex remained silent. The soles of his shoes grated against stone.

Agnew ostentatiously slipped a pen into the handle on the screen door, pulled, and went inside. The screen door slammed before we could follow.

Rex opened the door. With his hand.

We'd left the teal-painted main door ajar. Agnew pushed it farther open with his pen. I wanted to giggle.

Rex held the screen door for Summer and me, and then followed us into the cabin's main living area.

Staring up toward the little balconied hallway and the bedroom beyond it where the heap of jewelry had been before the police finished their investigation, Agnew growled, "Where's the watch and envelope?"

Summer pointed toward the kitchen. "The envelope is on the floor where it landed after it came unstuck from the bottom of that pan on the counter. The pan had been nestled with others in the bottom drawer of the stove. The watch is in the pan. We found the watch in an ice cream container in the freezer."

Agnew turned and stared at us. "Ice cream? The watch was in ice cream?" His voice sounded as strangled as his face was beginning to look.

"In rice," I managed. "Not ice cream. Someone filled an ice cream tub with rice and put the watch into it."

Agnew nearly ran into the kitchen. "Don't come any closer."
Summer and I stayed put.

Agnew might have wanted Rex to hold back, too, but Rex joined Agnew at the kitchen counter. I heard his quiet, "Is that the watch you were looking for?"

"Absolutely." Agnew patted his uniform pockets. "Do you have an evidence bag, Clobar?"

Rex pulled one from a pocket and deftly slipped the watch, and maybe a grain of rice or two, into the bag without adding fingerprints to the watch. He stooped and carefully slid the rust-spotted ecru envelope from the floor into another evidence bag.

From near the horseshoe of couches, Summer and I explained that we'd sifted through the rice with a fork and hadn't found anything besides the watch.

With much banging, Agnew pulled the other pans out of the stove drawer and turned them upside down on the counter. Apparently, nothing was stuck to any of them. Glowering, he picked up the fork and ran it through the rice.

Rex said mildly, "Investigators usually look into things like freezers and toilet tanks."

Cursing, Agnew ran up to the balcony. Rex followed him into the bathroom. Seconds later, I heard the lid of the toilet tank clank into place.

Summer and I exchanged grins, and then we both had to turn our backs to hide our snickers. Luckily, anyone would understand why we might want to gaze out toward the lake. The shaking shoulders might have been harder to explain.

Heavy footsteps rushed along the bedroom hallway. I glanced back. Agnew stomped toward the front bedroom where I'd found Pamela. With a determined look on his face, Rex stalked after him. Maybe Rex didn't trust Agnew any more than I did.

Had Pamela left that watch in the freezer, or had Agnew planted it there after his investigators were done? If he had, he must have wanted to blame the theft of the watch on someone. Pamela, maybe, but more likely Summer. However, he couldn't have been certain that anyone would have discovered that watch soon, or if when they found it, they would call the police. He'd have needed to return and "find" the watch himself in the same way that he could have returned to my yard and "found" the whorl after leaving it there himself, only Dep and I had beaten him to it.

I didn't like Agnew and wasn't certain that his alibi was a good one or that he hadn't killed Pamela, but the idea that his grandfather's watch might have been left in ice cream seemed to have surprised him and caused him a fair amount of anguish. I was almost certain that Pamela must have accidentally picked up the envelope with the pan and put the pan away without noticing the envelope.

A door in the front bedroom creaked open and then slammed. Agnew came out onto the balcony and complained, "One of the closet doors is locked."

Summer asked sweetly, "Would you like me to unlock it?"

As if to forestall Agnew, Rex quickly answered, "That won't be necessary. Just let us know if you find anything else or think of something that might help us."

Agnew's face verged on purple. "We're done here. For now." He marched along the balcony, down the four steps, through the living area, and outside.

More quietly, Rex joined us. "Sorry about the intrusion, Summer. Will you two be okay?"

Summer smiled at him. "Sure. May I toss out that rice and ice cream tub? Actually, I won't. I'll boil that rice until it's mush and then press it through a sieve and pinch it between my fingers and flatten it with a rolling pin until I'm positive it doesn't contain diamonds."

I stared at her in admiration for her craftiness, persistence, and creativity. And her optimism.

Rex threw back his head and laughed. "Sounds like fun. Let me know if you find any gems."

She beamed a smile toward him. "Okay. But first, Emily and I are going kayaking."

We all went out onto the little porch.

Rex glanced down toward the beach. Parts of the blue and yellow kayaks showed between shifting branches of pine and poplar. "Nice," he said. "I'd rather do that than . . ." He gestured toward Agnew striding down the flagstone path toward his SUV. "Than return to your police station."

Summer answered, "Emily will visit again when we have time for a longer paddle. You can, too."

He gave her a smile that made me glance at his left hand. No wedding ring, which didn't prove a thing. "I might take you up on that." He ran down the hill. Unlike me, he had no trouble reaching all of the flagstones without stepping onto the grass or moss-covered rock between them.

"Mmmmm," Summer said.

I felt a little guilty for not telling Rex about the key that had fallen out of the toy donut, but I wouldn't have wanted the others, especially Agnew, to overhear. I could explain it to Rex another time.

Summer and I watched until the two vehicles were out of sight. Laughing together because we, two amateurs, had found the envelope and Agnew's grandfather's watch after the investigators had completed their search, we went back into the cabin. We carefully poured the rice into a pot of water to soak and then washed and dried the baking trays and the fork and put them away. Summer replaced the magnifying glass in its spot in the cupboard, next to a glittery chunk of rock.

Outside, again, she locked the front door. "I never used to do this if I was only going to paddle around, but now I don't feel comfortable leaving it unlocked." She glanced toward the driveway. As far as we could tell, Agnew and Rex were long gone, and no one else was arriving.

Summer and I put on our life jackets and water shoes and clambered into the kayaks.

The sun was slipping behind treetops on the far shore. Above us in the light blue sky, feathers of clouds turned rosy.

We launched the kayaks. I pulled the foot pedals toward me, and then the kayak and the paddle felt just right. As usual when floating in a kayak, I felt almost weightless and carefree.

Paddling gently and economically, Summer led the way out of her family's little harbor and turned toward the stony lookout point. The rock cliff below the point was nearly vertical, explaining why even ripples had been audible from that side of the cabin. We passed the point and veered closer to shore, a tangle of brush between stone outcroppings and other coves similar to the Peabody-Smiths' harbor. Windows on buildings tucked among trees and rocks reflected the setting sun, some so brightly that I had to look away.

And when I did, I spotted a canoe in the middle of the river of brilliance flowing from the sun across the lake.

Had Gregory Tinsletter left, as he said he would, or was he hanging around Deepwish Lake and the cabin his late ex had rented? And if so, why?

Chapter 35

✣

The person in the canoe was silhouetted, dark against the gleaming water, and I couldn't tell whether it was a man, woman, or child. Whoever it was sat still, maybe watching us, maybe fishing, or maybe merely relaxing in the serene and lovely surroundings. The scene was almost an exact replica of one of Summer's paintings in The Craft Croft.

It took me a second to realize that the canoe had turned and was heading toward us.

In the sunlight, drops of water in shades of gold, silver, and copper cascaded from the canoe's paddle. That canoe was coming fast. I probably would have merely admired the canoer's skill if a woman had not been murdered in a cabin on that very lake less than a week before, but she had been, and her killer had not been caught.

And the canoer was quickly closing the gap between us.

In my experience, kayaks were lighter and more maneuverable than canoes, but I doubted that Summer and I could outrace this one.

Summer seemed unconcerned. She turned her kayak toward it. Telling myself to calm down, I followed.

As if they'd done it many times before, Summer and the canoer maneuvered their crafts to face each other while keeping the setting sun to their sides. I pulled up beside Summer. Half sunlit and half shaded, the three of us steadied our boats, and I got a good look at the canoer.

Surprisingly small and wispy considering her apparent strength, the woman wore a well-loved canvas hat with a drooping brim. Her thinning, plaid flannel shirt must have been around as long as the hat. She put a hand up to block sunlight from that side of her face. "It's little Summer, isn't it? But you're not so little anymore." The woman's voice cracked as if she seldom used it. Judging by the wrinkles I could now see, she had to be at least eighty.

Summer's laugh boomed out. "Hi, Ms. Murphy. No. I gave up on being little. This is Emily."

"She's not from the lake." Ms. Murphy said it with great certainty.

Summer's smile didn't fade. "She's a friend, visiting me."

"There was some excitement at your parents' place a week or so back." Again, there was no doubt in Ms. Murphy's voice.

Summer held her paddle straight up and down, keeping her kayak in place. "Yes."

I shielded the sunny side of my face. "What happened, Ms. Murphy?" Wavelets rippled against our hulls.

Ms. Murphy worked her mouth as if trying to figure out if it was proper to discuss lake business with someone who wasn't from the lake. "Lots of vehicles. I was out here when the first one came down your driveway, Summer. I might be eighty-six, but my hearing's as good as anyone's. That car came down slowly, like the new woman who was renting the place always drove. A few minutes later, another one just barreled down the driveway. I was sure it was going to plunge off the cliff and into the woods."

My kayak started pivoting toward shore. I turned it to face Ms. Murphy again. "Did you see it?"

"I couldn't see any of them. That point's in the way. Just

lights, but that was later. This second vehicle rattled and clanked like an old pickup truck with a bunch of tin pails rolling around in the back. Maybe five minutes later, it barreled back up the driveway. It rattled and clanked up to Peabody Lane and then sped away. It was soon out of my hearing."

I asked Ms. Murphy, "Did you hear voices?"

"Nothing noticeable, but another vehicle came along and almost tiptoed down that driveway, like someone would drive who'd never been there before. I can't remember for sure, but I think I did hear a woman call out, but friendly, like she was greeting someone. You should get your folks to fix their driveway, Summer."

"It's on their list. How long did the tiptoeing vehicle stay?"

"I don't know. About ten minutes. Did I tell you the burglar alarm went off? Or maybe it was a smoke alarm, I don't know, but it was loud, and sounds carry across this lake. I paddled closer, almost to your beach. I wouldn't have heard any voices over that noise, but it stopped, and I didn't hear anyone talking. Then it seemed like only a minute or two later, someone drove away in something that looked like it could have been a white car or truck. I couldn't see much of it between the leaves. Everything seemed fine, so I backed out into the lake again." She cleared her throat and went on. "I heard another vehicle, and a car door slamming, and the next thing I knew, sirens were out on the highway, coming closer. Then there were heavy vehicles coming down that driveway, and people shouting, and flashing lights so bright I could see them even though the sun was still high, all colors like police cars and firetrucks. They gave me a weird feeling right here." She tapped her chest. "I remembered it was time to take my pills, so I went home. Ever since then, until about this morning, there've been trucks and people coming and going and talking in loud voices, so I guessed something must have happened." She tilted her head and peered expectantly at Summer.

Summer seemed to study the bow of her kayak. "Something did. The woman who was renting the place for the summer died."

Ms. Murphy clicked her tongue against the roof of her mouth. "That was a silly thing to do. I guess she wasn't from the lake, either. Well, that makes sense, or she wouldn't have needed to rent from your folks. But she should have waited until autumn to die. There's so much she'll have missed by departing this world in June. Well, see you, girls. It's time for me to turn in. Will you be here in the morning?"

"No." I heard affection in Summer's voice.

Ms. Murphy lifted her paddle from the water. "You should. There's good fishing before sunrise. Be out here with your fishing tackle about five. You'll catch the best breakfast of your lives." Ms. Murphy thrust her paddle into the water and sped away.

My mouth must have been hanging open. Summer smiled at me. "We should go in before it gets much darker." While we'd been talking to Ms. Murphy, the sun had drifted behind trees on the other side of the lake.

We paddled back to the Peabody-Smiths' beach and overturned the kayaks on the sawhorses. I wanted to ask Summer about Ms. Murphy, but the woman was observant, and as she'd said, sounds carried across the lake.

Summer and I started up toward the cabin. When the point of land was between us and the lake, Summer murmured, "She's quite a character, isn't she?"

"I want to be her when I grow up. Only, not alone. With Brent." *And maybe our children . . .* "How long have you known her?"

"All my life. She was always like that. Full of energy and opinions, fishing every chance she gets, keeping her eyes and ears on everyone around the lake. We have binoculars in the cabin. She must have stronger ones."

"Is there a Mr. Murphy?"

"There was. He didn't come out here much, and they had no children. He died when I was a teen, and after that, she began staying out here all winter, too. But now, partly because of my parents' urging, she has an apartment in town. I suspect that she resists going there until the weather gets threatening."

"I can imagine! She obviously loves it here."

"She does. Anyway, I'm sure she didn't murder Pamela, and if the murderer escaped by boat, Ms. Murphy would have noticed."

I unzipped my life jacket. "It sounds like the murderer was driving something that rattled. I'm pretty sure the white car that 'tiptoed' was mine, with me driving cautiously, and I did shout a greeting or two before I went up to the cabin door. Brent arrived next, and then other first responders. Do you think she's told the police anything about what she saw and heard that night?"

"I doubt it. She didn't seem to know there'd been a death, let alone a murder. She might have a phone, but I bet she doesn't answer it or the door if anyone knocks. Besides, she's out in that canoe a lot." We stowed the paddles and life jackets where they belonged. Summer locked everything again and we sauntered to our cars in the twilight.

I unlocked my car. "I hope Pamela's murderer doesn't have an inkling that Ms. Murphy witnessed anything that evening. He or she might think Ms. Murphy knows more than she does."

"The person in the rattletrap probably didn't know she was out there on the lake. She can be stealthy in that canoe."

"She must have been nearby when I discovered Pamela's body, but I didn't notice her, and I didn't even think of looking out at the lake for help or an escaping murderer. I just had to get out of here."

"We should tell Detective Clobar what she said. Not Chief Agnew." Summer shuddered. "He's creepy. I'll call Detective Clobar. Unless you want to."

"He's all yours." I would give Summer a chance to tell Rex what Ms. Murphy had said before I called him about the key.

"I wish!"

I grinned. "Call him tonight and tell him that the best way to talk to Ms. Murphy will be to join you in kayaks out on the lake at five in the morning."

I was sure that Ms. Murphy, and everyone else who lived around the lake, heard Summer's laugh. "Great idea, Emily! You come too, and bring coffee, or he and I will do nothing besides stare blearily at each other." Her mouth twitched. "But that could be fun." She pointed at her driveway, now almost completely dark underneath overhanging trees. "I'll let you go first so I can help if you can't make it all the way up."

"Thanks for the vote of confidence."

"Anytime."

"And thanks for the kayaking."

"My pleasure. Thank you for coming out here and helping push the nightmares away so the place seems more like it did in the good old days. And come again!"

Promising that I would, I got into my car. I turned my headlights to their brightest and let my SUV tiptoe up that driveway. Summer stayed a good distance behind me, and then followed me along Peabody Lane and onto the highway. When we were almost in downtown Fallingbrook, she flashed her lights and turned onto a road of homes built in the 1950s.

I drove on. And thought about what we'd learned.

Based on what Ms. Murphy had said, Pamela's killer might have arrived and departed in a vehicle that rattled. Ms. Murphy had said it sounded like a pickup truck with something loose in its bed. She seemed confident about her hearing, and other vehicles she'd mentioned matched what I believed happened.

A pickup truck . . .

Daniel had been nearby that evening. Was the woman from his church wrong? Could he have left her trees long enough to drive down the Peabody-Smiths' stony, pitted driveway, kill Pamela, and drive away again?

Kayla also drove a pickup truck. Did her photos really prove she'd spent Sunday evening hiking around Falling-brook Falls?

Diana drove a car. Maybe she had access to a pickup truck.

But Ms. Murphy hadn't actually seen a pickup truck. Any vehicle, including my SUV, Agnew's SUV, Diana's car, or Gregory Tinsletter's van, could have made more noise than usual on that driveway.

I didn't know if someone had killed Pamela because he— I was still picturing Gregory Tinsletter—wanted the key that had been in Dep's toy donut.

Could Gregory be taking advantage of my absence to break into my house and search for the key? He wouldn't find it unless he fished through the laundry and checked the pockets of my shorts.

Dep was home alone.

I pushed harder on the gas pedal.

Chapter 36

❧

I backed into my driveway and pressed the button on the garage door opener. I parked in the garage, closed the overhead door, checked that the door into my enclosed yard was still dead bolted, and went out through the side. I locked that door and followed the walkway from the garage to the front porch.

The house looked fine. The lights I'd programmed to come on at dusk were burning. Dep sat watchfully upright on the windowsill in the living room.

I started up the porch steps, and Dep jumped off the windowsill. I opened the door. Her fur silky and warm against my bare ankles, she described in great detail her feelings about having been abandoned. I picked her up and made a quick tour of the first floor. The back door and all of the windows were securely locked. Dep purred.

I opened the sunroom windows to let the evening's fresh air inside and then called Brent and told him about finding the envelope and the watch. "And then Summer and I went out in her kayaks."

"Lucky you. I've been marking papers."

I told him about our conversation with Ms. Murphy. "Summer is calling Rex Clobar with that information."

"Great, but I'm taking notes. After I get back, Agnew can't keep me off this case. Rex is looking forward to having my help."

Obviously, Rex and Brent were communicating with each other, so I didn't tell Brent about the key. Rex might come take it away, and I might never figure out if it unlocked something in my house. Also, whether Pamela had meant for me to have the key or not, and according to Gregory, she hadn't, it had been in our office in Deputy Donut before Pamela was killed. Her murderer might never have seen the key or even have known it existed. It might not count as evidence in the case.

I would figure out as much as I could about the key and then call Rex and let him decide if it was relevant.

Brent and I talked about what we'd do after he returned, and then I let him go back to marking papers.

I paced the kitchen, thinking about a pickup truck with things loose in its bed. What had Kayla really been searching for in my yard? I knew very little about her, other than that she had first met my parents at their campsite in Florida.

My parents had spent every winter in that campground for years, and I kept the manager's phone number among the contacts in my phone.

The manager must not have been busy on a Saturday evening in June. She answered on the second ring. I assured her that my parents were fine and were returning to Cypress Knee in the fall if not sooner, and I described the rehearsal picnic they'd hosted.

The manager laughed. "That sounds like them. Everyone who sticks around here during the summer misses them."

"Speaking of other people from your campground, do you remember a camper named Kayla?"

"I certainly do. Nice young woman, a friend of your parents. She said she might go stay near them in Wisconsin this summer."

"She did, and she helped build my new garage."

"I gathered she'd known your parents for a while."

"Before last winter?" I tried not to sound surprised—or worried.

"That was the impression I got. When she first pulled in towing that trailer, I hurried into the office to help her, and she was staring at the map of sites on our whiteboard. I was almost certain that she was looking right at the plot where I'd written *W and A Young*. The plot next to it was empty, and she asked for that one. I told her that because her trailer was small, she could have a less expensive site, but she had decided she wanted to camp next to Walter and Anne Young. I hadn't written Walt and Annie's full names on the whiteboard, so I figured Kayla knew them. Looking back on it, I can't be positive, but I'm pretty sure she said, 'Walter and Anne,' not 'Walt and Annie.' I figured she didn't know them as well as I do." She laughed. "That would have been difficult. I've known Walt and Annie since young Kayla was riding around on tricycles!"

I laughed politely, managed to say a reasonable goodbye, and ended the call.

Absently, I went upstairs and turned on my computer. My parents had said that Kayla befriended them while they were at their Cypress Knee campsite. They hadn't said a thing about meeting her during previous travels.

They wouldn't have forgotten her.

From what the campground manager in Florida had said, it appeared that Kayla might have gone to Cypress Knee looking for them.

Why?

Had Kayla somehow learned about whatever it was that Hattie was going to give Tillie, the delightful young lady, and Kayla wanted to find it?

If, like Daniel and I, Kayla had searched obituaries, she could have read Hattie's address, and then she could have researched and found out who now owned 1212 Maple Street in Fallingbrook. And then by looking for Westhill in obituaries, she could have found Alec's.

I didn't have to look that one up. It was engraved painfully in my mind. It had mentioned Alec's parents and me, and it had also given my parents' names and stated that they divided their time between Fallingbrook, Wisconsin, and Cypress Knee, Florida.

Cypress Knee was tiny. My parents had told me that its folksy online directory listed the longtime summer residents, including my parents, and gave the rural route address of their campground.

Had Kayla hauled a camping trailer from California to Florida specifically to meet my parents and then use them to befriend me? That didn't make sense. If Kayla had wanted to talk to the owner of 1212 Maple Street, she could have simply rung my doorbell. She wouldn't have needed my parents as intermediaries.

Maybe it had been too daunting to knock on a stranger's door and say, "Excuse me, but I'd like to dig in your yard for treasure, like the gold and jewels that King John lost in The Wash in Norfolk, England, or relics from Viking settlements."

Even if Kayla had tracked down my parents in order to meet me and dig in my yard, how could that possibly be connected with the murder of Pamela Firston?

I'd seen Kayla drive back to her campsite Sunday evening after I'd discovered Pamela's body. Logan had been following her in his car. According to Rex, they'd been hiking and taking pictures. Why had they driven to the falls to hike the trails? One of the trails to the falls originated in the campground not far from my parents' campsite. Maybe Kayla and Logan didn't know that.

But why go there in two vehicles? Because of his work, Brent and I usually went places in separate vehicles, but last

Sunday, Kayla had not yet started working for my contractor, and Logan was a teacher and had the summer off. But couples didn't always go everywhere together. Maybe they'd arranged to meet at the falls that night for their hike.

Jocelyn jogged around those trails and had seen the couple that evening. I called her and asked, "Last Sunday evening, when you were jogging on the trails around the falls and saw Kayla and Logan hiking, did you jog through the parking lot?"

"Yes."

"Did you notice either of their vehicles parked there?"

"Yes, his car. I thought it odd that they drove such a short distance to go hiking, but I suppose they could have come from somewhere else. If her truck was there, I didn't see it, but I don't think it was. Why? Are you doing some sleuthing I can help with?"

"No. Rex is quite capable. He'll figure it all out. See you tomorrow!"

With Dep watching me, I fished my work uniform shorts out of the laundry basket. The key, rough with accumulated rust, had slid partway out of the pocket. I pulled it the rest of the way.

"Mew?"

I held it in front of Dep's nose. "Recognize this?"

She sniffed for several seconds and then rubbed her gums against the key.

"Yes, I know it came from your toy donut and probably smells like catnip, but what does it unlock? Maybe we can clean it up a little."

Dep went with me to the basement where she helped, in her less than helpful way, find a wire brush. With her supervision, I removed rust until I was able, just barely, to make out the insignia: three capital letters inside a shield like on a coat of arms. Although the letters were in an old-fashioned script, they made me laugh. They were L-O-L.

If I was right that the key had been inserted in a letter in

1949, the letters had been stamped onto the key long before the shorthand for Laugh Out Loud was devised.

It was late, but I told Dep, "Let's go up to the computer and see what we can find out about this insignia."

Meowing, she stood in my way at the base of the stairs. I picked her up. Her purr reached its loudest rumbles. I carried her to the second floor and let her sit on my lap while I searched for L-O-L on the internet. There were millions of entries, and I almost gave up. But when I added the words "insignia" and "key" to the search and scrolled through images, I found a photo of a key almost like mine. It had been made by a company that had existed in the early 1900s. Leck-O-Lock had manufactured lockable fuse boxes with the motto: KEEP LITTLE FINGERS SAFE.

I shouted, "Aha!" Dep jumped. I stroked her. "It's okay, Dep. Now I know where to search for Hattie's treasure."

When Alec and I were renovating, we had come upon an old, locked fuse box in the basement. The home had originally been lit by gas, but Hattie had apparently converted to electricity soon after the house was built. Later, the knob-and-tube wiring from the first installation had been removed except for a couple of white porcelain knobs still screwed to rafters in the basement. Homeowners had eventually replaced the fuses with circuit breakers. By then, Hattie was long gone.

Alec and I had joked about what we might find inside the old fuse box if we located its key. We had considered removing the fuse box, but it hadn't been in our way. It was an antique part of the house that, like the porcelain knobs, we'd left in place for atmosphere, at least until we turned the basement into more living area. We hadn't needed the extra space for two of us, and I certainly didn't need it for only one.

"Mew."

I amended my thought aloud. "Okay, for two of us. C'mon, Dep, let's have a look at that fuse box."

She galloped to the basement. I took the stairs relatively sedately.

The metal box didn't look terribly rusty, considering that Hattie must have stopped using it before 1949. Shining my phone's light on the front cover of the greenish metal box, I could barely make out the words LECK-O-LOCK, stamped on the diagonal in a square embellished with curlicues. The company's motto, KEEP LITTLE FINGERS SAFE, was below it.

At first, the key wouldn't go all the way into the lock. I returned to the workbench and brushed off more rust. If I had to, I would soak the key in oil overnight.

I warned myself that haste made waste.

I couldn't wait to find out what was inside the "treasure chest."

The key went in. I wiggled it and tried turning it.

Afraid of breaking either the key or the lock, I didn't force it.

No wires led to the box. I didn't have to worry about live electricity in or near the box. I muttered, "I can cut the box open if I need to. Maybe tomorrow."

Ignoring the inner voice that said I could let Rex have the key now and cut into the box later, I applied a little more pressure.

The key turned, and the front of the Leck-O-Lock fuse box swung open.

Chapter 37

✻

An envelope, about five inches wide and six inches long, had been wedged into the fuse box. The envelope might have originally been goldish amber, but time had browned it. I blew off some of the dust and tilted my head sideways to read the faded word on the envelope. *Homeowner.* The handwriting was similar to Hattie Renniegrove's in her letter to Tillie, but more confident and less shaky. Younger.

I smiled down at Dep, waiting patiently at my feet for me to finally take her to bed. "Homeowner? That's us. Let's see what's in the envelope."

With gentle fingers, I eased the envelope out of the metal box. I took the warped and brittle envelope to the workbench where I could examine it underneath strong lights.

Either it had not been sealed, or the glue had dried and lost its grip. I pulled out a sheet of stationery, probably once beige. A spray of faded red roses, an old-fashioned print that appeared to have been adapted from a watercolor original, decorated the top of the stationery.

I checked the signature.

Harriet Renniegrove had apparently been fond of writing letters. This one was dated 1935.

To *whoever finds this*, it began. *I have done every-thing I could to restore my sister's bracelet to her, but for reasons that will become clear, I have not been able to. I am therefore asking you to give it to her.*

My sister is Esther Renniegrove of 1211 Walnut Street, Fallingbrook, Wisconsin. She accused me of stealing a bracelet that our father gave her. Far from having stolen the bracelet, I had never, up to that point, seen the object in question.

Our father was the renowned archaeologist, Ernest Renniegrove, who unfortunately fell from a cliff to his death.

I do not believe he merely fell. I believe he was pushed, and I said as much to Esther.

"And who," she demanded, "do you imagine pushed him?" I should have known from her angry flush not to answer that question. She must have guessed what I was about to say.

"Why," I replied, "it had to be Otto Nobbuth."

She asserted, "That is not true! Otto fell trying to save Father, and Otto's dear body has never been found!"

I do not understand why Esther was and continues to be besotted with Otto Nobbuth.

What was I to do except retort the truth? "Your cad of a swain came here after that dreadful occurrence. One night I thought I heard the front door close softly in the house where you and I were staying in Falling-brook while we planned our new home." At that time, Esther and I were going to build a home to live in to-gether, at least until one of us should marry. I explained to Esther, "I rose and investigated. A man was walking rapidly from the house. I followed at a distance, and nearly caught up with him near the plot where we are to build our home. Imagine my shock when, by the light of the moon, I recognized Otto Nobbuth prowling around our newly acquired land." It was my misfortune to add, "He must have come into our house that night. That is probably when he stole your bracelet. And then he left Wisconsin and went off to start a new life where no one would know he murdered Father."

Esther cried, "He never did! He never came to Fallingbrook, let alone entered our house. You stole my bracelet. Father gave it to me, and you stole it for yourself. You have always been jealous of me because I was Father's favorite!"

I, of course, demurred. "I have never seen your precious bracelet." By now I was a little hot under the collar, myself.

We argued in this vein for some time, and then we came to an agreement. Instead of building one large home, we would build two smaller cottages. It was she who decided that a wall must surround hers. Likewise, I built a wall around mine.

In the intervening years, Esther and I have not spoken to each other except during that first year when, of necessity, we discussed the building of our homes.

And then, not long ago, during my gardening endeavors, I came upon the gold bracelet. Either Esther lost it, or my original surmise was correct. Her cad of a swain stole it, and then, with plans to dig it up later, buried it on the property that Esther and I once shared.

Although knowing she would continue to believe that I had stolen the bracelet, I telephoned her. She hung up when she heard my voice and did not answer her phone although I had the operator try her many times during the next week or so. I sent her a letter in the mail. The letter was returned, marked "Refused." And not opened. All of my subsequent attempts to enter into discourse with my sister were likewise rebuffed, which is why, dear person who must have discovered this letter and the bracelet in their hiding place, I ask you to befriend my wayward and stubborn sister and give her the bracelet. I cannot simply leave it in her mailbox. I don't know what she might do if she witnessed me setting foot upon her property.

Signed in good faith, etc. etc.,

Harriet Renniegrove

P.S. *I don't know why she referred to the object as a "bracelet." It would never have fit even such a light eater as my sister.*

P.P.S. *This fuse box served as a fuse box from the time when I electrified this house until, having underestimated the usefulness of electricity, I updated it and put in a more commodious fuse box. There is no danger of electrifying yourself in the removal of the contents of the box.*

P.P.P.S. *I plan to continue trying to give the bracelet to my sister; if you find and read this, it means I did not succeed before I departed, either this home or this life.*

I peeked into the envelope, and then to be certain that it didn't contain even a tiny bracelet, I turned it upside down over the workbench. Nothing fell out besides the crumbling corpse of a moth and a sprinkling of paper dust.

I asked Dep, "What can have become of this alleged gold bracelet? Was it a figment of Hattie's imagination, or did someone remove it and leave the letter behind to tantalize whoever found it next?"

"Meow." Dep sat at the foot of the basement steps and stared upward.

"Okay, okay, I'll cuddle you and take you to bed, but let's have another look first."

With the help of my phone's light, I peered into the fuse box. I thought I had emptied it, but there was something at the bottom, something covered in a layer of dust and the siftings of powdered rust.

It was a brown bag made of sturdy paper. I was surprised at the weight of whatever was inside it. I took the bag to the well-lit workbench.

The bag had been wrapped around something and taped shut. The clear outer layer of the tape drifted off, leaving a stain of dried adhesive. I unrolled the bag, opened it, and looked inside.

Another whorl?

I turned the bag on its side and slid it off the object.

It was not a bracelet. No human hand, not even a baby's, would have fit through the hole in the center. It was approximately the shape and size of a raised donut.

It might have been gold once, but it was encrusted with dirt, probably the way it had been when Hattie found it, except the dirt had dried and was flaking off. The metal warmed in my hand. Had I found a pound or more of gold in my house? I tried not to think about how valuable that amount of gold might be.

My heart beating faster, I looked over at Dep. "Wow."

She stared toward the top of the basement stairs. "Mew."

If the thing was gold, water wouldn't harm it. I rinsed it in the concrete set tub that was probably as old as the house. Most of the dirt came off, but bits of it stubbornly remained in the intricate, flowery designs engraved or stamped in the metal.

It was dark with tarnish. It had to be brass, not gold.

I muttered to Dep, who was now on the third step up from the basement floor and staring hopefully at me through the railing, "Pamela might have been killed for a chunk of brass."

"Mew." Dep stalked up two more steps and hunkered down, obviously still waiting for me.

"I'll just clean off more of this dirt so I can see the pattern, and then I'll stop, I promise."

I rubbed a soft cloth against the brownish metal "donut" under running water. The tarnish stayed, but when most of the dirt was gone, I dried the thing on another soft cloth and carried it back to the workbench.

The ornate designs were pretty. Studying the brass donut more carefully, I noticed words. They weren't easy to read, and I wished that Summer and her magnifying glass were with me. Finally, I made out: ANCIENT VIKING WHORL. SOUVENIR OF THE NEW ORLEANS WORLD'S FAIR, 1884.

That made me laugh out loud. "It's not gold, it's not ancient, it's not a Viking relic, and although it's probably a good size and heft to stabilize a spindle when spinning thick yarn, I doubt that it was ever used as a whorl."

Dep had stalked down the stairs and was again at my feet, looking up at me. I told her, "Its only value is as a souvenir of the 1884 World's Fair." I had to add, "Which is impressive. Also, there's a significant amount of brass in it. But poor Pamela! What a thing to die for. And what a thing for the Renniegrove sisters to lose each other's love and sisterly support over. Okay, Dep, I hear you." I scooped her up. "It's after ten, way too late to call Rex. We'll call him in the morning and tell him what we've found and also what Jocelyn said about Kayla's truck possibly not being in the parking lot at the falls Sunday evening." Carrying Dep up the stairs, I bit my lip. "And maybe give him the number of the campground manager in Cypress Knee. But for now, let's go to bed."

Dep wriggled in my arms. The whorl was heavy. I stopped in the kitchen and left the souvenir on top of the half wall between the kitchen and the sunroom.

Dep stared toward the open sunroom windows. "Mew."

Air wafting in from the garden was warm and fragrant. I closed the windows except for a crack and locked them in place so that, from the outside, they couldn't easily be opened farther. Now that my new garage door was installed and locked, raccoons were probably the only threat, and as far as I knew, none of them had ever climbed over that smooth brick wall.

Finally, I carried my impatient cat upstairs.

Knowing I could close them later if the night became chilly, I left my bedroom windows wide open.

It wasn't a cool breeze that awakened me.

Dep hissed. I felt her creep off my shins.

My eyes flew open.

In the dim light from streetlamps, I saw Dep sitting up straight on the edge of the bed and staring toward the open back window.

I felt like I'd heard something before Dep hissed, possibly a screech like the one the rear door of my garage made if it was opened slowly.

But that door was locked.

And even if it hadn't been locked, the large overhead door was. It would keep anyone from coming through the smaller door into my garden.

I lay still and listened.

Something hissed. Not Dep or other cats or raccoons, but humans, at least two people from the sounds of it, arguing in harsh whispers, one person shushing another.

Chapter 38

✻

In my shocked and suddenly awakened state, I wanted to force myself to believe that the two Renniegrove sisters had returned as ghosts and were bickering aloud over who had done what with the so-called bracelet.

I hoped I'd been dreaming those angry whispers.

And then I heard them again. At least two people were arguing in hissing whispers in my yard, underneath my bedroom's back window.

Dep jumped off the bed, onto the floor, and from there to the windowsill. Pressing against the screen, she peered down toward the yard.

It was just after two.

I tiptoed out of bed and leaned over my warm cat. For once, she didn't purr.

The moon, now heading toward its last quarter, wasn't high enough yet to cast light onto the ground. Haze hid the stars, and my yard was almost completely dark.

I couldn't see anyone. My open patio umbrella might have been hiding them, which would mean they were near my sunroom door.

I heard a slow, drawn-out squeak, as if someone were cautiously opening the sunroom's screen door.

In a maneuver almost worthy of Jocelyn's gymnastic skills, I did something between a belly flop, a somersault, and a flip across my tousled sheets and managed to land on my feet on the other side of the bed. I threw on my terrycloth robe and thrust my phone into the pocket.

Halfway down the stairs, I realized that I should have shut Dep into the bedroom. She probably would have yowled enough to scare the intruders away, which might have been a good thing. Instead, she sped past me to the first floor and then stood looking up at me with her fur puffed out and her tail switching back and forth.

I tiptoed through my unlit living and dining rooms.

Scanning what I could of my walled garden through the sunroom windows, I entered the kitchen even more cautiously.

The sunroom's screen door squeaked again, but someone must have let it go. It thumped, bounced, and hit the jamb more softly.

Two silhouettes, one pulling the other toward the garage side of my yard, appeared beyond the sunroom windows. Painfully aware of the way my pastel blue robe might be glimmering, ghostlike, in the dim glow of the numbers on the digital clocks on my stove and microwave, I stood still, barely breathing.

I hoped the people were leaving the walled garden, but they stopped near one of the slightly open sunroom windows. I picked up Dep to prevent her from going into the sunroom and leaping onto one of the wide windowsills to investigate. Still bent over, I crept to the half wall separating the kitchen from the sunroom. I crouched behind it, as close as I could be to the sunroom without going into it where I might be seen by whoever was outside the windows.

Although I was listening carefully, hoping to hear whatever I could, I jumped when a shrill whisper ripped through the night. "You can't break in!"

A deeper voice answered, still in a whisper. "I can, and I will. I have to."

"Why?"

"You'll thank me later. You have to help me now."

"No, I don't."

"Yes, you do. It was your truck, you know. Your truck could have been seen in places and at times where it shouldn't have been."

Your truck. A male was talking to a female about her truck. Logan drove a car, and Kayla drove a truck.

Kayla was trying to convince Logan not to break into my home. Still squatting, I nearly lost my balance. The cat struggling to leap out of my arms didn't help.

Kayla demanded, "What are you talking about?"

"Be quiet. You'll wake her up."

Lowering her voice only slightly, Kayla spat, "You . . . you said you were borrowing my truck that night to help someone move firewood. And then you said I should tell everyone that we'd been together that entire evening, hiking."

Logan retorted, "You're making things up. Let me go."

"No. You had time, Logan. While I was hiking by myself, you had time to drive to that woman's cabin, kill her, and come back to meet me."

"What if someone else makes up the same crazy story? Now you see why you have to help me."

"No! You can't hurt Emily."

"No one's going to get hurt. Just do what you're told." Logan's angry words jackhammered into the night. "All we have to do is get something back. It belongs to me. You help me get it, and then we can retire to a tropical island and live a life of luxury. You'll thank me."

"No! I'm not doing more favors for you. You think I didn't notice you leaving in my truck the next night and coming back when the night was almost over. What did you do that for? Did you come over here? You've . . . you've been trying to harm Emily all along. You planned this when we were still in California. That's why you sent me to Florida to worm my way into Emily's parents' confidence. They're good people. We can't hurt their daughter. Let's leave. Come on. If Emily has something of yours, just ask her for it."

"She's not crazy, but you are if you think anyone would give up a treasure just because someone asked."

"Then sue her for it."

"That would take too long." He added fiercely, as if he were speaking between clenched teeth. "Let go of me."

I heard a noise like a slap. "Ow!" Kayla's voice. Something heavy thudded onto the lawn.

I fumbled for my phone and entered a nine and two ones.

A woman's voice came on and asked much too loudly, "Do you need police, fire, or ambulance?"

I plunked down onto the floor. Still hugging Dep, who did not want to be hugged, I whispered, "Police, please. Prowlers are fighting in my yard." I gave the dispatcher my name and address and promised to stay on the line. The sound of flesh hitting flesh became louder. Gasps verged on screams. In an urgent whisper, I added, "I think the man is attacking the woman."

"Are you in a safe place?"

"Yes. I'm inside my house, but the man was trying to break in through my back door."

"Can you safely go out through the front and run to a neighbor?"

"I think so."

"Do that."

I made an agreeable noise, but how could I save myself and Dep while leaving Kayla, who had tried to protect me, alone with her murderous boyfriend?

I stood up and steadied myself with one hand on top of the half wall between the sunroom and kitchen.

My fingers closed around the heavy brass souvenir.

Chapter 39

Outside, my back garden was still almost totally dark. I couldn't see the two shadowy forms I'd noticed before I ducked behind the half wall, but I could hear them fighting. Both of them must have been on the ground.

I ran on tiptoe to the switch beside the back door and turned on lights to flood the entire yard. I unlocked the back door, wrenched it open, and shoved at the screen door so quickly that if it squeaked, I didn't notice.

Before I could grab her, Dep raced outside.

I was not far behind.

The screen door bounced against the jamb, echoing sounds I'd heard moments before. With my phone in my bathrobe pocket and the souvenir brass whorl in my right hand, I dashed around the outside corner of the sunroom. Dep streaked in the opposite direction and disappeared underneath overhanging forsythia branches.

As if lights hadn't come on and the door hadn't banged, Kayla and Logan rolled around on the grass pummeling each other. Logan was dressed in a burglar outfit—black jeans, black long-sleeved shirt, black shoes. He hadn't worn socks, and the greenish artificial light turned his ankles fish-belly white. The black stocking cap on the ground had probably fallen off his surfer-blond hair.

In contrast, Kayla wore a pink T-shirt over ruffled pink sleep shorts. The rhinestone-bedecked pink flip-flops nearby must have come off her feet. I noticed that the door into my garage was standing open but didn't have time to think about it more than to guess that Logan had broken into my garage and then into my yard.

He was yanking at Kayla's braids as if trying to pull them out of her head.

Hiding the brass whorl behind a fold of my robe, I yelled, "Stop it!"

Logan sprang to his feet, grabbed Kayla by the armpits, and hauled her upright. Her head lolled, but she raised it. Glassy-eyed, blinking, and gasping for breath, she stared toward me, but I wasn't sure she registered what she was seeing.

Logan held Kayla in front of him like a shield. He must have noticed that I was hiding my right hand and whatever it might be holding behind folds in the skirt of my robe. "Don't come closer," he warned, obviously struggling to keep Kayla from drooping out of his grasp.

I asked sensibly, "What's going on? Why are you here?"

Kayla managed, "He . . ." She gulped for air.

Logan told me, "You have something that belongs to me. My great-great-great-grandfather was an archaeologist who left something here in the care of the daughters of another archaeologist. I am the legal heir."

"What is it?" I couldn't keep sarcasm from creeping into my tone.

"A bracelet. The value is sentimental, only, something the other archaeologist gave him in gratitude for the work he did."

Archaeologist, I thought. Student of an archaeologist, more likely. And gratitude from Ernest Renniegrove for the work Otto Nobbuth did? Like wooing Ernest Renniegrove's daughter and then pushing Ernest off a cliff to his death in hopes of obtaining a treasure that might never have existed? I asked, "What makes you think I have a bracelet that belongs to you?"

"My great-great-great-grandfather left it with the woman who owned this plot of land. For safekeeping. I inherited it. It's mine."

"The woman who lived here in those days had a sister." Still keeping my right hand and the heavy souvenir whorl hidden, I pointed with my left forefinger. I didn't think its trembling could have been noticeable to the other two. "She lived back there, on the next street. What makes you think that the bracelet would be here and not on the other side of that wall?"

"Research. I'm a scientist, remember. I planned to look in both places. But after I got to Fallingbrook, I discovered that the two sisters ended up in the same nursing home at different times, that the family who owned that nursing home back then still owns it, and that a member of the youngest generation was fired from the company. I checked her social media. She had recently moved to this area. Bingo! Word of the trea—the bracelet must have gone down through her family like it did through mine. Guessing that she was also looking for the bracelet, I went to talk to her. She tried to prove that the bracelet was hers by showing me a letter written by the woman who built your house. Supposedly your home's first owner gave the letter to the grandmother of the woman I went to talk to, along with a key to something. It has to be the jewelry box where the woman who owned this house left the bracelet. And I knew that the house where the bracelet was had to be yours, because the woman I was talking to had written your name and address on the envelope where she'd hidden the letter. But she wouldn't tell me where she'd put the key."

"Many other people have owned this house since the Renniegrove sisters were alive. Any of them could have found and kept the bracelet."

"Illegally. It's mine."

"Tell that to the judge. You borrowed Kayla's truck to go talk to that woman, didn't you, and you borrowed it a second time so you could dig in my yard at three a.m. hunting for that bracelet."

"Three a.m.? That's the middle of the night, and so is this." With a sneer, he accused, "You've been half dreaming and half making things up."

"You left a donut-shaped stone in my yard that morning. And then you enlisted Kayla to search my yard with a metal detector for the so-called treasure."

Still hanging onto Kayla as a shield, he took a step back. "No one's going to believe your cute little stories."

"Don't count on it." I almost didn't recognize the coldness in my voice. "You already have a problem with your alibi for the night that Pamela Firston was killed. The detective showed me copies of the photos you took of each other, supposedly at Fallingbrook Falls, the night the woman was murdered. But you two switched phones for part of that evening."

Kayla's eyes had been glazed over. She opened them wide and gave me a tiny affirmative nod.

Logan dismissed my accusations. "That was so I'd have pictures of my girlfriend on my phone. Who wouldn't want that?"

Maybe someone who would use his girlfriend as a human shield, I thought. Ignoring his excuse, I continued to explain the theory I was developing. "A couple of the pictures from Kayla's camera had been taken from near the ground, pointing up toward the sky. You took selfies from that angle to prevent anyone from noticing that a lake, not a river, was in the background."

Logan arranged his face into an infuriating smirk of superiority. "My arm's not that long."

"You propped Kayla's phone against a rock or a stump, set the camera's timer, and then backed far enough away to make it clear that the picture wasn't taken at only arm's length."

"You're making this up."

"I'm not. I just now realized that I recognized the top of a pine tree above your head in one of the pictures. That tree leans. It's not at Fallingbrook Falls. It's outside the cabin where Pamela Firston was killed."

Again, Logan mocked me. "No one recognizes the top of a tree."

I managed to say calmly, "No one has to. The police have those photos and can match them to the actual scene. The alibi you concocted is going to backfire." I glanced at poor, terrified Kayla. Whatever she'd done or how many lies she'd told for her abusive boyfriend, she had tried to protect me before I came outside, and I needed to try to return the favor. I told Logan, "I'll give you a break. Leave Kayla here, and you take off." He could probably tell from the steely anger in my voice that he wouldn't get far before I sent the full force of the law after him.

"Not without my—" He broke off.

I lifted the brass whorl where he could see it in all of its tarnished glory in the floodlit, misty yard. "Is this what you're looking for? A couple of pounds of melted-down gold?"

Hands outstretched and greed shining in his eyes, he let Kayla go and started toward me.

As if she had no bones, Kayla slumped down onto the grass. I wasn't sure if she had truly fainted or had faked it, but I didn't have time to check.

Logan was only a few steps from me.

Chapter 40

✽

"*Yowl!*" Fluffed to the size of a young tiger, Dep raced out of the bushes and flung herself at Logan's knees. He staggered. Dep detached herself, landed on her feet, and fled toward the garage.

Logan regained his balance. With a low growl, he lurched toward me.

I turned my right side toward him and widened my stance. As if the whorl were a donut-shaped throwing toy, I backhanded it at him. Because of its weight, I put a lot of force into the throw.

Logan reached up a hand. "Hey! Whuh?"

The whorl grazed his hand and hit him on the forehead. He sagged down onto his side, draped over his prone girlfriend.

I ran to them and placed my fingers on the artery in Kayla's wrist.

A man yelled, "Emily? Are you okay?"

Carrying my puffed-up cat, Daniel pelted past the wide-open door and into the yard.

Kayla's pulse beat underneath my fingers. I gave her wrist a reassuring squeeze and then stood. I pointed down at Logan. "He was attacking her."

Daniel set Dep down in the grass and nodded at Kayla. "Is she okay?"

Kayla said in a small voice, "Yes." She eased herself out from underneath Logan and sat up. Her shoulders shook, and tears ran down her cheeks.

I felt for Logan's pulse. He moaned.

Dep positioned herself beside his face, arched her back, and hissed.

Kayla scooted farther from Logan. "Call the police. He hurt me and would have hurt you, too, Emily." Her sob came out like a hiccup.

I took off my bathrobe's belt. "They're on the way."

Daniel and I wound the belt around Logan's wrists and tied it tightly, but we needed something for his ankles.

Shirtless and barefoot, Daniel wore jeans, but no belt. Kayla sat trembling in the dewy grass. She wasn't wearing a belt, either.

I ran into the kitchen and came out with a stack of towels. Kayla, Daniel, and I knotted them together and tied them around Logan's ankles. "There," I said, "that should hold him until the police get here." I grabbed Dep and nestled her into my arms. "I don't think we need your ferocious guarding any longer, sweetie."

I took her into the sunroom. I planned to set her down, shut her into the house, and return to the three people on my lawn.

The doorbell rang.

Still clutching my warm but tense cat, I ran to the living room and turned on the porch light.

In apparently thrown-on jeans, T-shirt, and armored vest, Chief Agnew was on the porch.

I opened the front door.

Agnew growled, "You called about prowlers and someone having a fight?"

Did he have to sound so skeptical? Also, I wasn't happy

about my beltless bathrobe gaping over my nightgown while Dep's attempts to flee threatened to reveal more. Car doors slammed. In their uniforms, Hooligan and his temporary partner Tyler ran toward the house. Rex Clobar was not far behind them. He'd had time to put on a dark gray suit, but his shirt collar was unbuttoned and he wasn't wearing a tie. He'd driven an unmarked cruiser again and had parked behind Hooligan and Tyler's marked one. Chief Agnew's huge black SUV was in front of the line of vehicles, closest to the walkway to my porch.

I told the crowd of law enforcement, "They're out back." Turning on lights as I went, I led the way through the living room, dining room, kitchen, and sunroom to the back door. I gestured to the four men to go out onto the patio. Finally, I set Dep onto one of the sunroom's wide windowsills and went outside, leaving her inside to complain about missing the wee-hours gathering.

The ridiculously early morning was chilly. I pulled my bathrobe more tightly around myself and crossed my arms over it.

Daniel stood over Logan. The brass souvenir was in his hand, and his face was strangely fierce.

Kayla was again sitting in the grass, but she was now farther from Logan. She hugged her knees close to her chest and rested her face on them. Her pink T-shirt, ruffled sleep shorts, long, bony legs, and partially undone braids made her look especially young and vulnerable.

Agnew bellowed, "Westhill and Suthlow, what have you two done, now? Killed someone else?"

Kayla raised her tear-streaked face. "Emily threw that thing at him to protect herself and me. Logan wanted to break into her house, and when I tried to stop him, he hit me." She stumbled to her feet and stood wavering in the floodlit yard.

Hooligan was better prepared than the rest of us. He ran to her, supported her with one arm, and gave her a tissue.

Agnew yelled at Daniel, "Drop that weapon and raise your hands above your head."

Daniel complied. The heavy brass "whorl" narrowly missed landing on one of his bare feet.

Rex Clobar asked calmly, "What happened, Emily?"

I explained concisely. Kayla nodded.

Logan, however, suddenly shouted, "Help me up!"

Rex squatted beside him. "Stay still. You might be injured." He ordered Hooligan, "Call an ambulance."

Hooligan said quietly. "It's on the way."

Logan grumbled, "I don't need one. Just get me out of these ropes, or whatever, and let me go." He pointed the top of his head toward me. "She tried to kill me. I was only trying to retrieve what's legally mine. She has a gold bracelet that I inherited from my great-great-great-grandfather. It's lawfully mine." Our tying of the terrycloth belt around his wrists had been less than successful. He released his hands, levered himself to a sitting position, and reached toward the towels confining his ankles. "That other woman, Pamela, she knew where the bracelet was, and she had a key. All I wanted from her was the key, but she wouldn't let me search. And to show her that I meant her no harm, I was going to give her a stone relic from a Viking settlement that I also inherited from my great-great-great-grandfather, but she wouldn't take it. She wouldn't give me the key, and she attacked me with a cane. I had to defend myself. I put that stone relic in this yard for safekeeping. It's over there somewhere." He waved a hand in the direction of the forsythia. "That woman, Pamela, didn't want my antique stone relic, so may I have it back, please?" He looked appealingly up toward Chief Agnew, who was still standing over him, hands on hips.

Hooligan and his partner scribbled in their notebooks. Rex put down his pen and stared at Logan with something like sympathy.

My voice rang out into the silence. "I found the so-called

bracelet a few hours ago. It's not a bracelet, and it's not gold. It's lying beside Daniel's feet, Detective Clobar. It's solid, and it's heavy, but it's tarnished. Gold doesn't tarnish. It's probably brass."

Logan ranted, "It's gold and it's mine! My great-great-great-grandfather buried it here. He planned to return for it immediately, but people were working here, and he had to leave. He went to California and never managed to come back, so he willed the bracelet to his daughter along with a map of this neighborhood that showed where it was. I dug in Emily's yard but didn't find it, and my other guess, my best one, really, was that someone moved it inside to a box that Pamela wouldn't give me the key for. I stand in line to inherit the bracelet. I have every right to it!"

Maybe Kayla didn't recognize that Logan might have had a concussion and was therefore saying things he might later regret. She argued, "You did not have a right to borrow my truck to go visit that woman and hit her with your stone relic. You did not have a right to borrow my truck and drive over here to dig in Emily's garden. You did not have the right to threaten me if I didn't lie for you. You did not have the right to make me search for metal in Emily's yard, and you certainly did not have the right to borrow my truck tonight to try to break into Emily's house. To do what? Kill Emily, too, when she couldn't produce the treasure you think you inherited?"

Logan retorted, "I did inherit it. And you did not have the right to borrow my car tonight without asking. That's stealing. I'll have you charged."

Kayla shrugged. "I needed to follow you. You were driving my truck, which according to what you just said, you stole from me."

Daniel accused Logan, "And you had no right to tear part of a map out of a book that was probably worth more than the so-called gold." Daniel's voice shook.

Still sitting in the grass, Logan scowled up at Daniel. "I wouldn't tear up a valuable book. My great-great-grandmother did that, long ago, before the book had any value. She was going to hunt for her father's gold, but she didn't live long enough, and neither did my great-grandmother or my grandfather, so I had to. I have not broken any laws. I'm an upstanding member of the faculty of Fallingbrook High."

Behind me, I heard Hooligan mutter, "Losing your faculties."

I didn't think Logan heard Hooligan, which was just as well. With my own shock belatedly setting in, I had to turn away from Logan and Agnew to keep them from seeing my grin.

Chapter 41

Samantha and another EMT must have discovered they could enter my yard through the garage. They wheeled a stretcher through the doorway cut into the brick wall.

They removed a case of equipment from the stretcher, helped Logan onto the stretcher, and strapped him in. Rex read him his rights and told him he was under arrest for the murder of Pamela Firston.

Logan protested. "It was an accident!"

Kayla's cheek was bleeding and one of her eyes was swelling. I said urgently, "Kayla's hurt."

Leaving Logan with Hooligan, Tyler, and her EMT partner, Samantha helped Kayla to one of my patio chairs, had her sit down, and quietly questioned her.

Chief Agnew folded his arms over his armored vest and told Rex, "We need to consider more arrests. When we arrived, the man you just arrested had been assaulted. He was tied up, and Suthlow was standing over him and threatening him with another of his donut-shaped murder weapons. And those two women"—he aimed his chin toward Kayla and then toward me—"were nearby and not stopping Suthlow."

I objected. "Daniel didn't hurt anyone with that brass relic or with the stone one, either. Daniel hadn't arrived in my yard yet when I threw that brass donut-like thing at Logan. I didn't mean to knock him down. I only wanted to stop him from harming Kayla and me while we waited for help to arrive. We tied Logan up to prevent him from getting away."

Calling from the patio table where she was sitting with Samantha, Kayla confirmed that my story was correct. "And check Logan's pockets. When he came here early Wednesday morning to dig in Emily's yard, he must have stolen one of the sets of keys that my boss left for Emily in her mailbox. When I got here shortly after he did tonight, both the side and the back doors of the garage were standing open. Each of those doors came with a set of two keys. The keys match. They all open both doors. Did you find all four keys in your mailbox, Emily?"

"No. Only two keys. One set, I guess." Mentally chastising myself for not figuring out that doors might come with more than one key each, I stared pointedly at Agnew.

He didn't meet my gaze, and he didn't admit to having seen two sets of keys in my mailbox, or to having borrowed one of the sets.

Rex removed keys from Logan's pockets and said in his quiet way, "Irv, you'll follow the ambulance to the hospital so you can begin questioning Logan." Rex sorted through the keys. "These new brass keys could be yours, Emily. And here's Kayla's truck key." He took pictures of the keys, made notes, and then gave us our keys.

Samantha helped Kayla to her feet. "I'm taking Kayla to the hospital to be checked out. She'll ride in front with me."

Rex nodded as if he'd expected that. "Hooligan and Tyler will take Kayla's statement while she's being patched up, and I'll stay here to talk to Daniel and Emily, and then I'll meet you at the hospital to plan our next steps, Irv." Rex turned to Tyler. "Do you mind riding in the back of the ambulance with one of the EMTs and the arrested man? Hooligan can drive the cruiser you two arrived in."

Tyler grinned toward Samantha, who was supporting the much-taller Kayla with one arm around her waist. "Not at all. I hear that Hooligan's wife is a good driver."

Samantha guided Kayla toward Tyler. "You better believe it. Meanwhile, can you help Kayla to the ambulance? Or, Kayla, is that your cane back there on Emily's table?"

Kayla shook her head. One of her braids had completely unraveled. "No. Logan brought it with him tonight. He set it down on the table when he started trying to get in through Emily's back door. He said he found it Sunday evening in a pile of firewood he was helping move, but that was a lie. It must be the cane he said the woman used to attack him."

Someday, Dep would probably find Kayla's missing hair tie in the grass and convince herself it was prey.

Agnew looked over at the patio table. "Gold handle. Probably another thing that woman stole from her clients."

I had to defend Pamela Firston. "I doubt it. Remember the gold-headed cane that Hattie Renniegrove mentioned in her letter? That letter was probably written to Matilda Aimes, Pamela's grandmother. Maybe Hattie left the cane to Matilda or gave it to her."

Agnew growled, "Or this Matilda person stole it from the Renniegrove woman."

I had to admit that was possible. "But Pamela wasn't born yet and couldn't have stolen it from Hattie Renniegrove."

Agnew peered at the cane's handle and then grunted. "Doesn't look like real gold to me. Maybe gold leaf over copper. The gold is wearing through in spots." He straightened and asked Rex, "Are you going to bring that along as evidence?"

Rex's answer was terse. "Yes."

Logan shouted, "She attacked me with it!"

Agnew glanced at me. "Who?" He actually licked his lips.

Logan let me off the hook and firmly hoisted himself onto it. "That woman out at the lake, the woman who was trying to steal treasure that belonged to me."

Samantha and the other EMT wheeled Logan away through my new garage. Hooligan and Agnew followed them.

Kayla seemed reluctant to be close to Logan, but Tyler offered her his arm, and she placed her hand on it and let him escort her out of my garden and toward the ambulance.

Rex asked me, "Do you mind if I go to Daniel's house and question him first?"

I gave him a shaky smile. "That will give me a chance to shower and dress." And maybe regain some of my equilibrium.

Daniel faked a shiver. "And I'll be glad to get out of this damp and foggy night and put on a shirt. And maybe three sweaters and a coat."

I followed them into my new garage. Someone, probably Samantha or her partner, had turned on the light inside it and pushed the button that opened the big overhead door. It was gaping. I guessed it was lucky that I'd had the garage built big enough to accommodate my car with enough space to wheel a stretcher past it.

I told Rex, "Ring my doorbell after you talk to Daniel."

"Okay. I'm afraid your garage and the walled section of your yard are a crime scene, and you'll have to stay out."

I slapped my forehead. "Oh, no! After I finally have a garage and parked inside it for the first time!"

Rex was good at looking empathetic. "I'll have a look around your car, and let you know if you can move your car to the driveway, for now. I'll make sure we process the scene quickly so you can use your garage and yard again."

"Maybe you'll dig up some gold?"

He laughed. "Maybe. Can you go into your house through the front door, or did you lock it?"

"I didn't. I'll go in that way."

He sketched a salute. "See you in about fifteen minutes."

He and Daniel started across the street. I pushed the button that closed and locked the overhead door, went into the house, locked the doors, apologized to Dep, and ran upstairs for a quick shower. It was around three, but I knew there was no chance of sleeping again after Rex left. I put on my work uniform, added a bulky sweater, and started coffee.

Rex showed up with a large evidence bag.

I asked him, "Can you stand a cup of coffee this early?"

"I'd love it. I'll collect that cane and lock it in my cruiser, first."

When he came back in from his car, my kitchen was brightly lit, warm, comfy, and fragrant with fresh coffee. He sat at the counter and opened his notebook. I placed a mug of coffee in front of him. Answering his questions, I made toast, fried bacon, and scrambled eggs.

We ate. I apologized for not recognizing that one of the photos of Logan taken with Kayla's phone had not been taken at Fallingbrook Falls. "At the Peabody-Smiths' cabin, there's a pine tree with a curved trunk. It's near a bench on the point overlooking the lake, and it leans near the top. Logan must have propped his phone up and taken at least one timed selfie while he was at Deepwish Lake."

Rex's eyes opened wider. "I noticed that tree, but like you, I didn't recognize it from the photo. I'll go out and make a comparison to add to our evidence against Logan." Rex pocketed his notebook and pen. "Thank you, Emily, and thank you for the breakfast. I'm glad I gave Irv the job of going to the hospital."

"So am I." Following Rex to the living room, I shuddered. "I don't trust that man."

He opened the door. "Maybe you'll never have to deal with him again."

"I hope not. And I hope he can go teach that course, and Brent can come back."

"Don't count on it. Irv will need to finish up here, and I hear that the police college likes Brent and wants him to finish the course. Thanks again for everything." He left.

The sun would soon come up, and it was almost fully light outside. Flowers were opening, perfuming the air, and birds chirped and sang in the old neighborhood's tall trees.

I closed the door and picked Dep up. "I guess we can feed you, clean up our breakfast things, start some chili in the slow cooker, and maybe go to work a little early even though it's Sunday. I feel like making donuts. And maybe eating some, too."

"Meow," she said.

I stroked her. "Rex is probably right. Brent won't be able to come back immediately, but we'll see him next Saturday, at the latest."

Purr, purr, purr . . .

Chapter 42

Rex kept Chief Agnew busy on the Pamela Firston case, and Brent stayed at the police college to finish teaching the course. The investigators took only a few days to search my yard for evidence about Logan's assault on Kayla and his trespassing and digging in my garden, and then I was able to use my yard again. And my new garage.

On Friday morning, Rex came into Deputy Donut for a coffee and donut to go. He was on his way home. He thanked me again for helping capture Pamela's murderer. "You can fill in the holes that Logan dug," he told me. "Or dig more. We didn't find any gold, but you might." He gave me back the brass souvenir. No one was going to charge me for throwing it at Logan. "We have enough evidence against Logan to stand up in court. If he pleads not guilty to Pamela's murder, you'll have to testify."

"That's fine. It won't be the first time."

"No, and you're good at it. However, Irv Agnew has convinced himself that he suspected Logan all along and solved the case himself. You'll never get thanks from him."

"I wouldn't deserve them. All I did was hear Kayla pitching her voice loudly enough to alarm me."

"And instead of going back to sleep, you investigated."

"That was for my own self-preservation."

"Keep doing that."

"I'll try. Is Kayla in trouble for lying to you about being with Logan the evening that Pamela was murdered?"

"What do you think?"

"I think she is in trouble."

He nodded.

I added, "She said he threatened her."

"That will be taken into consideration. Also, the reason he'd given her for lying was that the person who had asked him to help move the firewood was doing it as a surprise for someone who wasn't at the campground but was on the way. It was all a story, but Kayla didn't know that. She had learned the hard way what happened when she disobeyed Logan. Also, she didn't hear about the murder right away, and when she did hear about it, she still believed the firewood story and it didn't occur to her that Logan might have murdered anyone. She said that even if it had occurred to her, she wouldn't have believed it. She didn't piece it all together until she followed him to your place and realized he was trying to harm you."

Sighing, I handed Rex the paper cup and a bag of donuts. I'd slipped in a few more than he'd paid for. He'd be on the road for a while.

I walked with him to our front door. He opened it. "Tell Brent hello."

"I will."

After work, Dep and I detoured to The Craft Croft. Summer was there. She crowed, "Guess who had me meet him out at the cabin a couple of days ago so he could take some pictures!"

Grinning, I asked, "Who?"

"That hot detective, Rex."

"I like him a lot."

"So do I. He brought me up to date on the case. Did you

have to solve it so quickly? He said he was going home to-day." She thrust out her lower lip, and then she grinned. "But yesterday afternoon, he came in here and bought a painting, one of that crooked tree near the lookout point at my parents' place on Deepwish Lake. He said that the picture might erase the bad vibes the place had given him when . . . when it was a crime scene. So, I invited him to come out some day, go kayaking with me, and erase those bad vibes entirely."

"I hope he never has to come back to Fallingbrook on business."

"Me, too. I reminded him that this is a great place to vacation, and he said he'd noticed, and he would come back sometime just to relax and chill. Then the smile he gave me!" Her own smile was huge.

Mine reflected it. "Your parents could rent him their cabin, and you can drop by often to make certain that everything is in perfect order. And you could go fishing with him at five in the morning."

Her laugh chimed through the shop. "I'd like that. Is Brent still out of town?"

"He finishes tonight, but he won't arrive until late. He's going straight to his place in the country, but he'll visit me tomorrow night. We'll grill steaks."

"You're blushing."

"Can't help it." And I could hardly wait to see Brent, too.

I loved working at Deputy Donut, but Saturday seemed to go on forever.

Finally, we finished cleaning up. I said goodbye to Tom, Olivia, and Jocelyn, and then Dep and I walked home in warm sunshine. At home, I had just enough time to change into a cool, sleeveless linen dress that matched the blue of my eyes and set the patio table, and then Brent showed up.

Our hug went on so long that Dep complained and had to be held between us so she could join the affection-fest.

We poured our drinks, took them outside, and sat at the patio table. Dep took possession of Brent's lap and gave me a sleepy but reproving look for letting her favorite man stay away for so long. Brent picked up the souvenir brass whorl. I had polished it until the brass was almost as shiny as gold. Maybe when it was new, the gleam had fooled Esther and her beau, Logan's great-great-great-grandfather, Otto Nobbuth.

Brent studied the brass donut. "How could anyone mistake that for a bracelet?" He slid it over the top of his ring finger. "It doesn't work as a ring either." He set it on the table and reached into a pocket. "This does, but it's platinum, not gold, and it's too small for me. The sapphire matches your eyes. Emily, will you—"

Dep popped up and widened her pupils, nearly hiding all of the green in her eyes. A paw rose tentatively toward the sparkling ring.

I gasped, "Hold on to that ring, Brent, before Dep gets it, and . . . and buries it!"

Brent gave me a lazy grin. "I've got it, but I have a better idea for where it should go." He took my left hand in his. "Emily, you know how I have felt about you for years. Will you marry me?"

Somehow, he understood my combination of inarticulate sounds, nodding, laughing, and crying. He slid the ring onto my finger.

Again, Dep had to be held between us during another long hug. Brent smiled down at her. "Is this okay with you, Dep? May I officially join the family?"

Purring, Dep reached up with one front paw, and softly patted his chin.

RECIPES

Cinnamon Twists

1 dab of butter
1 ½ cups whole milk, warmed to 111° F
1 tablespoon instant dry (powdered) yeast
3 tablespoons granulated sugar
1 egg, room temperature
4 cups all-purpose flour
½ teaspoon salt
6 tablespoons butter, just barely melted
vegetable oil with a smoke point of 400° F or higher (or
    follow your deep fryer's instruction manual)

(A mixer with a dough hook attachment is easiest for this recipe, but if you don't have a dough hook, mix as much as you can with your mixer and finish kneading by hand.)

Rub the dab of butter around the inside of a large bowl and set the bowl aside.

In a large mixer bowl, combine the milk, yeast, and sugar. Let sit for 5 minutes. Small bubbles will appear as the yeast begins working.

In a separate small bowl, whisk the egg until it's a uniform texture.

Whisk the beaten egg into the yeast mixture until it's blended.

Place the flour and salt into another large bowl and stir it with a whisk or a dinner fork.

Using a dough hook, stir the yeast mixture on low.

Running the mixer on low, add ⅓ of the flour mixture. Continue mixing, stopping to scrape down the sides of the bowl until the dough is a consistent texture.

Add another ⅓ of the flour mixture and continue mixing with the dough hook.

Add the melted butter 1 tablespoon at a time and continue mixing, stopping the mixer to scrape down the sides of the bowl until the dough is blended.

Add the remaining flour mixture and continue stirring on low until the dough begins to come together.

Increase mixer speed slightly and knead the dough until the dough forms a ball and begins cleaning the sides of the bowl. This takes only about 3 minutes.

Place the dough into the greased bowl and cover with a wet (but not dripping) kitchen towel. Allow the dough to rise to double in size. The time will vary depending on temperature and humidity.

Cover the bowl, wet towel and all, with plastic wrap.

Refrigerate 4–6 hours or overnight. The dough will shrink—there will be no need to punch it down.

Line a cookie sheet or baking tray with a silicone pad or parchment paper or use a nonstick cookie sheet, and set aside.

Form the dough into balls about 3 inches in diameter, leaving the balls in the bowl covered with plastic wrap.

One at a time, stretch and roll the dough balls into snakes about 10 inches long and ¾ inch in diameter. Fold the "snake" in half, twist the halves together, and pinch the ends together.

Place the twists on the parchment-lined baking tray and cover with the wet towel. When all of the twists have been created and covered, let them sit about a half hour for their second rising.

Heat the oil to 350° F.

Working in batches and not crowding the twists, fry them 1½ minutes on each side.

Drain on paper towels.

While the twists are still warm, coat them in cinnamon-sugar topping (below).

For the Cinnamon-Sugar Topping:
Mix ½ cup granulated sugar with 2–3 tablespoons ground cinnamon.

Tip: Place the mixture into a container fitted with a perforated lid for shaking, and sprinkle as much or as little of the mixture onto your cinnamon twists as desired. Keep extra on hand for sprinkling on raisin toast, French toast, pancakes, cereal, or any food you like!

Quick Cinnamon Twists

1 sheet of store-bought puff pastry. If frozen, thaw in fridge overnight.

1 teaspoon butter, softened

⅛ cup packed brown sugar

1 heaping teaspoon cinnamon

With a rolling pin, roll the puff pastry to smooth and un-curl it.

Cut the pastry into 9 equal rectangles.

Stir the butter, sugar, and cinnamon together. They do not need to be thoroughly blended.

Spread approximately 1 teaspoon of the butter, sugar, and cinnamon mixture in the center of each rectangle of pastry, leaving edges uncovered.

Fold the long edges of each rectangle to the middle and pinch them together to seal. Pinch the ends to seal them, too. You'll have a long, thin envelope containing the filling.

While gently stretching, twist each pastry. Some of the filling will end up on the outside. This is fine.

Arrange the twists on a parchment-lined baking sheet with an inch separating them to allow for rising.

Refrigerate the sheet of twists for 15 minutes.

Preheat oven to 400° F.

Bake for 15 minutes.

Remove from oven. Coat with the cinnamon-sugar mixture (see above) while they're still warm. Makes 9.

Quick Pesto and Mozzarella Twists

1 sheet of store-bought puff pastry. If frozen, thaw in fridge
  overnight.
approximately 3 tablespoons prepared pesto
approximately ¼ cup shredded mozzarella cheese
fresh basil leaves (optional)

With a rolling pin, roll the puff pastry to smooth and un-
curl it.

Cut pastry into 9 equal rectangles.

Spread approximately 1 teaspoon pesto in the center of
each rectangle of pastry, leaving edges uncovered.

Sprinkle approximately 1 teaspoon shredded mozzarella
over the pesto.

Fold the long edges of each rectangle to the middle and
pinch them together to form filled cylinders.

While gently stretching, twist each filled cylinder. Some of
the filling will end up on the outside. This is fine.

Form each cylinder into a circle and pinch the ends together.

Arrange the circles on a parchment-lined baking sheet
with an inch separating them to allow for rising.

Refrigerate the sheet of twists for 15 minutes.

Preheat oven to 400° F.

Bake 15 minutes.

Remove from oven. Sprinkle approximately 1 teaspoon
shredded mozzarella cheese on each twist.

Return to oven for 1–2 minutes until mozzarella cheese
melts.

Cool slightly, garnish with fresh basil leaves, and serve.
Makes 9.

Annie Young's Mustardy Potato Salad

Some of Annie's campground friends are allergic to onions, celery, and parsley. Luckily, none of them are allergic to mustard, so . . . she devised this potato salad recipe.

½ cup olive oil
¼ cup white vinegar
salt
8–10 medium potatoes
4 hard-boiled eggs, peeled
1–2 tablespoons yellow mustard
1 tablespoon yellow mustard seeds, or to taste
paprika—Annie uses smoked sweet paprika
chopped chives or sliced green onions if no one's allergic to
    them

Boil unpeeled potatoes until soft. Drain thoroughly and set aside.

In a large mixing bowl, make dressing by combining olive oil, vinegar, and ½ teaspoon (or to taste) of salt.

When potatoes are cool enough to touch, remove their skins and cut them into ½-inch cubes.

Toss the potatoes in the dressing in the bowl.

Slice the eggs and set aside the prettiest slices.

Chop the other slices and stir them into the potatoes.

Stir in the mustard.

Taste, and add more oil, vinegar, salt, and/or mustard to taste.

Stir in the mustard seeds.

Transfer the potato salad to a serving bowl.

Garnish with the prettiest slices of egg.

Sprinkle with paprika.

Top with chives or green onions, if using.

Walt Young's Fruit Punch

1 cup fresh fruit, sliced or diced
1 cup fresh or frozen berries
3 cups orange juice
3 cups cranberry blend juice

Stir together, chill, and serve.

Visit our website at
KensingtonBooks.com
to sign up for our newsletters, read
more from your favorite authors, see
books by series, view reading group
guides, and more!

BETWEEN THE CHAPTERS

Become a Part of Our
Between the Chapters Book Club
Community and Join the Conversation

Betweenthechapters.net